"It's *our* ~~baby~~
Yours as ~~much as mine.~~"

No! his mind screamed. The child she was carrying had nothing to do with him. He couldn't pretend otherwise.

He stared straight ahead, wishing she'd leave him to his numbness. He didn't think he could hold on much longer. His wife was pregnant with another man's baby. He felt sick.

And betrayed.

And *jealous.*

He stood up abruptly and headed for the door. *Jealous.* What kind of man did that make him, that he was jealous of his own wife's *ability* to conceive? Jealous because she was having the baby they'd always wanted—because she wouldn't have to *pretend* that she, not someone else, had created their child.

ABOUT THE AUTHOR

Tara Taylor Quinn knew nothing about artificial insemination until she began the research for *Another Man's Child*. On the other hand, she went through premature birth with a friend of hers, an RN, whose niece was born at five months. In fact, baby Stephanie's picture—complete with wires, tubes, tape and a warming bed—was beside Tara the entire time she wrote this book. Readers will be glad to know that Stephanie is a healthy child now.

Tara loves to hear from her readers. You can reach her at P.O. Box 15065, Scottsdale, Arizona 85267-5065.

Books by Tara Taylor Quinn

HARLEQUIN SUPERROMANCE
567—YESTERDAY'S SECRETS
584—McGILLUS V. WRIGHT
600—DARE TO LOVE
624—NO CURE FOR LOVE
661—JACOB'S GIRLS
696—THE BIRTH MOTHER

ANOTHER MAN'S CHILD
Tara Taylor Quinn

Harlequin Books

TORONTO • NEW YORK • LONDON
AMSTERDAM • PARIS • SYDNEY • HAMBURG
STOCKHOLM • ATHENS • TOKYO • MILAN
MADRID • WARSAW • BUDAPEST • AUCKLAND

ISBN 0-373-70729-0

ANOTHER MAN'S CHILD

Copyright © 1997 by Tara Lee Reames.

This edition published by arrangement with Harlequin Books S.A.

® and TM are trademarks of the publisher. Trademarks indicated with ® are registered in the United States Patent and Trademark Office, the Canadian Trade Marks Office and in other countries.

Printed in U.S.A.

For Michael Scott Gumser

It's the ties that bind,
and our knots are forever, little brother.
I love you.

CHAPTER ONE

THE WOMAN HAD A BODY that practically begged a guy to come out and play, a glint in her eyes that dared him to win.

And she was looking at Marcus. There was enough money among the businessmen she was addressing to buy the eastern United States twice over, but it was Marcus with whom she made eye contact.

He shifted in the cushioned armchair he'd chosen midway around the table. He knew Julie Winters. Had always admired her genius. She had a helluva mind for numbers and for manipulating those numbers, making her one of the most successful forces on Wall Street.

"In summary," she concluded, "independents are the businesses of the past. Diversify your assets. Scratch your own backs before someone else scratches it for you and leaves you bleeding."

She caught Marcus's eye. *I'd like to scratch your back, but I'll be gentle,* her glance seemed to say.

He had a sudden vision of Lisa's eyes when she'd looked up at him from the paper that morning. They'd had that sad, troubled, faraway quality he'd seen all too often in the past eighteen months.

The meeting was over. And Marcus had a question

or two for Julie. She'd quoted some figures he hadn't heard before, pertaining to the future of electronic advertising. Standing at the back of the room while he waited for her to finish, he admired the confidence with which she was dealing with one of his more overbearing peers.

That glint was back in her eyes when she finally approached him.

"Marcus! It's good to see you again." She placed a perfectly manicured hand on his forearm, her red nails glistening against his sleeve.

"You, too, Julie. Got a few minutes? I'd like to hear more about your predictions regarding warehouse to the consumer."

"I have another session to get to," she said, "but we could talk about it over dinner."

The woman's smile promised more than just dinner, and his body surged to life. *Tell her no, jackass. A few minutes to pick her brain is all you're after.*

He looked at his watch, the Rolex Lisa had given him when he was still the man of her dreams. "We could meet back here in the lobby at six."

"I'll be here."

Her bright red lips promised to make the evening one he'd remember. With one last look up and down his suited frame, she left the room.

He tried his damnedest not to carry the vision of her lush breasts and womanly hips, encased so seductively in that black-and-red business suit, with him as he headed to the last session of the day. He was a married man. Very much in love with his wife.

Except that every time he thought of Lisa, he saw

again the disappointment, the sadness he'd brought to
her eyes—to her life. He'd always been a doer, a prob-
lem-solver, but there wasn't one damn thing he could
do about that look in Lisa's eyes.

At five o'clock he was back in his room to shower
and change from his suit to slacks and a sport coat,
trading his staid navy tie for one a little more colorful.
He couldn't quite meet his reflected gaze as he took
one quick look in the mirror, but he refused to feel
guilty. He was going to a business dinner. That was
all.

He also avoided the picture of Lisa he'd set out on
his nightstand when he'd checked in that afternoon.
And he didn't call her as he'd promised when he'd
kissed her goodbye in their garage that morning, either.

He'd come to the convention, not only to deliver
his paper on multiple diversification, but to garner
enough space from his lovely unhappy wife to consider the consequences of his inability to give her what
she wanted most in the world. He'd sacrifice his life
to save his marriage. But there were some things he
just couldn't change.

The door of his hotel room slammed behind him as
if sealing his fate, even while he knew that there was
no earthly pleasure worth selling his soul for. But as
he walked down the hall, his mind flashed back to the
way Julie had looked at him, the way Lisa *hadn't*
looked at him since that diagnosis eighteen months
ago. These days all he saw in her eyes was that damn
sadness and disappointment. He pushed the button for
the elevator.

Julie was waiting for him as he stepped off the elevator, and her smile was as bright as the sequined halter dress she was wearing. Her eyes, dancing with pleasure, made another slow seductive tour of his body.

"Do I pass?" he asked, smiling as he took her arm to lead her to the glass-sided elevator that would whisk them to the top floor restaurant.

She rubbed her elbow against his side. "More than ever."

One soft breast brushed against him, and his body throbbed with sudden desire. She wasn't looking at him with the embers of a dying happiness in her eyes. He could give her exactly what she wanted without even trying.

Julie smiled politely as the maître d' led them to an intimate table for two alongside a wall of windows in the glass-enclosed revolving restaurant. Marcus felt carefree, full of anticipation, virile again, as he escorted her, knowing she was turning the heads of the other patrons. He'd always felt like that with Lisa, too, back when they spent enough time together to accommodate dining out.

"I have to admit, I'm surprised you agreed to have dinner with me," Julie said an hour and a half later. They'd finished the lobster he'd ordered, their conversation almost entirely business and even more stimulating than he'd expected, and had moved into the lounge area of the restaurant. His body was humming with the wine he'd consumed.

"You're a very beautiful woman. I find it hard to believe you'd ever question a man's desire to be with you." For just a moment his gaze caressed her. Down over her gleaming bare shoulders, her lush breasts to her slim waist, and back up to a mouth made for kissing.

"The last time we met, you didn't seem the least bit interested."

The last time. That conference in New York two years before. He and Lisa hadn't known then. "Times change." Marcus stared at the liquor he was swirling in his glass before setting it back on the table decisively. "You want to dance?" he asked abruptly.

"Yes." If she minded his brusque tone, she certainly didn't let it show as she took his hand. Along with desire, Marcus felt a surge of sympathy for her, this woman so cloaked in the aggression necessary to take her success from a man's world that she scared off the suitors she also craved.

The band was playing a romantic ballad, the perfect background for seduction. Marcus led Julie to a shadowy corner of the half-empty dance floor and brought her into his arms. Her skin was like satin as his hands came to rest on her bare back, her breasts soft mounds against his chest, tempting him. The sequins on her dress glittered under the muted lights. One dance. Just one dance.

They moved naturally together, swaying skillfully to the music. Marcus tried not to notice when her nipples hardened against him, or to see the smoky knowing look in her eyes. He'd have to stop if he acknowledged them. He wasn't the type of man who could cross that line.

Julie's lips parted, inviting his kiss. He pulled her

closer, instead, even though he knew she could feel his arousal. She moaned, pressing her pelvis against the hard resistance of his, burying her face against his neck. Her passion was so honest it threatened his control.

She was his for the taking. He could lose himself in her, bring her the satisfaction she so obviously hoped for. He didn't have a single doubt he could give her what she desired. That alone was the biggest temptation.

But still a forbidden one.

He'd known it was going to come to this. Julie had made no secret of the fact that she wanted him. So why had he accepted her invitation to dinner? Why had he asked her to dance? Why was he torturing himself?

He adjusted her body against him, trying to mold her softness so that she fit him better, to find that feeling of protectiveness that would come when she settled her head on his shoulder. He craved that feeling. Craved that surety that he could make everything right for her. That he could take care of her.

Marcus adjusted the woman in his arms again, but to no avail. She just didn't fit. She wasn't ever going to fit.

She wasn't Lisa.

And no matter how badly he wanted the release, he couldn't take it at Lisa's expense. He'd promised her his loyalty, and that, at least, was something he could still give her.

With a feeling of inevitability, he pulled back from the beautiful woman in his arms. He couldn't do it.

He couldn't take the pleasure she was offering. He loved Lisa too damn much.

"HEY, DOC, HOW'S IT GOING?" Beth Montague stopped outside Lisa Cartwright's office door in the medical complex connected to Thornton Memorial Hospital.

Lisa looked up from her desk and met her friend's searching gaze with a shrug.

Coming in and closing the door behind her, Beth planted one plump hip on the corner of Lisa's desk. "The kitten didn't help, huh?"

Lisa shook her head. "No more than the cruise, the summer home at the beach and the season's tickets to the theater." Instead of filling up empty holes, the cat's presence had pointed out what bottomless pits those holes had become. She and Marcus had both tried so hard to make the cat a reason to come home that they'd smothered it with attention. "The poor thing ran from us every time we walked in the door," she said, shaking her head again.

"Cats are that way sometimes," Beth replied. "Remember I told you about Corky, the cat we had when I was growing up? He'd only come out from behind the furniture at night. I used to wait up for him sometimes, and after he got used to me sitting there in the dark, he would crawl up into my lap and purr so loud I was afraid it would wake up my little brothers and sisters."

Lisa smiled. She'd heard a few stories about Beth's favorite childhood pet.

"Of course, he got a lot bolder as he grew up. Anyway, maybe you guys just needed to give the kitten more time. Cats are great companions.''

"It wasn't the cat, Beth. It was us." She hesitated, almost loath to admit the rest. "One night last week Marcus and I spent half an hour talking baby talk to the thing, trying to coax it out from under the bed to play with this new squeak toy Marcus bought. Suddenly we looked at each other, sitting on the floor in our work clothes acting like a couple of idiots, and it hit us what we were doing. And the worst part was, we couldn't even smile about it. It was just too...pathetic. So Marcus found another home for the cat the next day. A home where it's allowed to just be a cat.''

Beth's cheerful blue eyes filled with sympathy. "Okay, so you haven't found what works yet, but you will.''

"I wish I could be so sure." Marcus hadn't called after his meetings in New Jersey the day before as he'd promised. He'd phoned, instead just as Lisa was climbing into their big empty bed that night, and he'd been different somehow. Nothing she could name exactly, just a little distant, evasive, as he'd answered her questions about the day. She'd hung up with the unsettling knowledge that no matter how much she loved her husband, no matter how solid their friendship was or how completely she believed in them as a couple, their marriage was in serious trouble.

"Have you tried to talk to him again about the possibility of artificial insemination? It's the perfect answer, you know." Beth was a doctor, too, though not a pediatrician like Lisa, and she ran a fertility clinic at Thornton. Not only was she Lisa's friend, she was also the doctor who'd overseen the months of testing she and Marcus had been through in their attempts to have a child.

"I'm not going to mention it to him again," Lisa said. Her stomach became tied in knots just remembering what had happened the first time she'd broached the subject with Marcus. She'd already tried talking to him about adoption, she'd brought home pamphlets on fostering a child, and both times Marcus had refused even to discuss the issues with her. But he'd discussed artificial insemination, all right. She still remembered the stricken look on his face.

Beth's brow furrowed. "It sounds as if nothing else is working, hon. What could it hurt to talk about it to him again? The clinic's *designed* for couples in your position." Tragically widowed while still in her early thirties, Beth had never had children of her own. Now she spent her life helping others to do so.

"I can't, Beth. He'll just tell me that if I'm dissatisfied with what he can and cannot provide, then I'm free to leave him for someone who *can* satisfy me. The worst part is, I think he really means it. As much as he loves me, he would just let me go. He's so eaten up with self-hatred he can't even look at things with an open mind. And *I* can't hurt him anymore. He sees his sterility as his ultimate failure, and I can't continue to rub it in his face."

"Do *you* think he's failed you?" Beth asked.

"No!" Lisa had no doubts about that. "I'm a doctor. I *know* he had nothing to do with the fever that rendered him sterile. I love him, Beth, flaws and all. But…''

"But?"

"But I just can't see either one of us being happy without a child. It's what we both want more than anything on earth, what we've always wanted. Hell, Marcus and I were planning a nursery before we even planned our wedding. Every big decision we've ever made, every goal we've set, has been influenced by the family we'd planned to raise. I just don't see how we can keep a union that's been built on such a foundation from toppling over."

"Answer one question for me." Beth's eyes were piercing.

"Sure. If I can."

"Who do you love more, need more—your husband, or the baby he was supposed to give you?"

"That one's easy. My husband. He's my best friend. I can't imagine a life without Marcus."

Beth stood up, nodding. "Then you'll find your answer, Lis."

"Even though there's a part of me, a part that's been there as long as I can remember, who needs to be a mother, too?" Lisa asked the question softly, almost afraid even to say the words out loud.

Beth's eyes warmed with concern. Lisa knew how much her friend was pulling for her and Marcus. The three of them had formed an unshakable bond that first year after Beth's husband had been shot waiting in line at a fast-food restaurant. She and Marcus had insisted that Beth move in with them, and for six months they'd both taken turns sitting up with their friend on those nights when the demons had become too fierce for her to face alone. That had been more than five years ago.

"I understand your reluctance, Lis," Beth said now, "but you need to talk to him again. Have him come visit me. Maybe if he sees how much he'll be involved in the process, if he understands how scientific everything is, he'll come around."

Lisa smiled and nodded as her friend left, but she knew she wouldn't do as Beth suggested. She'd never known Marcus to look so beaten as he had the night she'd tried to talk to him about giving him a child through artificial insemination. She'd never seen him so angry. Or so hurt. No, she couldn't do that to him again.

TWO DAYS LATER when she unpacked Marcus's suitcase and found the shirt rolled in with his other dirty clothes, she was tempted to change her mind. She picked up the shirt slowly, staring blankly at the lipstick-stained collar for a moment, her mind masked with disbelief. It couldn't be.

Standing there, unable to move, to look away, she felt frightened—and stupid. Had Marcus…? Surely he hadn't… No. Of course not. He wouldn't. Not ever.

And then she remembered his phone call from New Jersey. Not only had he not called when he'd promised, he'd been strangely evasive.

She blinked, surprised when a tear splashed onto the incriminating collar. Had they come to this, then? Had they really come to this? Were their ties of friendship, their loyalties to each other, in jeopardy? Was the love she'd cherished for more than a decade going to slip through her fingers right along with her dream of having a child? She dropped the shirt as if she'd been burned.

And then just as suddenly picked it up again. The lipstick was still there. She could see it through the blur of her tears. She just couldn't believe it. And didn't know what to do about it. This happened to other women, other couples. Not to her and Marcus.

"Nothing happened."

Lisa jumped. She hadn't heard Marcus come upstairs.

"*Something* apparently did," she said, throwing his shirt in his face. It was too much. To lose Marcus on top of everything else was just too much.

He grabbed her arm as she pushed by him. "Nothing happened, Lisa."

She looked up at him, this man of her dreams, and even blinded by tears of anger and disappointment, she knew she still loved him. After ten years of marriage, after eighteen months of anguish, even after finding another woman's makeup on his clothes, she felt the impact of him clear to her soul. "Her lipstick's on your collar."

Marcus dropped her arm and bowed his head. "We had dinner—and one dance. That's all."

It was enough. She knew him that well. Wrapping her arms around her middle, she warded off the darkness that threatened to consume her. "You wanted her."

"*She* wanted *me*. And yes, I guess part of me

wanted her, too, wanted to be with a woman who didn't know I could only do half the job.''

A sob broke through the constriction in Lisa's throat, and she backed away from him.

"Who was she?" She willed herself to speak calmly.

Marcus swore and strode over to her, grabbing her arms, forcing her to look at him. "Nobody. She was nobody, Lis. Just a woman. Any woman who'd looked at me the way she did would probably have had the same effect. Which, in the end, was no effect at all. Because she wasn't you.''

"Was she pretty?" Lisa couldn't let it go.

"She was pretty, sure, but so are you. And you're the one I want to be with. You're my best friend, Lis."

She studied his face, his blue unblinking eyes. "Are you sure about that?"

"Absolutely."

His gaze bore into her, telling her things mere words couldn't, and suddenly some of the tension that had held her rigid, barely able to breathe, drained away, leaving her feeling weak and helpless. She sank against his chest.

He held her silently, his hand rubbing the back of her head soothingly as she soaked the front of his shirt with her tears. He was still wearing his business suit, and Lisa burrowed her arms beneath his jacket, taking comfort in his lean hard strength, letting his love console her, just as it had done for well over a decade. She needed him more than life itself. And she felt it all slipping away.

"I love you, Lis." His voice was thick through the whispered words.

"I love you, too."

But she knew that love might not be enough, not if he refused to believe in the strength of that love, not if he continued to blame himself for something he couldn't help and was convinced that she blamed him, too.

MARCUS LAY FLAT on his back, staring at the shadows the moonlight made on the ceiling as he listened to Lisa breathing beside him. He'd made love to her that night, giving her everything he had to give, and she'd been smiling when she fell asleep in his arms. But still, he knew that what he had to give wasn't enough. It was never going to be enough. Because no matter how often or how expertly he made love to her, he was never going to leave behind the seed of that love. He was never going to impregnate his wife. He wondered how long it was going to be until she started to think about leaving him for a man who could.

She stirred in her sleep, snuggling up against his chest, and Marcus automatically put an arm out to pull her close, settling her head in the crook of his shoulder. He used to love these moments in the night when he lay awake and cradled her, glorying in the knowledge that this gorgeous, intelligent, caring woman was his. Until he'd met Lisa, the only kind of affection he'd known had come in terms of discipline, respect and loyalty—necessary, but so cold. It had taken years before he'd really believed that Lisa's body curled warmly and lovingly into his was something he could count on for the rest of his life.

Now the feel of her against him was merely a reminder of how he'd failed her, of what he couldn't do, of things he couldn't make right.

Being careful not to disturb her, Marcus got up from the bed and went downstairs, hoping to dispel his demons with a shot of whiskey. But after the second shot, he knew the hope was in vain. He sat alone in the living room of the home where he'd grown up, where his father and grandfather had grown up before him.

He had it all. He'd taken the family shipping business and turned it from a solid respectable venture into an enterprise that far surpassed even his father's vision. Cartwright Enterprises had been through many transitions since its inception almost two centuries before. His early ancestors had made the family's first millions in whaling and sealing, and the generation following them were glorified Yankee Peddlers. His grandfather had expanded into imports and exports. Marcus's father had doubled the Cartwright shipping fleet before a car accident had taken his life—and his wife's, as well.

But in the eight years since Marcus had taken over, Cartwright Enterprises had become a business of the nineties. It owned several of the companies it had once shipped for. It was no longer just the middle man.

And like his father before him, Marcus had done it all for the son to whom he would one day pass his heritage. He was a Cartwright. One of *the* Cartwrights.

His ancestors, English gentry with everything but money, had come to the New World with dreams and determination. Through the early battles with Indians, the revolutionary war, the Civil War and both world wars, the Cartwrights had remained strong, determined and successful, each generation continuing and surpassing the achievements of the one before. And from the time he was old enough to understand, Marcus had worked hard to fulfill his responsibility to his birthright, to ensure that the breath of his ancestors, when he passed it on, would continue to thrive.

But unlike his father, who'd worked for financial power, Marcus had worked like a madman for another reason. He'd done it to buy his freedom, to have the time to be at home with his family when he had one, to make it to every school play, to watch each and every game, to attend all recitals, birthday parties and Christmas pageants. He wanted to make enough babies with Lisa to fill the rooms in the home he was born to, and to dispel forever the emptiness of his boyhood.

He didn't look back on those lonely years with any fondness. His parents had been interested in raising the Cartwright heir, not a child.

Marcus reached for the bottle and poured another inch of scotch. His mind turned to his sterility, and he tried for the millionth time to think about the alternatives Lisa had talked about soon after his diagnosis. But as hard as he'd tried, and God knew he'd tried, he just couldn't consider them rationally. He felt the rage coming, felt it in the sudden heat in his veins, in the tenseness in his muscles. *Why?* By what cruel twist of fate did *he* have to be the one to end the Cartwright line, to silence forever the voices of his ancestors? He who wanted children more than wealth, who understood their value in a way his father never had?

He'd worked hard all of his life, earning an honest living when, in his position, it would have been surprisingly easy to do otherwise. He gave to charities. He upheld the faith of his ancestors and never balked when there was a task to do. He'd never left a job unfinished in his life.

So why had he been robbed of the ability to do the one thing he wanted most to do? There were plenty of men out there who didn't want children, who fathered them without even knowing or caring. Yet it was Marcus who'd had that privilege revoked. *His* wife who had to look elsewhere to get his job done.

Marcus strode around the living room, trying to outdistance his demons. And as always, as the rage within him continued to boil, he was seized by the desire to just pack his bags and leave this town for a place where the Cartwright name meant nothing, where he could hide from his shortcomings—and his heritage. Where he could live out the rest of his days, if not in happiness, at least in peace. He'd have gone, too. If it wasn't for Lisa.

Marcus took one last swallow from the crystal shot glass, then hurled it into the fireplace where it shattered into a thousand glittering pieces, reminiscent of the dreams he had once been foolish enough to have.

CHAPTER TWO

DREAMS. LISA HAD always had two of them. One was to grow up, get married and have babies as sweet as her little sister, Sara, had been. Lisa had been an only child, a somewhat lonely child, until she was ten years old. And then Sara had come along, surprising them all, like a ray of sunshine that continued to shine in Lisa's heart long after her baby sister was gone.

Lisa's second dream, also a by-product of Sara, was to become a pediatrician. So at least she had realized one of the two. And as the weeks passed, she immersed herself more and more in her work. Marcus was never home anymore, and on the rare occasions when he wasn't working late, he kept busy in his den or out on the grounds, rarely smiling and hardly looking at Lisa at all.

So Lisa volunteered for an extra shift on call. She added to her already full patient load; she offered to cover for whatever physicians were on vacation or taking a long weekend to spend with their families. Anything she could do to stay busy, to keep her mind occupied, to ignore the fact that Marcus was slipping away from her. He still made wonderful love to her— Marcus had always had an incredible sexual appetite—but he didn't gaze into her eyes while they were making love anymore, nor did he linger in her arms afterward.

Pushing away the fear that had become her constant companion, Lisa pulled some recently delivered X rays from their folder, placed them up on the view box beside her desk and flipped on the light so she could study the results. Her heart sank.

Little Willie Adams's back was broken; he wouldn't be playing Little League any more this season, and probably not next, either. Depending on the damage to his spinal cord, he might never be playing it again. Reaching for the phone, she punched in the number for one of the best neurosurgeons she knew, all the while thinking of the little redheaded boy lying so still in the hospital bed across the street. Willie was one of the patients Lisa saw gratis, courtesy of state welfare. He was one of six kids, the only boy, that his mother was raising single-handedly. His father had run off before Willie was born. The one good thing in Willie's life was his success in Little League.

Lisa pulled into the gate at home two hours later, weary in body, but even wearier in soul. She'd spent an hour with Willie until Dr. Shea had come; she'd told Willie and his mother Willie's prognosis, she'd answered all of his mother's questions and watched Willie's face turn to stone, but she'd never seen him shed a tear. Considering the amount of pain he was in, that was amazing in itself, but to have just had his one hope of getting out of the ghetto snatched away…

Lisa left her Mercedes in the circular driveway, then trudged up the steps, her briefcase weighing on her exhausted muscles as she let herself in. It was late, long past dinnertime, and she knew Hannah, the part-time housekeeper who saw more of Lisa and Marcus's home than they did, had left hours before. She started to call out for Marcus, needing him desperately, but closed her mouth before she wasted her breath. He'd been out until midnight or later most every night lately, attempting to keep Blake's, a family-owned chain of department stores in Rhode Island, from going bankrupt. She didn't begrudge him the time. Not really. She knew her husband well enough to know how good it made him feel to be able to help save someone else's dream. Especially since he couldn't seem to save his own.

But that didn't stop her from needing him.

Taking her briefcase into the home office she shared with Marcus, she shrugged out of her suit jacket and rubbed the stiff muscles along the back of her neck. Sometimes she wondered if she was *meant* to be a doctor. She'd never been able to develop that impenetrable shell they'd talked about in medical school.

"Rough day?"

At the sound of Marcus's voice she whirled around, filled with the instant warmth that still came to her every time he walked into a room.

"Yeah." She didn't elaborate as she once might have, rubbing at her neck again.

He looked relaxed, wearing slacks and a polo shirt, instead of one of the suits he always wore to work. She wondered how long he'd been home and was instantly disappointed that she hadn't been here with him. The gorgeous Connecticut June weather was perfect for evenings sitting out under the stars, sharing a drink. Or more.

His eyes were loving, sympathetic, as he moved closer to her.

"You want to tell me about it?" He pushed her hands aside and began massaging her tense muscles with the expertise born of experience.

Lisa bowed her head, giving him easier access to her neck. "A patient of mine, an eleven-year-old boy, broke his back today playing baseball. He was sliding into home and the catcher fell on top of him."

"God, the poor kid." Marcus's hands continued to work their magic.

"He'd just had an offer from a city team. He's good, Marcus. And he's inner city. Baseball was his one shot out."

"He's young, Lis. He's got time to mend." Marcus pulled her fully into his arms and Lisa soaked up his strength, nestling her head into her usual place on his shoulder.

"He's paralyzed. The damage may be permanent." As she said the words out loud, words she hadn't yet had the heart to tell Willie or his mother, the dam inside her broke and she started to sob, not only for the stalwart little boy lying so still across town, but for the man who held her, for the permanent damage that long-ago fever had done to him, for the damage it was still doing to *them*.

Marcus held her until her emotion was spent. And then he started to kiss her, long, slow, tender kisses. The healing kind. Offering her forgetfulness in the one way that always worked. She clung to him desperately, and when they moved upstairs to their bedroom, arms wrapped around each other, she gave him all the love within her, all the passion only he could raise. He was her husband, her lover, her best friend. And just as she was going to do everything in her power to help Willie Adams, including footing his bills anonymously if she had to, she was going to do whatever it took to fix the problems between her and Marcus.

Her life's work was saving lives, but her life was nothing if she didn't have her soul mate beside her, sharing it with her.

WITH HER NEWFOUND RESOLVE still burning inside, Lisa approached her tenth wedding anniversary the following week with optimism. She checked in on Willie that morning, satisfied that he'd come through his second surgery better than they'd hoped, and then took the rest of the day off. She had some primping to do.

Stopping at the mall on the way home, she wandered through a couple of exclusive lingerie shops until she found just what she was looking for—a black pure-silk teddy. Marcus was a sucker for silk.

"Will there be anything else, Mrs. Cartwright?" the saleswoman asked when Lisa handed over her charge card.

"Is that lavender bubble bath?" Lisa gestured toward the display beside the counter.

"Yes, ma'am. It's not too overpowering, though, and it's full of moisturizers. I use it myself. Would you like to try some?"

"Sure, why not?" Lisa said, feeling a little decadent. These days she rarely had time for more than a quick shower, let alone a leisurely bubble bath, but her husband had always liked the scent of lavender. And she'd bet he could think of a few interesting things to do in a lavender-scented tub. He was wonderfully inventive.

She hurried home and stayed there only long enough to pack a few things for herself and a bag for Marcus. Telling Hannah not to bother with dinner, she jumped back in her car and headed out of New Haven. She knew exactly where she was going. Haven's Cove, the beautiful private resort on the coast between New Haven and Milford. It was the perfect place for her and Marcus to celebrate. If the memories they'd find there didn't remind them of all that they were to each other, nothing would.

She spent half an hour or more reacquainting herself with the grounds, glad to see that little had changed since the last time she'd been there, and then whiled away the afternoon in the salon, treating herself to the works. She was going to bring the hungry look back into Marcus's eyes.

At five o'clock on the nose, she sent a telegram to Marcus: MEET ME AT HAVEN'S COVE. I NEED LOVIN'. And then she waited.

Some of the best hours in Lisa's life had been in the cabanas at Haven's Cove. It was where Marcus had first told her he loved her. Where, months after they'd become lovers, she'd finally seen the knowledge of her love for him dawn in his eyes. Where he'd asked her to marry him.

And now she hoped he still believed in them enough to join her.

MARCUS WAS BEAT when he arrived back at his office. He'd just come from an afternoon meeting that had lasted twice as long as it should have. The Rhode Island department-store venture had to be pulled into the nineties if it was going to have any hope of surviving, and George Blake, the old gentleman who sat at the helm of the family business, while seemingly agreeable to every suggestion Marcus and his team made, was having a hard time letting go of the only way of life he'd ever known.

Marcus didn't *have* to take the time to consider the man's feelings. Not legally. But he couldn't just take over a man's life's work and leave him with nothing. He wanted Blake to understand the changes, to be able to continue to sit at the helm of his company after Marcus had him set up and running again. So he was taking the time to teach the man what it had taken himself four years at Yale, and three times as many in business, to learn. Or at least an abridged version thereof.

He'd realized halfway through the meeting what day it was. He'd been putting in so many long hours for Cartwright Enterprises the past couple of weeks that the days had all started rolling into one. Not that he minded. To the contrary. The only time he didn't have doubts about himself these days was when he was working.

But he still didn't know where the first half of the month had gone. Someone had mentioned a golf date when they'd taken a break for lunch, and it had suddenly dawned on Marcus that it was the middle of June. The sixteenth to be exact. His anniversary.

Or maybe it hadn't suddenly dawned on him. Maybe he'd been unconsciously trying to forget. He wasn't sure there was much to celebrate. Not for Lisa, anyway. Not anymore.

He'd had coffee with his wife early that morning and she'd read the paper just like every other morning, not giving any indication that she'd remembered what day it was. She sure as hell hadn't wished him happy anniversary as she had all the other years since they'd been married. And when he'd tried to call her at lunchtime, he'd been told she wasn't expected in her office at all that day. Which meant she was either out exhausting herself in the free clinic or volunteering her time at the hospital. Anything to stay away from home. Not that he blamed her. The emptiness there mocked him, too.

"A telegram came for you about an hour ago, and your other mail is there, too," Marge, his secretary of thirteen years, said as he let himself into his suite of offices on the top floor of Cartwright Tower in downtown New Haven. She'd been with him since his sophomore year at Yale, when he'd begun working his way up the ranks at Cartwright Enterprises. She'd been working for him the year he'd met Lisa; had been at his wedding, too. "There's also a stack of letters for you to sign, and Paul Silas wants you to give him a call."

"Thanks, Marge. Give yourself double overtime

this week and go home. You don't owe me all these late nights."

"It's okay, Marcus. The twins left a couple of weeks ago to take summer jobs at the University of Connecticut—they're getting ready for their freshman year—and the house is so quiet it's depressing. I'd just as soon be here as home."

"Where's James?" Marcus asked.

"He's in Florida for a month, overseeing the construction of a new shopping complex outside Orlando. I almost wish he hadn't been promoted to project manager."

Marcus smiled at his middle-aged secretary's uncharacteristic grumbling. "You don't mean that, Marge. You'd have to give back that boat he bought you last summer."

Marge grinned. "You're right. I don't mean it. But I'm telling you, Marcus, for once I think you and Lisa have the right idea."

"About what?"

"About not having children. It hurts bringing them into this world, they take years off your life with all the worry they cause, and then they just up and leave home, not caring that they're breaking your heart as they go."

"And if you could, would you trade away any of the past eighteen years with them, Marge?" he asked softly.

She smiled, her pretty features lighting up. "Of course not. Don't mind me. I guess I'll go home and bake some cookies. I promised the boys I'd send them some before the weekend."

"So why not take tomorrow off and deliver them yourself? Storrs is only an hour away, and you'll feel a lot better once you've checked up on them."

"Am I that obvious?"

"Maybe I just know you better than most," Marcus said, envying her sons. He wasn't even sure his folks had known he was gone when he left the family home for a dorm room at Yale.

"But what about the Rhode Island group?" Marge asked, frowning. "Aren't you all meeting here tomorrow?"

Marcus shook his head. "We postponed it until after the weekend. George wants a couple of more days to study the manuals for the computer system we're installing at Blake's. So take the day off."

"Yes, sir!" She was grinning from ear to ear as she tidied up her desk and gathered her purse.

Listening to her humming, Marcus headed on into his office and the tasks waiting there for him. Maybe the telegram was something urgent. Anything to take him away from New Haven and the empty house he knew he'd find if he went home. Of course, with all the time he'd been spending on the Blake venture, he had enough pressing work on his desk to keep him busy well past midnight. With that comforting thought, he opened the telegram.

MEET ME AT HAVEN'S COVE. I NEED LOVIN'.

Marcus stared at it, hardly daring to believe the words. But there they were, all neat caps, teasing him with long ago memories. Good memories.

He read it again. MEET ME AT HAVEN'S COVE.

I NEED LOVIN'. What full-blooded man could turn down an invitation like that?

Especially when the woman issuing it was Lisa?

The love of his life.

And when the man was feeling such incredible relief that the woman wanted to celebrate their anniversary, after all. He broke every speed limit in Connecticut as his Ferrari ate up the miles to Haven's Cove.

THE CABANA SMELLED of Lisa. It amazed him that after ten years of marriage, he could be aroused merely by the scent of his wife.

"Lis?" he asked, letting the door close behind him. He was eager to see what she had planned for them, prepared to change her mind if it wasn't bed in the next ten minutes.

"In here," she called from the direction of the bathroom.

Marcus shed his jacket as he headed across the room, the splashing of water luring him on. It sounded as if she was in the bath. As he recalled, the bathtubs at Haven's Cove were huge. He'd played out a few fantasies in one of them on their honeymoon.

They'd been so filled with dreams back then. Dreams that had turned to ashes. He stopped outside the door. Maybe this wasn't such a good idea.

"Marcus, come on. The water's wonderful," Lisa called, her voice husky with desire. It was all the invitation Marcus needed. All the invitation he'd ever needed. His wife to want him.

Lavender. The air was filled with lavender. Lisa was

sitting in the enormous porcelain tub surrounded by bubbles, a piece of skimpy black silk hanging haphazardly from the towel rack above her. Her dark hair was pinned up on her head, with a few wispy tendrils, damp on the ends, falling down around her face and shoulders. The glistening skin of the tops of her breasts was just visible above the white foam.

She'd never looked so desirable in her life. Not even the first time he'd seen her naked, when her young ripe body had been much more beautiful than he'd even imagined.

"Hi," he murmured, staring at her.

Her big brown eyes were sultry-looking, telling him she was his to command, to do with her as he willed. There was no sadness in them now. No disappointment lurking in their depths.

Marcus stepped out of his shoes and dropped the rest of his clothes in a pile at his feet in one quick move. Lisa's eyes widened, and for the first time in a long time, Marcus was proud of his body. Sexually, he knew no other man could please her more than he did. Because no man could love her more.

"I hope you didn't call for room service," he said, lowering himself, facing her, into the warm water.

She shook her head, her eyes filled with a hunger room service couldn't assuage. "I waited for you."

"Good." He slid his hands up her calves to thighs that were still as smooth as the day he'd married her, holding her gaze with his own. "Your skin's like satin."

She smiled slowly, the smile that had brought him to his knees the first time he'd seen it and kept him there ever since. For a woman who had come to him almost innocent, she had the art of seduction down to amazing perfection.

Skimming his hands over the sides of her hips, he found her waist and almost circled it with his big hands. Every time he felt her slenderness, her femininity, he was filled again with a need to cherish her, to protect her from whatever hurts life might throw her way.

He'd just never counted on being one of those hurts.

His fingers continued their exploration, up her rib cage to her breasts. He cupped their exquisite softness, knowing the feel of them, and yet finding their familiarity wildly exciting. They were his. *She* was his. Right here. Right now.

"You're as beautiful now as you were the first time," he said.

She reached for his swollen penis and caressed it. She chuckled softly, a sweet husky sound. "You remember that first time? I wanted you so badly it was driving me crazy, but I was scared to death you'd think I was easy."

Marcus smiled, too, remembering. She'd been such a contradiction, seducing him and crossing her knees at the same time. "All I could think about was getting between those gorgeous legs of yours. You'd been tempting me all summer, running around in shorts so short they revealed more than they concealed."

"They did not!" she said, pretending to take offense.

"Oh, yes, you were a little tease," he returned, and

then he immediately availed himself of the treasures the shorts had promised that long-ago summer.

Her hand had fallen away from his penis, and now she reached for him again. "Oh, Marcus, please..."

He gently pushed her hand away, completely caught up in his memories of the past, the invincible feeling he'd had the day he'd married her. "Not yet, my love."

"But..." She frowned up at him as he placed his finger against her lips.

"Let me." He spent the next hour, in the bath and then out on the bed, showing her how much he adored her.

Her eyes were slumberous with passion, with a peace he hadn't seen in months, when he finally entered her and found his own bit of paradise.

"I love you," she whispered in the aftermath, her body still clinging to his. Her words warmed his heart as thoroughly as she warmed his body.

"I love you, too," he said. He looked at her and saw she was smiling. And at that moment, Marcus had all he wanted. "Happy anniversary." They fell asleep, locked in each other's arms.

MARCUS STAYED IN BED with Lisa for most of the next twenty-four hours, loving her, laughing with her, debating with her about everything under the sun—except the life awaiting them outside the door of their cabana. They explored each other in ways they never had before, made love in ways that were achingly familiar and ordered whatever outside sustenance they needed from room service. He wanted to draw out their time at the cabana forever. To never let the honeymoon end. Because he was afraid of what came next.

As long as they were in the cabana, he was everything Lisa wanted. It was only outside those doors that he failed her.

"Can I ask you something?" Lisa said, looking up from the crossword puzzle she'd found in the morning paper that had been delivered along with their breakfast. She was dressed in his shirt from the day before, propped on a mountain of pillows in the middle of the bed.

He set the business section of the same paper down on the table beside him. "Sure," he said, but he *wasn't* sure. The shadows were back in her eyes.

"If you'd known ten years ago that we couldn't have a family, would you still have married me?"

"Does it make a difference?" He wished he was wearing more than the sweats Lisa had packed for him. He had a sudden urge to head back to the city.

She shrugged, laying aside her puzzle. "I think it might."

"I suppose, if you'd known then what you do now, if you'd been content with that knowledge, then yes, I'd have asked you to marry me."

"Why?" Her beautiful brown gaze bore into him, telling him how badly she needed answers, allowing him no choice but to give her the truth.

"Because even back then you were the best friend I'd ever had." He moved over to the bed, taking her hands in his. "I've never been able to talk to another person the way I can talk to you, Lis. I've never cared as much about another person's happiness as I do yours."

She smiled, but her eyes brimmed with tears. "Then where are we going wrong now?"

"It's not a perfect world, Lis. And you didn't marry me at peace with the idea of never having a family."

"But I would have, Marcus. You have to believe that. I care the same about you as you do about me. You're right, it's not a perfect world, and our lives aren't turning out to be the perfect fairy tale we envisioned, but we still have each other. Why can't that be enough?"

"Can you honestly tell me that you're content facing the rest of your life childless?"

Her gaze dropped to the covers across her knees. He had his answer. And so did she.

But she was looking at him again when she finally spoke. "I can tell you this, Marcus. I can't bear to face the rest of my life without my best friend." She began to cry.

Her tears broke his heart and he wiped them away with the pads of his thumbs. "Shh."

"I'm scared, Marcus. I'm so scared I'm losing you."

If truth be known, Marcus was more than a little afraid himself. "I'm right here, honey. And I love you more now than ever. We'll get through this, Lis. Trust me." Even as he said the words, he feared how empty they might prove to be. He loved her. More than life. But he was no longer sure he could make her happy.

AT TEN THAT EVENING Lisa's beeper sounded. One of her welfare patients had acute appendicitis, and Lisa had to rush back to town to perform an appendectomy.

But she took the memory of the past twenty-four hours with her, along with a large dose of hope. The bond between her and Marcus was too strong to be ripped apart. Somehow they were going to find a way to be happy together again.

She grabbed a couple of hours' sleep on the couch in her office after the surgery and then started her morning rounds. But only after calling Marcus and telling him how much she loved him. He was on his way into work, as well, but said he'd be home early that evening.

And he was. That evening, and several after that. But as the days passed, it was getting harder and harder for him to pretend he was happy there in that huge house. Its emptiness taunted him with what would never be. She knew it must, because it taunted her.

"Let's move," she said one night almost two weeks after their anniversary. They were both in their home office, working at their respective mahogany desks on opposite sides of the room, but Lisa had a feeling Marcus wasn't concentrating any better than she was.

He looked up from the page of figures he'd been

studying when she spoke. "Move? Move where?" he asked, frowning at her. "I've lived here all my life. Why would I want to move?"

Lisa told herself not to be intimidated by that frown, nor by his logic. They *had* to do something.

"That's exactly why. You've lived here all your life. Maybe we need a change."

He set his pen down on top of the papers in front of him. "What kind of change?"

"I saw this new development out on the edge of town today—you know where the old whaling museum used to be?" Lisa couldn't look at him as she continued, feeling herself starting to sweat. "It's called Terrace Estates and it's a beautiful gated community. The condominiums are larger than most single-family homes, and they're all set back from the street about a hundred feet, some more, with separate gated yards. There are three community sports complexes, a PGA golf course and even a couple of fine restaurants all within the community walls. And there's twenty-four-hour security, too."

"I didn't realize you had a problem with our security. Why didn't you tell me you're nervous here alone?"

"I'm not!" Lisa said, afraid to tell her proud husband the real reason she'd gone to see the new community. And even more frightened by the fact that there were things she could no longer discuss with him.

She and Marcus seemed to have made an unconscious agreement after they'd left Haven's Cove two weeks before to stop talking about what ailed them. It was as if by ignoring the problem, they could pretend it didn't exist. But it did exist, and Lisa feared that if they didn't do something soon, she was going to lose Marcus.

"What is it, Lis? I always thought you loved this place."

He sounded disappointed. "I *do* love this place. I always have. But Terrace Estates might suit us better." She sneaked a peek at him. He was still frowning, obviously confused. "It's an adult community, Marcus. I just thought we might be happier there."

He didn't say anything. But the tightening of his jaw told her he now understood her motive. He sat silently at his desk, his fingers steepled in front of him, his chin so rigid it could have been carved from stone. Lisa longed for him to look at her, to give her some hint of what he was thinking, what he was *feeling*. Day by day, he was closing himself off to her. And day by day, her heart was breaking.

"I'll take a look at it." She jumped when he finally spoke, his voice without inflection, and his eyes, when she met them, were just as empty.

"Tomorrow?" she asked, desperate enough to keep pushing.

"Fine. Set up a time."

They were the last words he said to her that night. Although he reached for her when he finally climbed into bed beside her sometime after midnight. And while she went willingly into his arms, she didn't find the joy she'd found there two weeks before. And once again, when he reached his peak, his gaze was locked, not on her, but on the wall behind her head.

CHAPTER THREE

"THE WALLS ALL HAVE double insulation to insure your privacy, in spite of the common wall between you and your neighbor. Of course, since we're all adults here, we find we have little problem with noise..."

The woman continued with her friendly sales pitch, but Marcus had a hard time concentrating on what she was saying. The four-bedroom unit she was showing them certainly appeared to live up to her praises, but for the life of him, Marcus couldn't figure out why anyone would want to live there. The Cartwright mansion might be empty, it might be quiet, but at least there he could breathe. The moment he'd driven Lisa through the ornate gates of Terrace Estates, he'd felt like he was suffocating.

They'd been stopped by a security guard immediately. Their names were on the visitor list and the guard sent them on through, but if they lived there they'd have to show a pass to the security guard every time just to get to their own home. Their guests would have to do the same. It reminded Marcus of a prison.

But if this was what Lisa wanted.

He looked at his wife as she followed the Terrace Estates representative into a double walk-in closet.

Lisa had come straight from work and was wearing the soft yellow suit he'd bought her last Christmas. The cropped jacket showed off her slim waist, and the short skirt complimented her long gorgeous legs, reminding him of the last time they'd been wrapped around him. She'd cradled him lovingly, but without ecstasy. He was losing her, slowly but surely.

"Marcus! Look at this closet! It's big enough to be another bedroom." Lisa sounded almost as enthused as the Realtor. Didn't the place seem as barren to her as it did to him? Had they really grown so far apart?

"It is large," Marcus replied, glancing inside. It seemed like a lot of wasted space to him. And it was along the wall the unit shared with the place next door. He couldn't imagine listening to some stranger scraping hangers along the clothes bar every morning. Couldn't imagine why anyone would want to.

"Oh, and come see the bathroom!" Lisa called from the other side of the master suite.

Marcus made the proper noises as she pointed out the sunken bathtub, the separate Jacuzzi and shower stall. Very nice, very modern, but he just didn't see how any of this was going to help things. Their problems went a lot deeper than empty rooms. Lisa was only fooling herself if she didn't see that.

"What do you think?" Lisa whispered to him as he peeked into the ceramic-tiled shower stall.

"We'll buy it if you want it." He'd never been good at telling her no.

With her hand on his shoulder, she turned him to face her. "Do *you* want it?" she asked, her big brown eyes filled with love—and doubt. The Realtor had tactfully disappeared.

"I want you to be happy."

Lisa's eyes filled with tears. "I *am* happy, Marcus. As long as I'm with you," she whispered.

Looking down into her lovely face, Marcus could almost believe her. "Then let's go home," he said, putting his arm around her as he walked her out. Her hand slid around his waist, pulling him closer, and he tried to convince himself that she wasn't ruing the day she'd fallen in love with him.

"Disappointed?" he asked, glancing over at her as they left Terrace Estates behind them.

She shook her head. "Relieved. I love our house. I'd have hated living there."

"But you'd have done it."

"Yes. But, oh, Marcus, it's just...I miss you. I miss the time we used to spend together." She stared out the windshield.

They'd been together almost every evening for the past couple of weeks, but Marcus knew what she meant. They were together in body, but in the ways that mattered, they were more apart than ever. Since their anniversary, they'd been hiding from each other—thinking before they spoke, weighing every word to make certain they didn't voice the thoughts that were tearing them up inside.

"Let's go to the club," he said suddenly. "We haven't gone dancing in months." He needed to hold her. Just hold her.

She turned to him, her face alight. "What a good idea! I'd love to."

He grabbed her hand, holding it under his on the gearshift between them. "Dancing it is," he said, and he turned the car along the road toward the country club. Disaster had been averted once more.

But as he drove her home later that night, as he took her upstairs, undressed her and made slow intimate love to her, Marcus was stabbed again with the guilt that was corroding everything good and dear in his life. What right did he have to deprive her of the family she wanted, the family she'd always dreamed of having? What right did he have to deny that family the chance to thrive under her great store of love? What right did he have to keep it all for himself?

None. No right at all. He simply wasn't ready to face the alternative. To live his life without her beside him. He'd been taking care of Lisa since the first day he'd met her, when she'd been trying to carry too-big boxes into her sorority house the August before her sophomore year at Yale. He'd taken one look, relieved her of her burden and decided then and there that she needed watching over. By him. He'd been watching over her ever since, this gorgeous woman who was physically weaker than he and therefore in need of his protection. But he'd known almost from the first where the real strength in their relationship lay. Within her. He drew his strength from the love she gave him so freely. And, God help him, he wasn't sure he could give that up.

He held her long into the night, listening to her breathe softly beside him. But sleep eluded him. His own selfishness left too bitter a taste.

LISA'S THIRTY-THIRD birthday fell on a Sunday in the middle of July, and for once she wasn't on call. Marcus woke her with a kiss when the sun was peeking over the horizon. He set a warming tray laden with two covered plates, a single red rose and an envelope on the night table beside her.

"Happy birthday, sweetheart," he said, kissing her once more before he straightened.

He was wearing nothing but a pair of cut-off sweats, and desire pooled in her belly as she ran her gaze up his long muscular thighs.

She lifted the comforter and smiled at him. "Come back to bed, Marcus..."

The omelets Marcus had made for them were still warm, if a little tough, by the time they got to them, but Lisa enjoyed every bite. Hannah provided enough deliciously cooked meals to get them through the week, but they cooked for each other on weekends. Lisa always enjoyed those meals the most.

She and Marcus sat across from each other on the unmade bed, the warming tray a table between them. Or rather, she sat. He was sprawled on his side, propped up on an elbow, taking up the whole length of the bed, and still naked.

"You're beautiful, you know that?" he said, munching on her last piece of toast.

"I'm glad you think so."

"I know so." He motioned to the envelope still propped against the bud vase on the tray. "That's for you."

Lisa reached for the envelope slowly, excited, but just a little afraid to see what was inside. Marcus wasn't a card man. In all their years together, he'd only given her two. One on their first anniversary and one for Valentine's Day. She still had them both.

The intent way he was watching her as she slid the card from the envelope only increased her trepidation.

The front was simple, an airbrushed picture of a sailboat. She opened the card.

Every day of my life, I celebrate the day you were born. Love, Marcus. He'd written the words in his familiar scrawl. The rest of the card was blank.

Tears filled Lisa's eyes as she read the words again. She hadn't realized how much she'd needed that reassurance.

She looked across at her husband, smiling through her tears. "Thank you."

Removing the tray from the bed, he tumbled her onto her back and showed her the truth of his words.

"HOW ABOUT WE MOVE this party to the shower? We have exactly half an hour before we have to be somewhere," Marcus said almost an hour later.

Lisa glanced at the clock. "Where could we possibly have to be at nine-thirty on a Sunday morning?"

Marcus just grinned and headed across the room to her dresser, pulling out a pair of white shorts and a blue-and-white crop top. "You ask too many questions. Now get your pretty rear into the shower and then into these clothes." He tossed them on the bed.

Two minutes later she heard him singing in the shower. With one last sip of coffee, she went in to join him. In spite of her efforts to draw him out, Marcus remained closemouthed about where they were going as he hurried her out to his Ferrari. Lisa giggled, enthralled with this playful side to her husband. Marcus hadn't been so lighthearted since before—

No. I'm not going to think about that. Not today.

"We're heading toward the ocean. Are we going to Angelo's?" she asked, naming her favorite Italian restaurant.

Marcus shifted the Ferrari into fourth and grinned at her.

"But, Marcus, we just ate breakfast."

He kept his gaze on the road, still grinning.

She thought about Angelo's succulent pasta. The bottomless basket of freshly made Italian bread. "I suppose we could walk on the docks awhile and work up an appetite."

If anything, his grin grew wider. The man was infuriating. Didn't he understand that she didn't want to spoil a perfectly wonderful meal by being too full to eat it?

"You don't want to walk on the docks?" she asked.

"I didn't say that."

"That's the problem. You aren't saying anything. Going to Angelo's is a wonderful idea. I *want* to go. I'm just not hungry yet."

"Did I say anything about going to Angelo's?"

He'd stopped the car at the marina. And right in front of her, bobbing in the deep blue ocean, was a sleek beautiful sailboat with a huge red ribbon blowing from the masthead. But the name, written in large gold print across the stern, was what finally reached her. *Sara.*

The name she'd chosen for their firstborn, in memory of her little sister.

"She's ours?" she asked, still staring at the boat. She'd always wanted to learn to sail. And Marcus had always promised to teach her. But somehow they'd never found the time.

"Happy birthday, Lis."

Excitement bubbled up inside her. Excitement and hope for the future. Their future. This was something they could do—together.

"Are we going to sail her today?"

"Unless you'd rather go straight to Angelo's," Marcus said, his eyes twinkling.

Lisa punched him in the arm, then threw her arms around his neck, kissing him full on the mouth. "Thank you, Marcus."

"You like her?" he asked, and she heard the hesitation in his voice. There it was again, his questioning his ability to please her. She just didn't know how to convince him that he still made her happier than any other person on earth. That it was something he did just by loving her. She cursed his parents for teaching him that he had to earn affection, for showing him that if he was ever cause for disappointment, he'd lose that affection. For convincing him that he was responsible for everything—even those things beyond his control. For making him doubt that he was worthy of his wife's love.

Lisa looked at the *Sara* again, the shiny white bow trimmed with royal blue. "It's perfect," she said, giving him another hug. She'd just have to keep showing him until he believed again.

"In that case, Dr. Cartwright, let me teach you how to sail."

They didn't go far, they didn't go fast, and at times, Lisa was more of a hindrance than a help, but she loved every minute of it. The boat was just the right size for a two-man crew, and Lisa was delighted when she discovered the cabin below, complete with a tiny kitchen, an even tinier bathroom and a queen-size bunk.

"We'll christen it soon," Marcus called down from the deck where he was busy maneuvering them toward Long Island Sound. Lisa smiled. He'd read her mind—as he often did.

She was exhausted but happy when they finally docked the boat in the slip just before sundown. She couldn't remember a day she'd enjoyed more. The Connecticut shoreline beckoned them, the lush green banks blending into the vivid blue sky as if rendered on canvas by a painter.

Lisa's skin was a little tender from so much time in the sun, her cheeks and hair were filled with salty ocean spray, her clothes were damp and wrinkled, and she felt great. She watched as Marcus went forward and secured the *Sara* to the dock. The wind had blown his hair into casual disarray, his polo shirt had come untucked from shorts that were no longer white, and his skin had a healthy golden glow. A secret little thrill washed through her as she watched him. He was gorgeous—all man—and he was hers.

A pretty young woman standing with a baby on her hip on the deck of the boat across the dock from the *Sara* smiled and waved when she saw Lisa on the deck. Lisa waved back just as a toddler came running up and clutched the woman's leg, saying something Lisa couldn't hear.

With a shrug and another little wave, the woman took the child's hand and led him away. Probably to the bathroom, Lisa thought. She wondered if the woman knew how incredibly lucky she was.

And she was so young. She couldn't have been more than twenty-two or -three. A whole decade younger than Lisa. And she already had two children. Lisa blinked back the tears that sprang to her eyes, quickly wiping away the couple that spilled over, cursing herself for her weakness. She lived a blessed life, with a man she adored. It was enough.

"Let's get this thing bedded down," Marcus said, his voice clipped. He'd come up behind her.

Lisa swung around, stricken. Marcus looked from her tear-filled eyes to the other boat, where the woman and her children had been standing only seconds before, and then turned away. His shoulders were as stiff as his Puritan ancestors'. Lisa knew he'd seen the whole thing.

Cursing herself again, Lisa ran her hand along his back. "Marcus—"

"Leave it, Lis."

He didn't look her way again as he instructed her on furling the sails.

Lisa helped Marcus secure the Sara in the slip, eager to learn everything she could about caring for their new boat, but much of the glow had gone from her day. Marcus was beating himself up again, and this time it was her fault. Suddenly thirty-three felt ancient.

A MONTH LATER Marcus gave Lisa another surprise, though he wasn't there to share it with her. She went in to see little Willie Adams again, the eleven-year-old ball player with the broken back. She'd talked to Marcus about the boy weeks before, and he'd agreed that they would finance the boy's treatment, but so far, Willie's physical-therapy sessions had been a complete waste of time. She'd been particularly worried because the boy's lack of progress stemmed more from his defeated attitude than it did from his injury.

But when she entered his room at the hospital that morning, he was wearing a baseball glove and tossing a ball between it and his free hand, in spite of the cast that kept most of his torso immobilized. His red hair was combed into place for the first time since she'd admitted him, and he was grinning from ear to ear.

"How you doing today, Willie?" Lisa asked, taking the chart from the end of his bed to see what could have brought about such a miracle. Had the boy regained some more feeling in his legs? And if so, why hadn't she been called? She'd left instructions to be informed the minute there was any change.

"Hi, Doc. Watch," Willie said. He shoved the covers down past his toes, and slowly began to rotate his right foot. And then, a bit more quickly, his left.

Lisa watched, her heart thumping. *Finally*. Now he had hope.

"That's great, Willie!" she said, as the boy started on his right foot again. "How does it feel?" She ran her hand over the boy's leg.

Willie shrugged, his freckled face breaking into an

embarrassed grin. "I guess I can feel it a little better," he said. "It kinda hurts."

Lisa helped him settle the covers back over his partially paralyzed limbs. "Well, don't overdo it, buster," she said. A week ago she'd been begging him to try to sit up.

"But I gotta work hard, Doc. Danny Johnson says that if I'm better by next summer, I can come to his Junior League training camp."

"Danny Johnson?" Lisa asked, suddenly understanding—and falling in love with her husband all over again.

"He's a pitcher for the Yankees, Doc, the best, and he runs a camp for promising teenage baseball players every summer."

He'd also gone to college with Marcus. "Teenage players?" Lisa smiled at the boy. "You won't be thirteen until the summer *after* next."

Willie grinned. "I know. Ain't it great? I'll be the youngest guy there, but Mr. Johnson talked to my coach and he says I'm ready."

Lisa replaced the chart at the end of Willie's bed. "Then we'll just have to make sure you're better by next summer, huh?" That gave them a year. And as there was no longer any sign of permanent damage to Willie's spine, she figured they could just about make it.

Lisa tried to wait up to thank Marcus that night, but by midnight, she knew she was going to have to go to bed without him. Again. She was on call starting at six the next morning, and her young patients deserved to have her well rested. It wasn't their fault that her husband would rather be in meetings with strangers than at home with her. In the month since her birthday, he'd hardly been home. And he hadn't touched her at all.

"SOMETHING TELLS ME this is more than just a friendly visit," Beth Montague said when Lisa took a chair in Beth's office late the next afternoon. The office was light, airy, with a white carpet and a lot of blond wood. And comfortably cool, despite the August heat.

"I'm losing him, Beth."

Beth was silent for a moment, her gaze darting toward the framed picture on the corner of her desk. Lisa knew it was a picture of John, Beth's late husband, and that her friend could fully understand the pain of losing the man you loved. "Have you tried talking to him?" Beth finally asked, her eyes unusually somber.

Lisa shook her head. She'd been reading a pamphlet about artificial insemination when he'd come in late one night a little over a week ago, and the frozen look on his face had been haunting her ever since. "It's a little difficult to talk to someone who's never around." Her throat thickened with tears. For weeks he crawled into bed at night long after she was asleep and was up before she awoke.

"John and I couldn't have children, either. Did I ever tell you that?"

Lisa's head shot up. "No! I thought you'd just been waiting until the clinic was up and running."

Beth shook her head, glancing again at the picture of her husband. "We were genetically incompatible. I miscarried a couple of times after we were first married, but neither one of us expected to hear the doctor tell us that I'd probably never carry a baby to term, and that if I did, chances were it would suffer severe defects.''

Lisa was shocked. She'd never guessed. Beth and John had always been so cheerful, so obviously happy with their life together. "How did you get over it?" she asked.

Beth shrugged. "It was hard at first, of course. But we'd both come from big families, and neither one of us had ever had a burning need to produce a child. Quite the opposite, as a matter of fact. We appreciated the peace we found alone together. But still, having a family was the natural course of things, so we'd decided to do it while we were still young—that way we'd have a lot of golden years afterward. Naturally, when we were first told we couldn't have children, we suddenly wanted them a lot. But once we got used to the idea of a whole lifetime of golden years, it wasn't so bad. We had more time for each other than our friends did—their time was taken up with feedings and diapering and pacing the floor with crying infants. As it turned out, I'm thankful for every moment of that time.''

Lisa gaped at her friend. "You amaze me, you know that? You've been through so much, but you're one of the most cheerful and optimistic people I know.''

"Well, look at my life." Beth waved a hand at the room around her, the walls adorned with plaques, commendations and many many baby photos—Beth's success stories. "How can I not be happy? I have a job I love, friends enough to chase away the loneliness, enough money to do what I want to do—and I have memories of a love most people are never lucky enough to find. But then, you know all about that once-in-a-lifetime love. You and Marcus are in with the lucky few."

Lisa nodded.

"And that's why I can't just sit back and watch you two fall apart."

"I can't watch it, either, Beth. Which is why I'm here." Lisa smoothed a wrinkle from the skirt of her pale blue suit. "I've got to do something. A lot of Marcus's problem is that he knows how badly I wanted to have a child, and he thinks his inability to give me one is cheating me out of my life's dream. I'm sure that's why he won't consider adoption. He seems to think that would be shortchanging me, raising another woman's child when I'm perfectly capable of giving birth to my own."

"I guess that makes some sort of sense," Beth said. She leaned her forearms against the edge of her desk and folded her hands in front of her ample chest, just as she had the day she'd told them that Marcus was sterile.

"He's against artificial insemination, too, of course, but you know Marcus," Lisa rushed on. "He'd make a wonderful father. And with insemination he wouldn't have to feel guilty anymore. He wouldn't have to feel like I've been cheated."

Beth spread her hands wide. "That's what I've been telling you all along, Lis. I've thought artificial insemination was your answer from the first, but it's not me you have to convince."

Lisa sat back hard in her chair. "I know. So how do I convince my husband that it's a good thing to impregnate myself with another man's seed?"

"You're a doctor, Lis. You know that part of it is little more than a medical procedure, like getting someone else's blood. We have blood banks. We have sperm banks. Legally, and every other way that really counts, the baby would belong to Marcus."

Lisa knew that. She crossed one leg over the other. "How is the donor selection actually made?"

Beth pulled what looked like a homemade catalog from a pile in front of her and tossed it to the outside edge of her desk, just within Lisa's reach. "You look through there and you pick one."

Lisa took the catalog, opening it slowly. She scanned the first couple of entries. "These listings are incredibly thorough," she said, glancing up at Beth. She'd expected to see physical characteristics, medical history, maybe even an IQ, but the records also contained notations of schooling, of likes and dislikes, habits.

"But remember, they only represent the final product of one particular genetic toss-up, mixed with an unknown environmental upbringing. There are no guarantees."

"No, of course not." Lisa continued reading. If only she could find one with eyes of Marcus's particular shade of blue, with his rich brown hair and quick mind.

"The one on page forty-nine is probably what you're looking for. If I didn't know better, I'd say Marcus was the donor."

Lisa shut the book. "I'm not really in the market."

Beth rocked back in her chair. "Fine. But if you ever decide you are, page forty-nine's there."

Shaking her head, Lisa tried to make herself think clearly, to not let herself hope for—or want—something she couldn't have. "Page forty-nine. It's really that impersonal, is it?"

"Yep."

"But what about the donors? Couldn't one come back looking for his child?"

Beth shook her head. "Not here they can't. In the first place, a donor must sign a waiver before the process is ever begun. And then, as soon as all medical tests are administered and the man is cleared for donation, all records are destroyed."

"Destroyed? They aren't locked in some cabinet somewhere or sent out into cyberspace?"

"We destroy them, as is the common practice at most fertility clinics."

Lisa folded her hands, rubbing her thumbs together. Back and forth. Back and forth. "So what happens after a donor is chosen?" She was just curious. It was fascinating what medical science could do.

"The mother has a physical, blood tests for HIV, rubella and so on."

"I just had my yearly last week, and I've been having that blood work done each year since Marcus and I first started trying to have a family,'' Lisa said.

Not that it mattered. She couldn't seriously consider any of this. Not without Marcus's support. She folded her arms across her chest.

Beth smiled. ''I thought you weren't in the market.''

''I'm not.'' She couldn't be.

''Well, if you were, you'd need to get out your ovulation kit again, back to the old basil thermometer every day. And as soon as you begin ovulating, you have an ultrasound done and a blood test to show your hormone level. Then come to see me within the next twelve to thirty-six hours. But remember to give me at least an hour to thaw page forty-nine.'' Beth grinned.

''That's really all there is to it?''

''For you it is. The important forms have already been signed.''

''They can't be.'' She knew Marcus had to sign a waiver, allowing her to have the procedure done. Because, legally, married to her, the baby would be his responsibility, too.

Beth pulled a thick folder from a cabinet behind her. ''Remember that first time you two came in here— professionally, that is?''

Lisa remembered back to the day she and Marcus had first come in for testing. They'd been so full of hope. Beth had asked them if they were willing to do whatever it took to have a baby. They'd both replied with an emphatic yes. And she'd given them each a stack of papers to take home, red tape that could slow down the process if they had to stop and sign for each procedure. They'd signed them all that night and Lisa had returned them the next day.

"There wasn't anything about…"

"Yes, there was. I have his signed waiver right here." Beth pulled a sheet of paper from the file.

Frowning, Lisa leaned forward. It was Marcus's signature all right. "But he wouldn't have…"

Lisa thought back to that night. Marcus had gone into the office the minute they'd arrived home. He'd come back out with the completed stack of papers in record time and tossed it on the hall table, as if it wasn't the least bit important. He'd just wanted to be done with it, so sure that they weren't going to need anything but the basic tests to set their minds at ease, certain they'd conceive as soon as they quit trying so hard. He hadn't read the papers.

"It's notarized," was all she could think of to say, still staring at the form. The other information had been typed in. Marcus had simply scrawled his signature across the bottom.

Beth was nodding. "I had it done here, along with a stack of other things. At the time, I really didn't think we were going to need it."

Lisa remembered Beth saying much the same thing that first day. She'd thought that having the tests would simply help them relax and let nature take its course. It was probably the only thing Marcus had heard that whole afternoon. The only thing he'd wanted to hear. Which was another reason it had hit him so hard when they'd finally learned the truth. Until that point he hadn't even allowed the possibility of sterility to enter his mind.

"He didn't read what he was signing," Lisa finally said.

"Were you with him?"

"No." She'd been in the bathroom, drying tears she didn't want him to see. Because she'd had a feeling, even if he hadn't, that they had a problem. She was a doctor, and her instincts had been crying out for months. Oftentimes a couple couldn't conceive while trying too hard because they made love strictly to have babies. She and Marcus had always made love because they couldn't stop themselves.

"Then you don't know that he didn't read it, Lis. It's possible that he read what he was signing and, dismissing it as an impossibility, signed it, anyway, just to avoid further discussion. Marcus has always thought he could control the world, or at least his part of it."

Lisa smiled sadly. "He's always been able to until now."

Beth's eyes softened. "So what's it going to be, Lis? Are you going to pull out that ovulation kit?"

Lisa looked at the paper again. At Marcus's scrawl across the bottom. Unable to speak through her tears, she shook her head.

CHAPTER FOUR

OLIVER WEBSTER was worried. His thirty years as a professor of law at Yale had in no way prepared him to deal with the problems facing his daughter's marriage. He had no idea how to help Lisa and Marcus, what to even suggest to them. But he knew someone who might have more answers than he did. Lisa's friend, Beth Montague. He had a hunch just talking with Beth would make him feel better. It usually did.

He stopped by her office on his way home from his volunteer shift at the hospital. He'd been taking a stint every week since Barbara had died, having found during his wife's prolonged illness how badly the hospital was in need of volunteers. Helping other people who were suffering as she had made him feel a little closer to Barbara. But lately he'd been looking in on Beth on a fairly regular basis, as well.

Her office door was open and she was sitting behind her desk engrossed in a textbook that looked as big as his law tomes.

He tapped lightly on the door. "Am I interrupting something?"

"Oliver!" Her head shot up, her studious expression replaced with a welcoming grin. "I was wondering if you were going to stop by. How were things on the ward this afternoon?''

It pleased him that she remembered his schedule. "Rosie Gardner's back in. She's developed an infection at her dialysis sight, but they've got it under control.'' He shoved his hands into the pockets of the tweed jacket he wore even in the heat. "I, uh, wanted to talk to you about something. Do you mind if I sit down?''

"Of course not. Have a seat.'' She came around the desk and joined him. "What's up?''

"I'm more than a little concerned about Lisa and Marcus. The last time we had dinner together, all three of us, was two months ago. They're both working themselves to death.''

Beth grimaced, her round features serious. "I know.''

"The thing is, I know what the loss of a child, or the loss of the ability to have a child, can do to a marriage.'' It chilled him even to think about that time in his life.

"I know you do.'' Her eyes brimmed with sympathy.

"Eighty percent of the marriages that go through it fail afterward, did you know that?''

"I didn't, but I'm not surprised. I also don't think Lisa and Marcus are in that eighty percent.''

Oliver smiled, feeling better already. "Somehow I didn't think you would. And I remember John saying that once you'd made your mind up about something, everyone involved may just as well accept it as fact.''

Though Beth's husband had been several years his

junior, he'd enjoyed his conversations with his younger colleague. It was through Oliver's connection with John that Beth and Lisa had first met. During one of her mother's bad spells, Lisa had accompanied Oliver to a university function where John and Beth were in attendance. Lisa had just started her residency at Thornton Memorial Hospital at the time, and Beth had immediately taken her under her wing.

"So, are we going to have dinner or do you have to hurry off?" Beth asked. Her plump cheeks had a way of dimpling when she smiled that made him feel like smiling, too.

"Dinner, most definitely," Oliver replied, offering her his arm. He refused to dwell on the twinge of unease he felt as he escorted Beth out to his car. There was absolutely nothing wrong with the friendship he and Beth had developed over the past year. Neither of them was looking for passion; each respected that the other had already had that once-in-a-lifetime privilege. But neither had mentioned the friendship to Lisa, either. Oliver wasn't sure how his daughter would feel about his befriending a woman almost young enough to be his daughter.

Almost, but not quite, Oliver reminded himself as he sat across from Beth at their favorite Chinese restaurant. At fifty-three, he still had a lot of years ahead of him. And if dinner once a week with a woman who made him smile made those years happier ones, where was the harm in that?

"I GOT ALL THE FIGURES you needed, Mr. Cartwright. A couple of the properties look promising for Cartwright warehouses. The rest I'd leave alone."

Marcus glanced up from the report he'd been study-ing to find his long-haired executive assistant at the door to his office. "Thanks, Ron. Leave them there on the table, will you please?" He returned his attention to his report.

"Yes, sir." Ron Campbell did as he asked and then hesitated by the door.

Marcus looked up again. "Was there something else?"

"Not really, sir. It's just that, I hope you don't mind my asking, but you and Mrs. Cartwright aren't plan-ning on moving, are you, sir? That property you had me check in Chicago is residential."

Marcus swore silently, tired to the bone. He should have done that investigating himself. He knew how thorough Ron was, too thorough to simply call for terms as Marcus had asked him to. Which was the reason Ron had reached such an elevated position within Cartwright Enterprises at the tender age of twenty-five, in spite of his ponytail.

"We're doing a lot more business in the Midwest. I thought it might be beneficial to have a home there," he said. "Even the nicest hotels get old after a while."

Ron nodded and left, not looking completely satis-fied, and Marcus couldn't really blame him. He trav-eled to Chicago once, maybe twice, a year. Certainly not enough to warrant a home as nice as the one he'd had Ron check on. But Ron didn't need to know that Marcus wanted the house so that he'd have a place to go when he gave Lisa her freedom. A man of action, he wasn't sure he was going to be able to exist in their current stalemate much longer. More importantly, he didn't think Lisa could, either.

LISA COULDN'T SLEEP. She'd been restless ever since she'd stopped by Beth's office earlier that day, but the restlessness solidified into guilt as soon as she climbed into bed and turned out the light. Rolling over to Marcus's empty side of the bed, she flipped on his bedside lamp and flopped back down to hug his pillow to her breasts. She kept thinking about page forty-nine, and every time she caught her mind dwelling on that anonymous specimen, she felt as if she was being unfaithful to her husband.

Where *was* Marcus, anyway? It was almost one o'clock in the morning. She needed his arms around her to chase away the uneasiness of the day, to surround her with his love and convince her they weren't falling apart.

Beth and John had overcome childlessness quite successfully, happily, even. Surely the love she and Marcus shared was every bit as strong. Still clutching Marcus's pillow, she rolled over and looked around their room. Elegant to the core, it could have been showcased in *House & Garden* magazine, and probably had been when Marcus's parents were still alive.

But her gaze didn't fall on the matching Queen Anne furnishings or the professionally decorated walls and floor. She glanced, instead, at the little gold jewelry box Marcus had bought for her at an antique fair on their honeymoon, at the Norman Rockwell original she'd surprised him with for his thirtieth birthday, at the numerous photos on her dresser and his. At the *his* and *hers* rocking chairs they'd laughingly picked out together when they'd gotten engaged. They'd planned to rock their babies in those chairs—and grow old in them together.

But there weren't any babies to rock. And Lisa wasn't putting much stock in their growing old together, either. Not lately.

The light was still on and Lisa was lying awake in their bed when Marcus finally came in, pulling off his tie, almost an hour later.

"Hard night?" she asked softly.

"This dragging George Blake into the nineties—I don't know who it's hurting more, him or me," Marcus said with a self-derisive chuckle, sitting down to untie his shoes.

"He's still fighting you on things?" Marcus looked like he'd aged ten years in the past twelve months. There were new lines on his forehead and around his eyes.

"Sometimes. But it's even worse when he doesn't. Today he was as docile as a lamb, and I hated to see it. The man built an empire from a single five-and-dime store. He didn't do that by sitting back and taking whatever comes. And every time I have to tell him that his way won't work anymore, every time he nods and gives up without a fight, I feel like I'm killing part of a legend."

Lisa watched him unbutton his shirt. She loved Marcus for caring about an old man's feelings, but she hated seeing him beat himself up over it. "He didn't work his entire life to have the Blake's department stores go bankrupt.''

"You're right, of course.'' Marcus stepped out of his slacks and tossed them on the valet. "It's just been a long day.''

Padding naked to the bed, he clicked off the light and slid in beside her.

"Thanks, Lis. I was beginning to feel like the big bad wolf.''

"You're a good man, you know that, Mr. Cartwright?'' Lisa asked, taking him in her arms automatically, before she remembered that they weren't doing that anymore. She tensed, afraid he would push her away.

"I bet you say that to all the guys, don't you?'' he teased, reminiscent of the old days when he'd been completely confident in his ability to give her whatever she wanted. But tonight, as he leaned over to kiss her, there was no sign of the arrogance that usually accompanied the remark.

It had been so long since Marcus had touched her that Lisa's entire body responded to that first stroke of his lips. The blood surged in her veins. Her nerves sang in anticipation—and relief. She'd obviously misread the last month of abstinence. Marcus still wanted her; he'd just needed her to come to him. Another first. But one she could live with. Pushing the thoughts of the day from her mind, she gave herself up to the magic that only Marcus could bring her.

This was all she needed. All either of them needed. They could make it through anything else when they shared a love this passionate.

It took her a moment to realize that Marcus wasn't sharing her passion. His body was ready, she could feel his rigid penis against her thigh, but he'd stopped kissing her and was pulling her gown down where it had ridden up over her hips.

"What..." Her voice trailed off as he pulled away from her and lay back, his shoulders propped against the headboard.

"I'm sorry," he said.

The words sounded so final.

She sat up, facing him. "Marcus? What's wrong?" Had something terrible happened that he hadn't told her about? Something more than George Blake's coming-of-age? She wanted to turn the light back on, to see his expression more clearly than the moonlight coming through the window allowed, but fear held her paralyzed.

"We can't go on this way, Lis."

She wasn't ready. "What way? What are you talking about?"

"Us. Our lives. Both of us working ourselves to death, neither of us happy."

Lisa had to touch him, to draw her strength from him, just as she always did when life looked as if it was going to be more than she could bear. "I love you," she said, putting her hand on his thigh, soaking up his warmth.

"And I love you." His hand covered hers, his fingers wrapping around her knuckles. "But don't you sometimes wonder what your life would be like with someone else? Honestly?"

Lisa snatched her hand away, attacked by a vision

of that lipstick on his shirt collar. Did he think *his* life would be better with someone else? That his need to fill his empty house with a passel of children would just vanish?

"No," she finally said slowly, firmly. "I've known since the moment we met that you were the only one for me." There was no room for pride in the desperation she was feeling; maybe that would come later, but for now she wasn't going to give up on all that they were together without a fight.

"But back then, we thought I could give you everything," he said. "And while I *can* still provide your creature comforts, we've got to face the fact that I'll never be able to give you the one thing you want most to have."

Relief flooded through her; another woman wasn't the problem. "You're wrong, Marcus," she said softly, rubbing her hand along his thigh again. "*You* are the one thing I want most to have. You always have been. That hasn't changed. And it never will."

With a muffled oath Marcus stood up and pulled on a pair of sweatpants. "We can't keep avoiding the issue here, Lisa. You can't tell me you're happy, that you've been happy these past months. I know you too well. And I can't continue to get up at dawn every morning to avoid the sadness I know I'm going to see in your eyes."

Lisa sat frozen. Feeling nothing. "What are you suggesting?"

He ran his fingers through his hair, his frustration spilling over into the room he paced. "I don't know what to suggest, or I'd have done something long before now. It looks to me like we've tried everything there is to try, Lis. And it's just not working. Maybe it's time to face the fact that there's nothing *to* do, nothing that will make this better for both of us. Hell, I didn't want to get into this tonight." He strode over to the window, a lion caged.

"Are you telling me you want a divorce?" she asked. She'd never felt so numb.

"No! Yes. I don't know, Lis." He turned to look at her, his blue gaze piercing. "How *do* you know when it's over?"

Somehow she held his gaze without flinching. "I'm not sure. I never thought it would be."

"Every time I look at you, I know I've failed you," he said, finally coming back to sit on the edge of the bed beside her.

She cupped his face. "Oh, no, Marcus. Never. Never have you failed me. Not in any way that matters. What's happened is not your fault."

He took her hands from his face, then held one on his leg between both of his. "It's not just my sterility, Lis." He tapped their hands against his thigh, accenting each word. "It's the rest of it, too. My inability to consider any of your options. I wanted to. God knows I've tried to consider adoption, but I just can't get past the rage I feel every time I think about your having to just make do. I just can't accept a lifetime of pretending, not for me, but especially not for you."

"Adopting a child wouldn't *be* pretending. We'd be his real parents, Marcus. He'd belong to us, just like we belong to each other."

"You can try to make it sound pretty, Lis, but it

wouldn't be the same as having a baby come from
your own body, feeling your belly swell with his
growth, nursing him. Those are the things I'd be denying you. Things I know you want so badly that not
having them makes you cry." He paused. "Things
you're perfectly capable of having with someone
else."

Lisa cursed all those times she and Marcus had
dreamed aloud together about the family they'd have,
cursed the intimate longings she'd confessed to him.
"I only wanted those things with you, Marcus, not
with anybody else. It wouldn't mean anything with
anybody else."

He stood up again. "Of course, you think that now,
honey, because you have no idea who might be out
there. You haven't looked. But how long do you think
it will be before you start to wonder? How long before
these empty rooms start getting to you like they're
getting to me?"

Telling herself to stand, to be strong, Lisa slid off
the bed and faced the man she couldn't live without.

"Can you tell me, honestly, that you want your freedom?" she asked. "That this…this thing between us
has killed your love for me?"

She could see his self-deprecating smile even as he
hooked his hand around her neck and pulled her to
him. "Sometimes I wish it had, honey. It would be
much easier to leave you to the life you deserve if I
didn't love you so damn much. But I guess you can
add selfishness to my list of shortcomings, because,
God help me, so far I can't seem to walk out that
door."

The knot in Lisa's stomach loosened a little. "Thank God," she said. Her eyes filled with tears, which overflowed and spilled down her cheeks, wetting his chest.

He crushed her to him and held her tight. "If I were any kind of man, I'd let you go. I'd free you to find someone else." The words sounded as if they were being dragged from him.

Lisa looked up at her husband, took in his strong handsome features despite the shadows and the blur of her tears. "You are the best kind of man, Marcus Cartwright. Don't you ever doubt that."

"So what are we going to do, Lis? We're right back where we started."

"I don't know," Lisa said. But deep inside, she did know. She knew what she was going to have to do—not just for herself, but for Marcus. Because she knew her husband, his sense of honor. Eventually he would let his misplaced sense of failure convince him to leave her, to release her to what he saw as a happier life for her. But she also knew that when he did that, he'd have no life at all. He'd never have the chance to be the father he was meant to be. The father *he* wanted to be as much or more than she wanted to be a mother. He'd never have the family he'd been dreaming about all his lonely life.

Not unless she took the decision out of his hands.

SICK WITH ANXIETY, with guilt, with the million doubts that had been whirling around inside her all week, Lisa once again walked into Beth's office. She was ovulating. According to the results of the blood test, her hormone level was optimum. It was time.

Beth glanced up as Lisa came in, took one look at her face and came around the desk. "Hey, there's no reason to rush into this if you aren't ready, Lis," she said, placing a hand on her arm. "It's not too late to back out, try again next month if you want to. Or not."

Lisa thought of Marcus's death grip on her that night a week ago. She didn't know how much time she had left.

"What? And waste poor thawed-out page forty-nine?" she joked. She had no intention of backing out on what might be Marcus's only shot at the life he'd worked so hard for.

Beth smiled, but her eyes were filled with concern. "Seriously, Lis. I'm starting to feel as if I've pushed you into this. It has to be something you want deep in your heart. I don't need to remind you we're talking about the possibility of another life here."

The thrill that shot through Lisa at the mention of that life was all the incentive she needed. "I'm ready, Beth. Now quit being a mother hen and hurry up and make me a mother before I have a premature bout of morning sickness."

Beth nodded. "Okay. Everything's ready. Right down the hall. But if you want to change your mind, just say the word."

Lisa found it oddly amusing that Beth was the one getting cold feet.

LISA LOST HER lunch. But not until she'd waited the obligatory couple of minutes after Beth, clad in a white lab coat, had finished injecting her with the seed she hoped would create a new life for her and Marcus. She'd even managed to get herself back into the pale peach suit she'd donned that morning, in spite of the row of tiny buttons on the jacket. It was when she'd slipped the paperwork Beth had given her into her purse that she'd had to dart for the bathroom.

She wished she could lose the memory of the past half hour as thoroughly as she'd lost the contents of her stomach. She felt as if she'd betrayed the vows she'd made to Marcus on their wedding day.

She'd almost yelled at Beth to stop when Beth had told her she was about to pass the specimen. But her mind had been too filled with Marcus's desperation when they'd finally gone back to bed that night a week ago, as if, through sheer strength of will, he could make everything right for them. The frenzy with which he'd made love to her had convinced her more than anything that he knew it was only a matter of time before he forced himself to leave her.

But the same sense of honor that would force him to go would also force him to stay once he learned she was pregnant. Wouldn't it? He'd stay long enough to fall in love with their baby, to see that Lisa was right, that what she'd just done was their route to happiness. Wouldn't he?

Lisa's stomach turned over again as the panic she'd been holding at bay all week finally got the better of her. What if she'd just made an irrevocable mistake? What if Marcus didn't accept this baby as his own? What if he couldn't forgive her for what she'd just done? Oh, God, what if she lost him, anyway?

Leaning over the toilet bowl in the clinic's bathroom a second time, Lisa held her hair back and was sick again.

"Lisa? You okay in there?"

"Fine." Lisa tried to inject some conviction into her voice. Being sick had always terrified her.

A key scraped in the lock and Beth's face appeared around the edge of the partially open door. Apparently Lisa hadn't been convincing enough.

Her friend was inside the lavatory with the door shut behind her in a flash. She felt for Lisa's pulse.

Lisa smiled at her friend's show of concern. "I really am fine, Beth. Just not used to handling the big stuff on my own. Marcus is usually around to carry half the burden." Beth checked her pulse, anyway. "I hadn't realized just how much I'd come to depend on his opinion when I'm making a decision. I really like having him there to confide in."

"So you still haven't told Marcus about this," Beth said.

Lisa shook her head.

"And you're sick with guilt."

"That and a few other pressing emotions. Like panic."

Beth nodded. "A little bit of panic is to be expected, even when a couple has been planning this together for months. Having a baby's a big step."

There it was again. That tiny thrill that was like nothing else Lisa had ever felt. A baby. A new life. A son or daughter to fill the empty rooms in Marcus's house. In his life. And hers.

"Do you think it'll take?" she asked Beth, rubbing her hand over her flat belly.

"The first time? Maybe. Chances are, though, it won't."

Lisa didn't think she could go through this again. "It won't?"

"Only twenty percent conceive the first time out."

Twenty percent. Lisa started to feel sick again, though for an entirely different reason. Did she have enough time to wait another month? Would Marcus give her that long before he did the gentlemanly thing, the honorable thing, and walked out on her?

Could she live with him for another whole month without telling him what she'd done? Could she go through this again?

"How long till we know?" she asked.

"We can do an early detection in a couple of days. It'll be two weeks before we'll really know for sure. But, if you're so inclined, you can have a blood test done each day, since you're here, anyway. That way you'll know for certain the first second it's possible to tell."

Two weeks. Could she wait two weeks? Lisa didn't think it was possible. She also didn't see where she had any other choice.

THAT AFTERNOON Lisa did something she'd never done before. As soon as Hannah was finished for the day, Lisa called Marcus at work and left him a message to come home. Then she showered and changed into a sexy black lace nightie and waited for him to arrive. Twenty minutes later she heard him at the front door.

"Lisa?" he called the moment he stepped over the threshold. "What's wrong—" He stopped abruptly as soon as he caught sight of her coming into the foyer. She was barefoot and practically naked, her hair a wild tangle around her shoulders.

Wrapping her arms around his neck, Lisa pulled his head down for a scorching kiss before he could ask any more questions. She'd startled him. Good. She could feel his confusion in his kiss, in the way it took him just a fraction of a second to respond. She poured every ounce of passion she had into that kiss, giving him all her love, promising him it had always been, and always would be, his alone.

His briefcase dropped to the floor at their feet as he scooped her up into his arms and carried her into the living room, falling with her on the thick velvet couch.

"I think I'm glad you called," he murmured into her ear as he worked his way around her neck, leaving hot little kisses in his wake.

"Me, too." He had no idea how glad, how badly Lisa needed to wipe away the thought of another man's seed in her body.

Their lovemaking, there on the couch, was more intensely passionate than Lisa had ever known. It was almost as if Marcus sensed her desperate need for him, and it triggered an answering need in him. And when, sometime later, he finally exploded inside her, Lisa knew it was then that their baby had been conceived. Because it was only after Marcus's love had mixed with that tiny bud of life inside of her that she could relax enough to accept the seed of another man into her womb.

He had a second orgasm before he finally led her upstairs to their bedroom, and while Lisa rode the waves with him every inch of the way, she couldn't help being aware, that second time, of a difference in Marcus's touch, an edge that had never been there before. She wasn't sure what it meant.

"I could get used to coming home early," he said later, holding her against him in the middle of their bed.

"Mmm. Me, too. 'Course the neighbors might begin to talk about the steam coming off our roof every afternoon."

Marcus chuckled, a warm rumble beneath her ear. "People have always talked about us, Lis. They can't figure out why I prefer to spend my free time with you rather than out hitting a little white ball around a bunch of manicured grass."

"Hey! I take my share of it, too. I'm always the odd one out when the girls get together in the cafeteria to complain about picking up their husband's dirty socks."

He pulled her closer. "I guess we're luckier than we think sometimes, huh?" he asked, but he didn't sound convinced.

"We sure are," Lisa said, believing the words, but knowing full well that luck, like their love, may not be enough to save their marriage.

She lay awake in his arms long after he'd fallen into an exhausted sleep. She continued to be besieged with moments of sheer panic, when she imagined the disgust, the breach of trust she'd see in Marcus's eyes once he knew what she'd done. She prayed over and over, in those moments, that the seed hadn't taken, that Marcus would never know how she'd betrayed him.

But as her mind grew weary, her thoughts drifted to her old dream, the one where Marcus was holding their baby in his big strong arms, cradling it against him, protecting it. And always in the dream, Marcus's eyes were filled with love, his voice echoing with laughter.

The dream vanished suddenly when, out of the darkness, it finally came to her what had been different about Marcus's lovemaking that second time. He hadn't held her as if he was protecting her, but more as if he was letting her go.

As if he'd been saying goodbye.

CHAPTER FIVE

RON CAMPBELL stuck his head into Marcus's office one afternoon almost two weeks later. "The house is yours, Mr. Cartwright."

"Thanks, Ron." Marcus hated the place already.

The young man came into his office and sat down in one of the huge maroon chairs in front of Marcus's desk, handing Marcus a fax with the final figures on it, along with a copy of the deed.

"They're overnighting the keys. You should have them sometime tomorrow."

"Fine. As soon as they arrive, I'd like you to fly out and get it furnished for me." He'd live with whatever choices Ron made, though judging from the ponytail hanging down the young man's back, Marcus had a feeling their tastes were very different.

"Of course. I can do it this week if you'd like. Should I consult Mrs. Cartwright on her preferences?"

Marcus shook his head, already feeling the overwhelming loss that was going to leave him incomplete for the rest of his life. "She's got a lot on her mind right now. Just go ahead and use your own judgment."

Oh, Lisa. How am I ever going to live without you?

MARCUS LEFT WORK early that Friday. He'd just received a telephone call from Ron telling him the house would be ready the following day. He couldn't stall any longer. He waited only until he knew the housekeeper would be gone for the day and then packed up his briefcase. He wasn't sure how soon he'd be back.

"You okay?" Marge asked, a concerned frown marking her matronly brow as Marcus told her he was leaving and wouldn't be back before Monday.

"Fine." Truth was he'd never felt worse in his life. But he was finally doing something. It beat these past months of procrastinating.

Marge couldn't seem to let it go, and her words stopped him as he was about to step through the door. "You're sure nothing's wrong, Marcus?"

He sighed. "Nothing a day or two of rest won't fix."

"So why the new house in Chicago?"

He opened his mouth to tell her. She'd know soon enough, anyway. But the words just wouldn't come. "We've doubled our Midwest holdings in the past two years. It's time to have a base there."

"You haven't kept me here all these years for being stupid, Marcus. I just want you to know that I'm here if there's anything I can do."

Warmed by his secretary's words, he nodded and left. There wasn't anything Marge could do. There wasn't anything *anybody* could do.

Meaning to go straight home and get it over with, Marcus found himself heading toward Yale, instead. With Oliver Webster only a couple of blocks away, it wouldn't be right if he left without saying goodbye.

Walking across the sixteen-acre village green, bordered on three sides by churches as old as New Haven, and by Yale on the fourth, Marcus was surrounded by monuments of his ancestors. Straight in front of him was Center Congregational, the church his great-great-great grandfather had helped build with his own hands.

And when Marcus turned, Yale yawned before him, a huge testimony to the few men, Harvard graduates, a Cartwright among them, who'd had a dream, and the determination to see it through. Not only had they founded a new university, they'd fought the battle to see Yale permanently settled in New Haven, rather than one of the larger towns in the new Connecticut territory.

That was the stock from which Marcus had come, doers all. They'd passed on their determination from generation to generation, producing heirs to carry on the tradition of excellence. Each generation of Cartwrights had fulfilled that responsibility. Until now. Until Marcus. The Cartwright line was going to end with him.

Striding across campus as if he could outdistance the voices of his disappointed ancestors, Marcus hardly noticed the bustling students around him, the comfort of the warm late-summer day, the beauty that the coming fall promised to be with the abundance of huge maple trees surrounding him. He reached his father-in-law's office in record time.

Oliver's door was windowed, and looking in, Marcus couldn't help but smile, though it was a smile tinged with sadness. Oliver was sitting behind his huge oak desk surrounded by books of every shape and size—on the floor around him, lining the shelves along the walls, even on the chairs across from him. With his spectacles on, his brow furrowed, Oliver looked like every student's worst nightmare of an intimidating college professor. Few people knew just what a softy Oliver Webster really was.

Marcus knocked on the door.

"Come in," the older man called gruffly, not looking up from the volume in front of him.

"You got a minute?" Marcus asked.

"Marcus! Of course, son, come in. Have a seat."

Oliver was dressed as usual in a tweed sport coat, slacks and a skinny tie that had been out of fashion for more years than it had been in. Marcus felt a rush of affection for his father-in-law, unlike any feeling he'd ever had for his own father.

"This is difficult," Marcus said, seated in front of Oliver's desk, his elbows on his knees. He looked up at his father-in-law, at the understanding in Oliver's eyes, and suddenly felt a dam burst inside him. "I'm making your daughter miserable, Oliver. I can't remember the last time I saw joy in her eyes. These days they're either unhappy or attempting to mask unhappiness."

"Give her time, son. She'll come around."

Marcus shook his head. He couldn't allow himself to buy into false hopes any longer. "Time isn't going to change our problem. It only seems to be making it worse. These past couple of weeks Lisa hasn't just been unhappy. She's been edgy, nervous. She's hiding her thoughts from me." That was what had finally convinced Marcus to give Lisa her freedom. He couldn't bear it that his wife no longer felt she could confide in him, that he was losing her friendship along with everything else.

"Come to think of it, she's been that way the few times I've seen her, too," Oliver said, frowning. "Maybe we should have a talk with that girl, huh?"

"She and I have done all the talking we can do." Marcus shook his head a second time. "Talk can't change what's ailing us, Oliver. You know that as well I do. Lisa was meant to be a mother, and she's not going to feel fulfilled and happy until she is one."

"Have you two talked more about adoption, then?"

"Again, there's no point. I have no intention of forcing Lisa to settle for someone else's child when she's perfectly capable of having her own. I won't rob her of the experience of feeling her baby kick inside her, of having him nestled at her breast or seeing herself when she looks in his eyes."

"The way my daughter feels about you would more than compensate her for missing those things."

"I'm not so sure about that. But even if it does now, for how long? What if we find out, too late, that it doesn't compensate at all?"

Oliver spread his hands wide. "Do we ever have such guarantees?"

"It's a moot point, regardless," Marcus said, standing. "Because while Lisa needs to be a mother, I am not meant to be a father."

"What nonsense is this?" Oliver stood, too, facing Marcus. "You'd make a wonderful father."

"Apparently the good Lord doesn't agree with you." Marcus held up his hand, warding off Oliver's next words. "Say what you will, Oliver, but I've thought about this long and hard. Hell, sometimes it feels as though I think of nothing else. And the only conclusion I come to is that I'm not meant to be a father. It's the only thing that makes my sterility bearable—the thought that maybe I'm sparing some poor kid a bad life."

"I'd be more willing to bet that any child you fathered, by any means, would live a blessed life," Oliver said softly.

Marcus forced himself to look the older man straight in the eye. "I've failed Lisa. Our plans together have become impossible dreams. I do not intend to go on failing her."

"What are you saying, son?" Oliver asked, his brow furrowed.

"I've bought a house in Chicago. I plan to stay there until the divorce is final—maybe forever if Lisa wants our house. I certainly have no need for it."

Oliver fell back into his chair, stunned. "You're walking out on her?"

"Of course not," Marcus said quickly. "I'll be there for her until the day I die, if she needs me to be. I'm simply giving her the freedom to find another man to build her dreams around. I hope, in the long run, I'll be making her happy again."

"And this is what you want? For another man to father Lisa's children? You trust another man to teach them, to provide for them, to love them?"

Marcus sat back down, knowing he'd lost, even while Oliver was still fighting for him. The thought of Lisa in another man's arms made him want to kill. But what kind of man would he be to deny her the chance? Didn't loving her mean making her happy? And if that meant freeing her to find the dreams he couldn't give her, what choice did he have?

"I trust Lisa to choose a man who would be worthy of her children," he said, the words cutting a wound clear to his soul.

"You're determined to do this?"

"I am."

"What about your own happiness, son?"

"I'll be a lot happier than I am now just knowing she's happy again."

Who the hell am I kidding? he thought. *If I get through the next twenty-four hours, it'll be a miracle.*

FEELING LIKE A MAN convicted for a crime he didn't commit, Marcus walked slowly up the front steps of the house he'd grown up in. The late-August heat was sapping his strength, but he wouldn't take off his jacket. He couldn't afford to get comfortable. Just a little bit longer, and he could crawl away and begin the long arduous chore of healing his wounds. One thing was for sure. He was going to be healing them alone.

The house was silent when he let himself in. He was glad he'd waited until Hannah was gone before confronting Lisa. He couldn't stand to think of someone else overhearing the demise of his marriage.

"Lis? You home?" he called, dropping his keys into the little brass tray on the side table.

"In here," Lisa called from the living room.

She was sitting on the couch, her legs tucked up

under the skirt of her pale blue suit, hugging one of his mother's brocade throw pillows to her chest. She avoided his eyes when he walked in, killing his last hope that there was another way. His decision was right. It was necessary.

"Our time's up, isn't it, Lis?" he asked, forcing himself to sit down and handle this calmly.

Her gaze flew to his face, stricken, but she looked away again immediately, still hiding from him. He wondered if it was relief she was hiding. She'd probably been ready to do this weeks ago, but knowing Lisa, she'd never be the one to leave him. She'd stand beside him until the end if he asked her to. And as soul destroying as Marcus knew that would be, he was tempted, even now, to ask. If she'd just look at him.

"I bought a house in Chicago," he said. "I can move in anytime."

"What?" she cried, her expression shocked. He had her full attention now. "You're moving? You can't move."

"I thought you'd want this house, but if not, we'll get you another. You can have whatever you want, Lis. What's mine will always be yours. The divorce won't change that." Even as he said the words he wondered if he was trying to hold her with the one thing he'd always known people wanted from him— his money. "Unless you want it to, that is," he added. *Smooth, Cartwright, real smooth.*

"Divorce?" The blood drained from her face. "You're asking for a divorce?"

She wasn't supposed to take it so hard. He wanted

her to be thankful for her freedom, to make this just a little bit easy on him. "It's the only answer, Lis."

She jumped up from the couch. "It's no answer at all! You can't divorce me now. I'm pregnant!" she hollered, throwing the pillow she'd been holding at him.

The pillow hit Marcus in the face and dropped into his lap. Did she say pregnant? Lisa was pregnant? He saw the confirmation in the still way she held herself, the strained look in her face. Relief rushed through him. Profound relief, leaving him weak. He didn't have to leave.

And then it hit him. The baby wasn't his. Couldn't possibly be his. Nor could it be some anonymous donor's; he knew he had to sign a waiver for that to happen, and he hadn't, had he? Somewhere in the back of his mind he wondered if he'd make it to the bathroom in time to be sick. He'd known Lisa wasn't happy. And he'd have bet his life on her fidelity. *Who the hell is this man who'd laid his hands on my wife?* He'd not only lost Lisa's friendship, he'd lost her loyalty. And suddenly nothing mattered. Nothing.

"Who's the father?" he asked, because it seemed like something he should say, not because he ever wanted to know. The deed was done. The whos and whys no longer mattered.

The part of him that was outside the entire scene, watching dispassionately as his life crumbled around him, saw Lisa fall to her knees in front of him. And that same part felt her clutch desperately at his hand with both of hers. It saw the pain in her eyes and wanted to reach out to her, make her pain go away.

But he sat frozen. His love for Lisa, his marriage of ten years, had been a mockery. He'd thought these last couple of weeks of living with Lisa and knowing he was losing her had cost him more emotionally than anything else in his entire life. He'd been wrong.

"Oh, Marcus, I'm so sorry," Lisa was saying. She was crying, too. His slacks were becoming damp with her tears.

He watched her silently, saw her wrenching display of emotion, afraid of how much he was going to feel if he allowed himself to feel.

"I...I didn't mean for you to find out this way," she said brokenly. "I had everything all planned. Oh, Marcus, I did it for you. I love you so much. Please believe me—the last thing I wanted to do was hurt you."

"I'm not hurt," Marcus said. It was true. He wasn't feeling anything at all.

"When you said that about a divorce, the news just came tumbling out. I'm so sorry, honey. There is no father other than you. I haven't been with anybody but you." She looked up, and her big brown eyes, so full of love, implored him to understand. "I was artificially inseminated, Marcus."

He didn't react. All he felt was confusion. She did this without his knowledge or agreement? Or had he... Numb, Marcus just stared at her.

"After my birthday and that horrible conversation we had about knowing when it was over," Lisa went on, "I knew it was only a matter of time before you convinced yourself I'd be happier without you. But you're wrong, Marcus. You're the other half of my—

self, and no other man, and no baby, either, is ever going to complete me the way you do.''

She paused, still gazing up at him, as if waiting for his reaction. When Marcus continued to stare at her silently, she started to speak again, but had to pause when fresh tears choked her. Marcus watched as she blinked them away, swallowed and began again. ''I also know that if you left, *you'd* never be happy again, either.''

Marcus flinched, almost overwhelmed by a pain that was frightening in its split-second intensity. And then it was gone. His happiness wasn't her problem.

''I know you, Marcus,'' she said, her voice firm for the first time since he'd walked in the door. ''You'd have lived out the rest of your life alone, never knowing the greatest of joys, only the greatest of sorrows. And I love you too much to see that happen. So I went to see Beth.''

He said nothing.

''I chose a specimen that matched you completely—brown hair, blue eyes, six-one, 186 pounds—''

''I weigh 180,'' Marcus said. It mattered somehow.

''—even the same blood type,'' she continued, as if he hadn't interrupted. ''It was just one little vial in a bank, Marcus, sort of like blood in a blood bank...'' Her voice trailed off, her eyes still pleading with him to understand.

Rage consumed Marcus, blurring the sight of his wife on her knees in front of his chair. She had another man's seed in her womb. She was his wife, but she had another man's child growing inside of her. He clenched every muscle in his body, willing himself to remain controlled, to keep a hold on the violence shuddering inside of him.

"Say something, Marcus. Please say something." She was crying again. And begging. And no matter what she'd done, he couldn't bear to see her like that.

"You went to Beth," he said, concentrating on that piece of information. His wife had betrayed him, but he was apparently still the only one who knew the delights of her body. At the moment, that small victory hardly seemed to matter.

"She's the only one who knows," Lisa said, her voice contrite.

"What about Oliver?" Marcus asked, thinking of his visit to his father-in-law that afternoon. Had Oliver known?

Lisa shook her head. "Only Beth."

Marcus nodded. He didn't know what else she wanted from him.

"It's our baby, Marcus. Yours as much as mine."

No! his mind screamed. The seed she was carrying had nothing to do with him. He couldn't pretend otherwise.

"You're as much a part of the reason for this baby's existence as I am, Marcus."

She wasn't going to rationalize this one away with pretty words. There was too much at stake.

He heard her crying again, but he didn't look at her. He didn't dare look at her.

"Th-that night I called you home. We made love. That's when our baby was conceived, Marcus. I know. Until *your* love was inside me, I couldn't accept the sperm Beth had given me. My body was rejecting it. Until you.''

More pretty words. Marcus didn't trust himself to speak. He stared straight ahead, wishing she wouldn't touch him, wishing she'd leave him to his numbness. He didn't think he could hold on much longer.

She ran her hand along his forearm. ''Eighty percent of women who are artificially inseminated by a donor don't conceive the first time. But I *knew*, Marcus. That night I knew we'd made a baby.''

Thinking back to that night, to the intensity with which he'd made love to her, remembering how he'd poured his heart and soul into her, Marcus felt used.

And betrayed.

And jealous.

He stood up abruptly and headed for the door before he gave himself another reason to hate himself. *Jealous.* What kind of man did that make him, that he was jealous of his own wife's *ability* to conceive. Jealous because she was having the baby they'd always wanted, that she wouldn't have to *pretend* that she, not someone else, had created their child.

He heard her call after him, but he couldn't slow down. He had to get out of there before he did something he'd regret.

HE DROVE FOR HOURS with no idea where he was going. He didn't care. He just kept driving. Thoughts whirled through his mind, torturing him. Lisa's dream was coming true and his was not, never would. She was moving on without him. They were no longer part of the same whole. He thought he'd prepared himself to face that eventuality. But nothing could have prepared him for the agony that ripped through him now, making him yell out into the silence, bringing tears to his cheeks.

He was surprised to find them there. He hadn't thought himself capable of tears. Hadn't cried since he'd been a young boy, forgotten at boarding school during the first two days of summer vacation one year. It had taken the school that long to locate his parents in Europe and for them send someone to pick him up.

Lisa was having a baby. *Another* man's baby. A stranger had been able to do for her what he could not. No matter how he looked at it, the fact was like acid, eating him up inside.

He drove faster and faster, until the roads became blurred and he was skidding around corners. Finally he checked himself into a run-down motel for the night. It had everything he needed. Which meant no phone.

LISA SPENT THE NIGHT alone, wandering through the rooms of Marcus's family home, touching his things, looking at pictures of the many generations of Cartwrights and worrying herself sick about the man she loved more than life itself. She needed desperately to lean on her best friend, to talk to him, to try to make sense of a world spinning too rapidly out of control— but he'd just walked out on her and she didn't know if he was ever coming back.

When the minutes stretched into hours and it became obvious that Marcus wasn't coming home for dinner, Lisa showered, changed into a pair of jogging pants and one of his Yale sweatshirts, fixed herself some toast and made herself eat it. She was having Marcus's baby, and she was going to take care of it for him, even if he didn't want it. This child would be a Cartwright just like all the other Cartwrights who had left their mark on this town. He would have the same strength of character, the same determination, the same ability to dream. She would make sure of it.

BETH MONTAGUE stayed late at the office on Friday. She always had things she could do, lab reports to go over, dictation to finish, but the work on her desk wasn't what was keeping her there. Oliver was in a meeting at the hospital. He was lobbying for new dialysis equipment for the ward where Barbara had spent so much time during the last years of her life. Beth wondered if it was wrong of her to hope he was still going to stop by after he was done fighting for his wife's cause.

And she worried about what he was going to think when he found out what she and Lisa had done. Would he blame her for her part in Lisa's decision?

The phone on her desk was eerily silent. She'd been waiting all afternoon to see how things had gone between Lisa and Marcus. Why hadn't Lisa called?

Beth picked up the phone to call her friend, but then put it back down. This was a special time for Lisa and Marcus, to be shared by just the two of them. If things went as well as Lisa had hoped, that was. And if they didn't…

Beth's gaze alighted on the picture of her husband. Dear, sweet, absentminded John. How she'd loved him! How she missed him! What would he think of her, interfering like this in her friend's business? She glanced at her watch and then at the door again. What would he think of her sitting here like an adolescent on the off chance her friend's father would stop by?

John's image seemed to be looking at her. She knew he'd say she should have left Lisa and Marcus to deal with their problem on their own. And as usual, he'd have been right. Oliver was going to think the same thing.

John would also consider her kind to befriend his lonely colleague. Though he'd wonder why, if she wanted Oliver to stop by, she hadn't just asked him to. Funny how much older Oliver had seemed than she and John when John and Barbara had been alive.

Barbara. Lisa's mother would have been thrilled to learn she was finally going to be a grandmother. She wouldn't have given the artificial means of conception a thought, other than to be thankful that the option was available. And eventually, with Barbara's help, Oliver would have seen things that way, as well—

"Hi, am I interrupting?"

Beth jumped guiltily at the sound of Oliver's voice. "No, of course not. Come on in. How'd the meeting go?"

Oliver shrugged his broad shoulders. "These things take time. But we're making progress."

He smiled at her and Beth smiled back, telling herself it was natural to feel that little flutter in her stomach. He was an attractive man, that was all. Any woman would find him so. Besides, she was still in love with John.

"Are you free for dinner?" Oliver asked, coming farther into her office.

"As a matter of fact I am." Beth collected her purse, glad to have what time she could with him before he found out about Lisa. She was too keyed up to be alone, in any case. And Oliver was safe. He'd never see her as more than his daughter's plump cheerful friend.

"Has Lisa been to see you again?" Oliver asked. He was looking at his daughter's folder on the top of Beth's desk. "I thought all that was done."

Damn. She'd had the folder by the phone in case Marcus called her. He was bound to have questions once he knew. "Uh, just the usual follow-up," she said now, grabbing the folder. It wasn't her place to tell him what was inside. Oliver was as old-fashioned as the tweed jacket he was wearing. She wasn't sure he'd approve of what his daughter had done or of Beth's role in it. If she had her way, he'd never have to know—except that, of course he would. Oliver knew Marcus was sterile.

Oliver frowned. "What follow-up? It's been more than a year and a half. Is something wrong with her? Something she's not telling me?"

"No! She's fine," Beth said, speaking with her hands, as well as her voice. And as she did, a single piece of paper, the only one not yet fastened in, today's lab report, slipped out of the folder in her hand and fluttered to the floor.

She and Oliver both went for the report, their fingers colliding as they reached it at the same time. Startled at the warmth of his touch, at her inappropriate response to it, Beth snatched back her hand. Oliver picked up the report.

He slumped down in the chair in front of her desk, reading. "Oh, my God."

Beth sat down beside him, looking at the paper still in his hands, wishing she'd been more careful. "It looked like their only hope, Oliver. She seemed convinced it was the right thing to do."

"You don't understand," Oliver said, glancing up at Beth, his brow furrowed. "This makes it all so much worse." He paused. "Because he's leaving her."

"What?" Beth's stomach knotted with dread. And guilt.

"He came to see me this afternoon. He bought a house in Chicago. He wants a divorce. He said he was freeing her to have a family with someone else." Oliver glanced again at the paper in his hand. "He never said—"

"When this afternoon?" Beth interrupted.

"Midafternoon. It was before my three-o'clock class."

"He didn't know." Sick at heart, she thought of the child she'd helped to create, a third life that was now going to suffer—unless Lisa's news would be enough to stop Marcus from leaving. Or would it just send him from her faster?

"He didn't know?" Oliver frowned down at the report.

Beth was surprised at the tenderness that welled up inside her as he struggled to assimilate the truth. She reached over and squeezed his free hand. "She came to see me. We did it all right here."

"Ah." Oliver glanced away, obviously embarrassed, but he didn't look angry. "And it worked?" Was that hope she heard in his voice?

"It worked the first time. I don't know which of us was more shocked."

"I'm going to be a grandpa."

Relief flooded Beth as she heard the boyish wonder in his voice. She sent up a silent prayer that Marcus had been even half as glad to hear the news.

CHAPTER SIX

LISA WAS AFRAID to leave the house. Afraid she'd miss Marcus, afraid he might clear out his things and be gone when she wasn't there. But by Saturday noon, after phoning both the police and every hospital she knew of in a two-hundred-mile radius of New Haven and reassuring herself that Marcus hadn't been in an accident, she was just plain afraid. Where was he? And worse, was he going to even come back?

She didn't call Cartwright Enterprises. She didn't want to hunt him down. She also didn't want to know if he wasn't there.

Forcing herself to keep busy, she spent the afternoon baking and decorating sugar cookies, made from her grandmother's recipe. They were Marcus's favorite kind, and cookies were one thing Hannah never baked. She took a couple of cuts of beef tenderloin filets out to thaw. Marcus loved her filet mignon.

And all the while she worked, the vacant look in Marcus's eyes as he'd sat frozen in their living room the day before haunted her. After more than ten years of loving him, she couldn't begin to guess what he was going to do. She'd hurt him. In his eyes, she'd betrayed him. She'd hoped his finding out that they were finally going to have a baby would make up for the fact that she'd had herself inseminated without telling him. She'd thought it would make a difference to him once he understood that she'd taken another man's seed out of her love for *him*. She'd been wrong. Dreadfully wrong.

And yet, she couldn't regret the tiny life that was even now forming in her womb. Because she knew, in the depths of her soul, that this baby was a product of the love she and Marcus shared. That it was *their* baby, conceived in love.

She talked to Beth on the phone, assuring her friend that everything was fine. She couldn't bring herself to admit that Marcus was gone. That she had no idea when or even if he'd be back. But she couldn't keep up her pretense for long, so she told Beth she'd call her on Monday. Beth sounded delighted for Lisa and Marcus, eager to let her friend go, obviously believing that Lisa and Marcus wanted to be alone. And they were. Just not together.

Oliver called her early Saturday evening, just as she sat back down on the couch after looking out the window, watching for Marcus, for the hundredth time that day.

"Everything okay there?" he asked.

"No." She'd eaten the filet herself, although she'd had to struggle to swallow every bite. "But it will be." *It had to be.*

"Marcus came to see me yesterday, Lisa."

"He did? When? What did he say?" Did her father know where Marcus was?

"That he'd bought a house in Chicago. That he was

leaving you to find someone else, someone who could make your dreams come true.''

Oh. Tears blurred Lisa's eyes. "I'm already pregnant, Dad.''

The silence on the other end of the line was unnerving, but Lisa pushed on, anyway, telling her father about the artificial insemination and that she'd had the procedure without her husband's consent.

"Don't you think he had a right to know beforehand?" She hadn't heard reprimand in her father's voice since she'd been a teenager.

"Of course he did.'' She held back her tears, afraid that once they started falling, they'd never stop. "I can't believe what a mess I've made of everything. But I knew he was thinking about leaving. He'd convinced himself it was the honorable thing to do, to free me to have the life I always wanted. I tried to talk to him about artificial insemination before, several times. He wouldn't even discuss it.'' Suddenly all the frustration from her unsuccessful attempts to convince her husband of the truth, that he gave her the life she'd always wanted, came pouring out.

Her father listened to her silently.

"Marcus is a proud man, honey,'' he said when she'd finally emptied herself of pent-up anguish. "A man used to providing whatever is needed. He's having to take a whole new look at himself, at who and what he is—and what he isn't. He's doing what he thinks is best.''

"So you think he's right to leave?" Lisa asked, incredulous.

"No, honey, I don't. That man loves you to distraction, and I know how happy he makes you."

"Happier than I've ever been in my life. Which is why I went to see Beth. I had to do something, and that seemed like the only answer left. This way Marcus wouldn't feel as if he was cheating me out of anything, and he could still have the child he's always wanted."

"I take it he didn't see it that way."

"He didn't really say *how* he saw it. He just got up and walked out." She twisted the phone cord around her finger, watching her fingertip turn red.

"So what happened when he cooled down and came home?"

"He hasn't come back yet."

Lisa heard her father take a deep breath. "Lisa, are you certain Marcus wanted to have children, that he wasn't just trying to have a family for your sake, to please you?"

"I'm positive." She unraveled the cord from her finger. "Marcus talked about wanting children almost from the time I met him. He's a Cartwright, Dad. He feels it's his duty to have children. But it's also something he wants very badly. He needs to fill this house with the laughter he never heard growing up here. Which is why I know he'll be a wonderful father."

"He doesn't think so."

Lisa sat up straight, suddenly cold. "What? Whatever gave you that idea?"

"He told me so himself yesterday. His sterility has left him feeling inadequate, maybe even a little insecure. And the way he's compensating for that is to assume that perhaps he wouldn't have been any good as a father. This way, by his not having children, he's saving some poor kid from an unhappy childhood."

"But that's ludicrous!" She felt sick to her stomach, and it had nothing to do with morning sickness.

"Sterility can do strange things to a man, honey. Especially a man as proud as Marcus. In order to accept it, he needs to understand why this has happened, and the only conclusion he's been able to reach thus far is that he isn't father material."

"Oh, my God!" Lisa gasped, reeling from the ramifications of her father's news. *What have I done?*

"Marcus is strong, Lis. He'll come around. Give him some time."

"I never would have had the insemination if I'd known that. Never. I did this for him, Dad. Because I couldn't bear the thought of him leaving me to have my wonderful life with someone else while he sentenced himself to a life of loneliness. But now it sounds like all I've done is sentence him myself." She wiped at the tears streaming down her face. She couldn't stop them now.

"Did you tell Marcus all that?"

"Of course."

"And?"

"It didn't seem to make any difference."

"What did he say, honey?"

"Nothing." Lisa's voice broke. "I explained everything. I told him how much I loved him, and he walked out, anyway. I haven't heard from him since."

"And you've been there all alone since yesterday?"

"I don't know when he'll be back, and I don't want to miss him." She sniffled and wiped her eyes. "I'm just glad I'm not on call." For the first time in years, Lisa hadn't even been thinking about her job.

"I'm coming over," Oliver said, sounding the way he had when she was a kid.

Lisa smiled in spite of her tears. "It's okay, Dad. I'm a big girl now. I made this mess, and somehow I'm going to have to live with it. Besides, I'd rather be here alone when he comes back. I might only get this one chance to turn him around. But thanks."

Oliver harumphed and then fell silent for a few moments. "He'll be back, you know," he finally said.

"I know."

"But I can still come over and stay with you until he gets there. Lord knows you have enough rooms in that house of his."

"Maybe. If he's not back by tomorrow. Just for dinner or something," Lisa conceded. She'd be grateful for her father's presence.

"You'll call if you need anything?"

"Of course."

"So...I'm going to be a grandpa?" Lisa heard the emotion in his voice. At least *someone* was happy about her news.

"Yeah."

"And you're feeling okay?"

"Beth says everything looks great."

"Congratulations, sweetie." His soft words brought a fresh wave of tears to her eyes.

"Yeah. You, too."

"Lisa? For what it's worth, I think you did the right thing. Marcus had already made up his mind to free you, give you a chance at your dreams. Now you've given him a chance to have his, too.''

LISA MADE IT through the second long night comforting herself with her father's words, but as the weekend wore on with still no sign of Marcus, no word at all, she finally called his office only to find out from security that he hadn't been in all weekend. She could no longer hold her panic at bay. What if something had happened to him? What if she'd hurt him so badly he'd done something foolish? What if he hated her so much their marriage was over? What if he never came back?

By Sunday afternoon Lisa was sitting on the bathroom floor in their master suite, dressed in a pair of jean shorts and one of Marcus's old T-shirts, her stomach tormenting her as thoroughly as her rambling thoughts. She prayed she wasn't going to be sick, not while she was alone. She knew her fear of being sick was irrational, that it was a direct result of the days of her little sister's illness, the many times she'd watched helplessly as the medicine they'd given Sara had made the four-year-old violently ill.

She'd watched—hiding in the bedroom closet—as her baby sister died. And she'd sworn to herself then that she was going to be a pediatrician when she grew up. She was going to cure little kids like Sara so they didn't have to suffer so. And she was going to have a house full of children, too, so she could hear Sara's laughter again.

But as much as she wanted this child, as thrilled as she was every time she thought about the life growing inside her, the pregnancy meant nothing without Marcus....

HE FOUND HER in the bathroom, asleep on the floor, when he finally returned home just after three on Sunday afternoon. She looked so fragile to him, so waif-like, that he knew he'd made the right decision. The only decision.

A stab of guilt shot through him as he realized how exhausted she must have been to have fallen asleep on the cold tiles. He should have phoned.

"Lis?" he said softly.

"Marcus..." She sat up, instantly awake.

"I just wanted to tell you I'm home."

Her beautiful eyes were shadowed as she stared up at him. "To stay?"

Marcus nodded. He wanted to tell her that he wasn't angry with her anymore, to take away the fear in her eyes, but he couldn't lie to her.

"You're sure?" she asked, still sitting on the floor.

He nodded again.

She leapt up and threw herself against him, her arms wrapping around his neck. "Thank you, God," she whispered. "Thank you."

Marcus held her close to his heart, where he knew she belonged. She still fit him perfectly, as if the child she carried was nothing more than a bad dream. Then her slender frame began to shudder, and the shudders turned to sobs. His arms tightened. He'd been wrong to leave her hanging all weekend with no word from him. He knew how emotional Lisa was, how deeply she felt everything. How much she'd worry.

But she'd been wrong, too! Even as he held her, he felt the bitterness of her betrayal. The pain of her deception. The jealousy. She'd accepted another man's seed into her womb.

Anger surged through him anew, and it took everything he had to continue holding her. He tried to concentrate on his love for the woman in his arms, wondering how much time would have to pass before the destructive emotions he felt would be gone, dreading the possibility that he would be living with them for a very long time. Perhaps for the rest of his life.

Surely loneliness and empty walls would be better than that.

He knew why Lisa had turned to artificial insemination, understood that her intentions, if not her actions, were honorable. She'd been trying to save him from himself. He could hardly fault her for that when he'd been presumptuous enough to attempt to do the same thing with his plans to leave her. But his plans would still have left the opportunity for them to live their lives together if she'd ultimately chosen to come back to him. He had been going to free her, yes, for a time. Free her to find out if he was what she still wanted, sterility and all. His plans had left the choice up to her.

But her plans had taken away *his* choices.

Which was one of the reasons he'd come back to her. She was pregnant. He was her husband. He would stand by her. Because he was an honorable man. Because she needed him. And because he loved her so damn much that, even pregnant with another man's child, he still wanted her. But he would never accept her baby as his own. He couldn't. It wasn't his. Not in thought, and certainly not in deed.

"I did it for you," she said against his neck, her voice wobbly with her tears.

"I know."

"I love you so much."

"I know."

She pulled away to gaze up at him. "I never meant to hurt you like that, Marcus. Never. I'm so sorry."

"Shh." He pulled her close again and kissed the top of her head. "It's okay, Lis. I understand. Everything's going to be all right." He wanted it to be. He was going to try his damnedest to make it be. Except that, deep inside, he was afraid nothing was ever going to be right again.

OLIVER HAD IT BAD. He wondered if fifty-three was too old for a midlife crisis. He was thrilled at the thought of being a grandfather, of holding Barbara's grandchild in his arms. But maybe the fact that he was going to be a grandfather was *bothering* him, too—subconsciously. Maybe that was why he was suddenly finding himself thinking about the woman across the table from him at odd times during the day.

She looked so cute in her short-sleeved red dress, like a juicy ripe tomato.

"Lisa was in today. It's great to see her so happy," Beth said, devouring her salad.

"It is," he agreed, though he suspected his daughter had some rough times ahead of her yet. "I haven't seen much of Marcus, though, have you?"

"No." She frowned. "Come to think of it, the last

couple of times I stopped over, he was nowhere around.''

Oliver's heart sank as he nodded. He'd noticed the same thing. He'd just been hoping it had been coincidental, a matter of bad timing. ''Has she said anything to you about him?''

Beth put her fork down. ''No. Why? Is something wrong? I thought he was happy about the baby.''

''Well, he left her when she first told him she was pregnant.'' The confidence just slipped out naturally, as if he were sitting here with Barbara and they were discussing their daughter, just as they'd done through every other crisis in Lisa's life. Except that he knew full well that the woman across from him wasn't Barbara. And he wanted to confide in her, anyway.

''He what?'' Beth said, her eyes wide with shock.

''He was only gone for a weekend, and according to Lisa, everything's been fine since he came home. But I know my son-in-law. He's honorable, he loves my daughter, and he's also one of the most stubborn individuals I've ever met. And if he's still got it in his head he isn't meant to be a father...''

Beth paled. ''He doesn't want to be a father? Then why did he put himself through all those tests?''

''It's *because* of the tests. The results, I mean. Men like Marcus tend to approach the crises in their lives logically, and he's determined that maybe he wasn't meant to be a father at all, that perhaps it's best he's sterile because he may be inadvertently saving a kid from an unhappy childhood.''

''But that's so wrong.'' Beth frowned. ''He had a fever when he was a child that wasn't attended to quickly enough. I told him that. His parents had left him with a nanny who was more interested in her boyfriend than in Marcus, and by the time his parents returned home from a trip they were on, his fever had been too high for too long."

Oliver put down his fork. "I knew nothing of this."

"I don't think Lisa knew, either, until I asked Marcus if he ever remembered having a high fever. He made it sound like it was no big deal."

"I suspect that my son-in-law learned very early on not to expect much from his parents."

They were both silent for a minute, and Oliver wondered why it was that some parents never understood that children were gifts to be cherished, not brushed aside. And why some people who were meant to be parents had that chance snatched away. He thought of his little Sara, of the few precious years they'd had with her, and couldn't imagine having missed a single moment of her life. How he still ached for a glimpse of her laughing eyes.

Beth touched his hand, bringing him back to her. "You think Marcus is still working himself to the bone?"

His hand tingled where she'd touched it. "Probably."

"So the baby hasn't helped their problem at all."

Oliver hated to hear her sounding so despondent. "It's helped. It's helped Lisa. She's smiling again, dreaming again. And if nothing else, seeing Lisa happy will help Marcus."

"But how long is she going to be happy if *he* isn't?" Beth asked.

That was a question Oliver couldn't answer.

"I SAW THE GREATEST MOVIE over the weekend," Beth said later, over dessert. By some unspoken understanding, they'd steered away from the conversation of Lisa and Marcus through the rest of dinner.

"What'd you see?" he asked, pushing aside the guilt that accompanied his thoughts of Beth more and more these days, guilt that grew with his eagerness to hear whatever details of her life she wanted to give him.

But all the while she told him about the movie, Oliver was wondering who she saw it with and then wondering why it mattered to him. He must be crazy. Beth Montague was almost young enough to be his daughter. She was the wife of his dead colleague. His daughter's best friend. She hadn't even had children yet, and he was going to be a grandfather. And she wasn't Barbara.

So why, when she smiled at him, did he feel like kissing her?

BETH SHOWED UP at Lisa's office the next afternoon, interrupting Lisa's dictation.

"I thought Wednesday was your early day," she said, propping her hip on the edge of Lisa's desk.

Lisa put down the mike from her dictaphone and shut off the machine. "It is, but Marcus is working late tonight, so I'm taking the time to get caught up on all this." She motioned toward the charts and correspondence littering the top of her desk.

"He's working late again? He was working on Friday night when we went looking for baby cribs. I thought the idea was that you'd both stop working yourselves to death."

Lisa shrugged. "I have. And he will. Just as soon as he gets this Blake deal done."

"I don't know, Lis." Beth frowned. "There will always be other deals."

"Of course there will, but this one is far more than just business to Marcus. He really cares about the old guy." She filled Beth in on the difficulties Marcus was having with George Blake.

"You sure that's all it is?" Beth asked.

Lisa loved her friend, and she was glad Beth cared, but sometimes she wished she didn't care quite so much. "He just needs time, Beth. I knew it would take him a while to come to grips with the baby, and I'm willing to wait. *I* had a chance to prepare, but it came as a complete shock to him."

"I kind of expected to hear from him."

Lisa, too, had hoped that Marcus would contact Beth. He usually liked to have a handle on everything. She sighed. "He doesn't say much about the baby yet, but he's fine with it."

Which wasn't entirely true. Marcus never said *anything* about the baby. And he hadn't completely forgiven her yet for her duplicity in conceiving it. He also hadn't made love to her since she'd told him she was pregnant. But she was completely certain that he was as committed to their life together as she was. The rest would come with time, just like her father said. It had to.

MARCUS WAS HOME for dinner the very next night. Hannah had left a casserole in the oven, and Lisa served it in the kitchen. She and Marcus had been eating in there for years, preferring its homier atmosphere to the formal dining room Marcus's parents had insisted on using for every meal when they were home.

"Do you remember Sue Carrin, that ditsy blonde who pledged my sorority our senior year?" Lisa asked Marcus over dinner.

"The one with the big—"

"Marcus!" Lisa laughed, cutting him off.

Marcus looked up from buttering his roll to grin at her. "Well, if she was going to make out with her boyfriend where someone could trip over them, she should have kept her top on."

"And if you were going to try to sneak in my window after curfew, you should have been watching where you were stepping."

"How was I supposed to see them? She and Skinny were behind the bushes! He was panting so hard the lenses in his glasses were all steamed up. Poor Skinny, it was probably his first real kiss, and I had to go and ruin it for him. I wonder what ever happened to him."

"He married Sue. I ran into her at the hospital today. She was bringing her mother in for cataract surgery."

"I'll be damned. Little Skinny Whitehall married Big Bazookas—"

"Stop it!" Lisa said in mock outrage. "Sue's a very

nice woman. You're just mad because you got caught trying to besmirch my virtue. And I guess Skinny's not so little anymore. He's made quite a name for himself as a computer-systems consultant, with a couple of nationwide firms on his client list.''

"I ought to put him in touch with George Blake," Marcus said, no longer smiling.

Lisa pushed her plate aside. "George is still holding things up?"

"Yeah, but I don't blame him, Lis. I'd do the same thing if our positions were reversed. Still, he questions every move we make. It's so damned frustrating. A merger that was supposed to take weeks is taking months.''

Lisa reached across the table to lay her hand over his. "George Blake is lucky he found you."

"I'm not sure he'd agree with you, but it's too late to pull out now. So, what's for dessert?"

They had their choice of chocolate cake or apple pie. Neither sounded good to Lisa, but she sat with Marcus while he had a piece of each. She wanted to ask him which one of them was eating for two, but wasn't sure he'd see the humor.

"By the way, our two-month obstetrical appointment is next Thursday morning at ten o'clock," Lisa said as she cleared the table after dinner. "Is that okay with you?"

Marcus was rinsing dishes at the sink where they'd leave them for Hannah to do in the morning. He stopped and turned to look at Lisa, his expression blank.

"I just..." she said hesitantly, "that is, you always said you wanted to be a part of things..."

Marcus turned back to the dishes. "That was a long time ago, Lisa. I'm not a part of what's going on with you now."

Lisa's stomach knotted. "'What's going *on* with me?' I'm having a baby, Marcus. *Our* baby."

He turned off the water with such force Lisa was surprised the faucet didn't break off in his hand. "We need to get something straight here," he said, facing her again.

Lisa backed up a step. She'd never seen him this angry.

"The child you are carrying is not, and never will be, *ours,*" he said through clenched teeth.

Lisa stared at him, her world teetering dangerously.

"When I said I wanted to be a part of every aspect of our child's birth, that included the conception."

She fell back another step. He hadn't forgiven her. He wasn't *ever* going to forgive her.

"I'm sorry," she said, anyway, feeling his pain, as well as her own.

"I spent the first twenty years of my life pretending that I had a father, Lisa. I cannot spend the next fifty pretending that I *am* one."

"What're you saying?" she asked, feeling a chill, afraid for the baby growing inside her.

"The child you're carrying is yours. I want no part of it."

He couldn't mean that! "Then why are you here? Why'd you come back? What have these past weeks been?" she cried.

"I'm here because you are my wife, and because, in spite of everything, I find that I still love you as much as ever."

She felt the blood drain from her face. This couldn't be happening. Never in her worst nightmares had she considered that Marcus would want her but not their baby. That he would continue to live with her, love her, but reject the child she was carrying.

"You're his father," she whispered, still not quite believing that she wasn't misunderstanding Marcus somehow.

His eyes filled with a pain so intense Lisa felt it clear to her soul. "No, Lis, I'm not," he said, his shoulders slumping as he turned and walked out of the room.

Lisa sank into a chair at the kitchen table, cradling her stomach, and the tiny life it harbored. It would have been better if Marcus had left her. Because as long as he was coming home to her, caring about her, she didn't think she could leave him. But neither could she bring her baby into a home where he wasn't wanted, where his own father could ignore him as if he didn't exist.

"It's okay, little one," she whispered, rubbing her stomach soothingly. "Your daddy'll come around." *Please God.* "He'll love you more than any daddy ever loved a child." *He will. I know he will.* "See, there's something about your daddy I haven't told you yet. He's never had much love in his life, so the one thing he's always wanted more than anything is a family to love. And you're it, little one. So hang in there. And don't worry, your daddy never stays angry for long.''

CHAPTER SEVEN

"DAMN!" MARCUS SWUNG the Ferrari around and headed back toward home. He'd forgotten the marketing textbook he'd promised to bring with him when he met with George Blake later that day. Impatient with his lapse, with the lack of concentration that had been plaguing him all week, he pulled around the circular drive to the front of his house, barely looking at the lushly landscaped lawn in front of him. Although fall used to be his favorite time of year, this year the leaves had changed colors without him even noticing. The crisp October morning was wasted on him.

Work had always been able to distract him, if not heal what ailed him. But ever since Lisa had asked him to accompany her on her first prenatal checkup, he'd been eaten up with corrosive emotions. All of a sudden the pregnancy was a reality, something he could no longer ignore.

He hated the anger that burned within him—and the panic. Lisa was going on with her life without him, and there was nothing he could do about it, no way for him to catch up. He knew it and she knew it. She watched everything she said around him these days, choosing her words so carefully it made him ache. He could feel their closeness deteriorating, knew they were in danger of becoming nothing more than wary housemates and yet was powerless to prevent that from happening.

Because he couldn't involve himself in Lisa's changing life. He was already so plagued with if onlys he wondered sometimes if he'd ever again know peace of mind. He might just as well have gone with her to the damn doctor's appointment the day before. He'd done nothing but sit in his office and torture himself with wasted dreams the entire time he'd known she was there.

Lisa's pregnancy had become a constant reminder to him of everything he'd always wanted, everything he could never have. He was so damn envious he couldn't think straight.

And he was scared to death that Lisa's baby was going to look nothing like Lisa.

Unlocking his front door, he hurried into the office he shared with his wife, hoping to be in and gone before she heard him. He made it a practice to leave the house before she was up and around these days. It was just easier that way. Easier to keep his emotions under wraps, easier to ignore the changes in his wife's body, his wife's life.

He hadn't made love to Lisa, either, not since the day she'd told him she was expecting a child. He didn't trust himself to touch her. He was afraid of what might happen if he let his guard down, if he let himself be vulnerable, if he let himself feel everything he always felt when he made love to her. He wasn't sure what other emotions might be unleashed or what he might do if they were.

He was also unsure how much lovemaking she could do in her condition, and he didn't want to ask. It just seemed better not to talk about that.

Grabbing the textbook from a shelf behind his desk, he was on his way out the door when he heard the sounds of retching upstairs. Lisa was sick.

Taking the stairs two at once, he made it up to the master suite just in time to hear Lisa throw up a second time. How long had she been suffering like this?

Without thought, Marcus dropped the textbook on his dresser, tore off his jacket and hurried into the bathroom. He wet a washcloth at the sink, then crossed to her and hunkered down, wiping her face and forehead, holding her hair back when the spasms came again.

"I'm sorry," she finally said, tears wetting her lashes. She took the cloth from him and buried her face in it.

Marcus rubbed her back, admiring her strength. He knew how frightened she was of being sick to her stomach. "Shh. You don't need to apologize, Lis. It's me, remember?"

She nodded, saying nothing, only looking at him. He hated the uncertainty he read in her eyes.

"This happen often?" he asked.

She shrugged. "Not so far."

But maybe later. As her pregnancy progressed. There it was again. The wall he slammed into every time he was with his wife these days.

"Are you gonna be okay now?" he asked, feeling awkward. After all, this had nothing to do with him.

Lisa nodded.

Marcus got to his feet. "I, uh, guess I'll be going then. I just came back to get a book I forgot."

Lisa stood up, as well, and moved to her sink. "Have a good day," she said, reaching for her toothbrush.

Marcus stood there for a second longer, wishing there was some way he could make everything right again. He missed her so much. "Yeah, you, too," he finally said, stopping in the bedroom to shrug back into his suit jacket.

"Marcus?" Lisa poked her head around the bathroom door.

"Yeah?"

"Thanks."

Marcus nodded and left, his day suddenly a little brighter.

LISA WAS SICK again that evening after dinner, and several more times during that next week. The violence and frequency of her vomiting started to alarm Marcus. He'd been waiting to leave with her in the mornings since the first time he'd found her sick, and after the fourth morning of nausea in a row he was an old hand at soothing her through the episodes. But while he quieted her fears, his own grew. It seemed to him that these bouts of nausea were far more than normal morning sickness.

"I want you to talk to Dr. Crutchfield today when you get to the hospital, Lis," he said on Wednesday morning while they both got ready for work. It was the middle of the last week in October, Lisa's ninth week of pregnancy. "You're sick all the time now."

"It's perfectly normal," Lisa said, chuckling. She opened her eyes wide to apply her mascara.

He couldn't tell, looking at her now, that she'd been so violently ill only half an hour before. She looked healthy. Better than healthy. She was glowing. Still...

"I can't believe that every woman goes through this every time she's expecting, Lisa."

"Some women just have it worse than others," she said, continuing with her lashes.

Why was she taking this so lightly? Few things in life scared him, but the thought of something wrong with Lisa, seriously wrong, scared the hell out of him.

"I'd still feel better if you talked to the doctor," he said.

Lisa met Marcus's gaze in the mirror, her eyes amused. "I *am* a doctor, if you..." She stopped midstream when he stared, stone-faced, back at her. "You're really concerned, aren't you?" she asked, surprised.

"Yes," Marcus admitted, refusing to apologize for that.

"I'll stop by and see her this morning, Marcus. I have office visits until eleven, but I'll go over straight after. Okay?" She smiled at him, looking about sixteen in her slip and bare feet, with her makeup only half-on.

"Okay." Marcus smiled back. God, how he loved her.

"IF LISA CALLS, put her right through, no matter what," Marcus told Marge as he walked into his office later that morning.

"Nothing's wrong, is there?" Marge asked, getting up to follow him. She stood in his doorway, a mother's worried frown on her brow.

Marcus had not yet told anyone about Lisa's pregnancy. He hadn't wanted to face the inevitable questions, the role he'd have to play in order to protect his wife's privacy. And his own.

But no matter how much he resented the position Lisa had put him in, her condition wasn't something he was going to be able to hide much longer. "No. As a matter of fact, she's pregnant," he said, trying to sound happy about the situation.

Marge was so effusive in her congratulations Marcus felt more like a fraud than ever, but he accepted them because he had no other choice. He tried to measure up to her expectations of a happy father-to-be. And by the end of the morning every other member of his immediate staff had been in to congratulate him. He found it increasingly wearing to keep up the pretense, but it warmed him to see how much genuine affection his coworkers seemed to have for Lisa and him. He hadn't expected everyone to be so excited. His paychecks guaranteed their loyalty. Not their well wishes.

It warmed him far more when, shortly after eleven, Lisa called to say that everything was just fine with the baby and her. He brushed right by the part about the baby, giddy with relief to hear that Lisa was in perfect health. He'd been more worried than he thought.

He forgot himself long enough to go out and share the good news with Marge.

"It sounds to me like you need to read up on the next seven months, Marcus, if a little morning sickness throws you so off kilter," Marge said, grinning at him.

Marcus considered her suggestion. Maybe he *should* find out just what the next months were going to bring. He'd had nothing to do with creating Lisa's condition, but her bouts with morning sickness had brought home to him how precarious an actual pregnancy could be, the risks it posed to the expectant mother's health. Lisa's health. He wanted to know more about it.

"Could you recommend some good books about it?" he asked his secretary. Having something to concentrate on, something positive he could contribute, something he could *do*, felt good.

Marge picked up her purse and headed for the door. "I'll stop at the bookstore when I'm at lunch," she said, still smiling at him.

Marcus grinned back. Finally. He had a purpose, a way to regain some of the inner balance he'd lost when his wife had become pregnant with another man's child.

BETH KNEW where Oliver lived. She wished she didn't. That it wasn't so easy for her to find him on this, the darkest of days, made even darker by the Thanksgiving holiday that followed so soon after.

It wasn't right that she reach out to him this way. Lisa would probably be expecting her to call, maybe even expecting her to spend the day with her as she had the year before and the year before that. Nothing had been said this time. But Lisa knew.

Beth almost turned her BMW around to head back

to New Haven. It was a gorgeous Indian-summer day, a gift she should be thankful for. She could drive up to East Rock, spend the day at Eastrock Park, as she used to do all those weekends when John was glued to textbooks. Surely she could outdistance her memories among the 650 acres of gorgeous Connecticut countryside. She had no business dropping in on Oliver. None whatsoever. Except that she was certain he could make her feel better. Beth's eyes blurred with tears. She blinked them away so she could see the road in front of her.

When had she come to rely on Oliver for her emotional equilibrium? How had she come to need him without even knowing it? And could she take comfort from him without making a mess of things?

She turned into the neighborhood where Lisa had grown up, finding the rambling house easily. She'd been there last Christmas, guests of Lisa and Marcus. It had been then, celebrating that emotional holiday, that she and Oliver had first connected. They'd both been celebrating with only half a heart, having lost a part of themselves when they'd buried their spouses.

Which was why, on this day in particular, Beth was drawn to her best friend's father for comfort. Oliver wouldn't just sympathize, he'd *know*.

Pulling up to the garage behind Oliver's house, Beth parked, grabbed her purse and got out of the car. There was nothing wrong with her coming here like this. It meant nothing more than a person seeking comfort from a friend who understood.

So why had she not told Lisa where she was going? Why had she purposely not gone home to change after church in an effort to avoid Lisa's phone call? And why had a swarm of butterflies taken up residence in her abdomen?

"Beth! What a wonderful surprise," Oliver said when he answered her knock. "I was just deciding what to fix for lunch. Come join me."

That was it. No questions asked.

Following him back to the kitchen, she dropped her purse on the counter, then looked over his shoulder as, together, they inspected the contents of his refrigerator. She felt better already.

Deciding on cheese-lettuce-and-tomato sandwiches, they prepared lunch together and ate it out on his covered patio, enjoying the unusual warmth of the day. The lush green acre of his backyard, lined with the spectacular autumn foliage of dogwood, was enchanting. In the spring the yard was filled with the pink and white blossoms of mountain laurel, as well as colorful rhododendron shrubs, the perfect accompaniment to the orchids that had been Barbara Webster's pride and joy.

"This was just what the doctor ordered," Beth said, finishing the last of her sandwich.

"Kind of convenient, don't you think, to be able to give your own orders?" Oliver smiled at her.

The pleasure he was taking in her presence was almost enough to soothe her tattered emotions. Almost.

"John was killed six years ago today." The words came out of their own accord, as if they'd been fighting for release. And she supposed maybe they had, going by the number of times they'd repeated themselves over and over in her head since she'd awakened, alone, early that morning.

"Ahh." Oliver's expression, his voice, was filled with instant understanding, and warmed with a huge dose of empathy. "I remember when we got the call at the university... Come." He reached for her hand. "Why don't we sit in the gazebo. I go there sometimes when I'm feeling blue. It seems to help."

Beth walked with him to the gazebo in one corner of his backyard. She'd been there before, of course, but always with Lisa. Surrounded with flowers except in the cold winter months, it had a slatted roof open to the sun and to the many birds that came to perch on the feeders Oliver had built. It was the most peaceful place Beth had ever been.

"Were you with him when it happened?" Oliver asked, sitting with her on one of the benches along the inside of the gazebo. Though the little building allowed in the sun's warmth, Beth's hands were cold, and Oliver rubbed them gently with his.

She'd had no idea how much she'd needed the contact, the touch of another person. "Uh-huh," she said, watching a couple of birds hover around one of the larger feeders hanging from the ceiling of the gazebo, but seeing, instead, her husband's blood on the tile floor of the hamburger place. They'd only stopped there for a quick bite before heading out to the country to look at homes. That day had been filled with sunny promise, too, just like this one.

She could still hear the shrieks of the women and children around them, the shouts of the men who'd tried to help, still feel the frantic flurry as everyone ran, trying to escape the gunman's next bullet. They needn't have worried. He'd turned the next one on himself.

Beth hadn't even realized she'd been speaking out loud until Oliver put his arm around her, pulling her into the comfort of his embrace. "I'm so sorry, my dear, so sorry. Shh. Don't cry."

It had been a long time since Beth had been cuddled, since she'd had someone to lean on. Burying her face against the solidness of Oliver's chest, she clung to him, allowing the sobs she'd been holding in check all day to burst free. The nightmare of that day would be with her always, but it almost felt as if she'd be able to bear it as she sat there with her head against Oliver's chest, listening to the strong steady beat of his heart.

"Thank you," she said, pulling away just enough to lift her head, to gaze into his warm brown eyes.

"Hush." He placed a finger against her lips. "You don't need to thank me. You've helped me more than I can ever say."

His gaze left hers to travel down to where his finger was still touching her lips. With no thought to what she was doing, Beth wet her lips, tasting the saltiness of his skin.

She saw the look in Oliver's eyes change, recognized the intentness of his gaze. Dazed, she watched his head lower and knew only that she wanted him to move closer, that nothing had felt so right in years.

Still, she was shocked by the first touch of his lips, by the warm connected feel of a man's mouth against her own, caressing her own. It had been so long. Too long.

Unable to deny him, to deny herself, Beth parted her lips to his. Her heart beat a passionate tattoo, and her belly flooded with wanting. Losing every ounce of the maturity of her thirty-eight years, she felt like a teenager again.

She gave kiss for kiss, clinging to him as he caressed her back with sure hands. Her senses swam with the taste of him, the bristly feel of his beard against her skin, his musky scent.

She wasn't ready when he slowly pulled back from her.

"I'm not going to apologize," he said, looking into her eyes, desire smoldering in his.

Beth melted under that gaze, felt cherished and alive. She wanted to lean her head against him again, but wasn't sure she should.

She shook her head, instead, bringing herself back to reality. "You don't have to apologize," she said, surprised to hear how breathless she sounded. "I needed comfort. You offered it." She told herself that was all it had been. That was all it *could* be. They'd both already given their hearts—to someone else.

"And I'm almost old enough to be your father," Oliver said, setting her away from him. "I can assure you, Beth, it won't happen again."

Beth nodded, glad for the reassurance. He was her friend's father. And she loved John. The feelings Oliver had evoked in her were just an outcropping of her longing for her dead husband. A natural emanation of her emotional neediness.

And his. Because as much as she missed her John, he missed his Barbara, too.

THE DAYS GREW SHORTER. Thanksgiving arrived, a quiet affair spent with Marcus and her father, eating out at the country club as Marcus's family had always done. Beth spent the day with her cousin in upstate Connecticut.

Willie Adams took his first steps the day after Thanksgiving, well on his way to recovery; but when she ran over to share the good news with Beth, her friend seemed almost distant, as she'd been ever since the anniversary of John's death. Lisa had tried to reach her all day that Sunday, knowing how difficult the anniversary was for Beth. But to no avail. When she'd asked Beth about it afterward, Beth had been evasive.

Lisa was thrilled about the changes in her body, evidence of the baby growing inside her. She'd tried to set up a dinner date alone with her father, needing to gloat over her progress with the only other family member who cared to hear about it, but Oliver was unusually busy, unable even to meet her for lunch. She'd had to satisfy herself with a shared coffee break at Yale the afternoon after Thanksgiving, and then only because she'd shown up at his office unannounced.

She was no longer on call at the hospital, agreeing with Debbie Crutchfield that it would be much healthier for her baby if she got her full night's rest. Nevertheless, she missed the excitement of administering emergency aid.

And then there was Marcus. The man made her happier—and sadder—than she'd ever been in her life. He also infuriated her, frustrated her and sometimes just plain made her laugh. He'd become a mother hen, watching her every move, denying her even the simple privilege of rinsing the dishes with him, insisting, instead, that she sit at the table while he did the task himself. He monitored every bite she ate, which meant her occasional hamburger and french-fry binges had to happen during the workday when she was usually too rushed to savor them. And he locked the doors and turned off the lights at nine-thirty every night to ensure she got her sleep.

She hated the unnecessary inactivity he was forcing on her, but she loved the attention he was giving her, or rather, giving her pregnancy. If only he'd be as attentive to her other needs. Because each night, after he saw her settled into bed, he went back downstairs to the office to work, sometimes not coming to bed until the early hours of the morning. Many nights Lisa lay there alone, awake, waiting for him to finally join her, her body taut with need, wanting nothing more than to feel her lover's arms around her, his body hard and demanding inside hers.

But she waited in vain. Marcus always eventually climbed in beside her, but he never took her in his arms. Other than the chaste kisses he gave her when he left her in the morning and returned home at night, he didn't touch her at all.

In the old days she'd have talked to him about it, just as she'd have argued with him about most of the constraints he was putting on her activities. Now she was just so damn grateful that he was taking any interest at all that she kept her dissatisfaction to herself. She was afraid to rock the boat, afraid that she'd push him right out the door again. And that the next time he wouldn't be back.

She missed his friendship most of all.

Lisa stumbled getting up from the kitchen table the night after Thanksgiving. Marcus's arms shot out, catching her against him, and her senses flamed. She wanted him so desperately she was almost embarrassed by her need. Rather than stifling her desires, pregnancy seemed to have heightened them. The instant hardening of Marcus's body told her in no uncertain terms that he still wanted her, too.

Acting purely on instinct, Lisa moved against him, silently inviting him to make love to her. It had been so long.

He pushed her away.

"I have work to do," he said, retreating to the office.

Only the fact that he'd left the dishes for her to rinse told her she hadn't just imagined his shudder of desire. For some reason, Marcus was denying himself something he wanted as badly as she did. He'd had to run away to stop himself for taking her up on her unspoken invitation. But the knowledge did little to ease the ache inside her.

"WHEN'S YOUR NEXT doctor's appointment?" Marcus asked the following night over dinner. They were at their favorite pizza parlor, sharing a cheeseless pizza, because Marcus said cheese had too much fat.

Lisa froze, her slice of pizza six inches from her

mouth. "Why?" she asked, remembering his reaction the last time she'd had an appointment.

"I think I ought to accompany you."

Excitement spun through her. "You're sure?" she asked him. They'd had a wonderful day aboard the *Sara*, although it was too cold to take her out for a sail—and too dangerous, according to Marcus, for Lisa. They'd spent the day bundled up in sweaters and jeans, picnicking and playing cards in the cabin down below, almost as if nothing had ever come between them.

He nodded. "There're a couple of things I want to ask her."

"I have my end-of-first-trimester check on Thursday morning at ten," she said, too relieved to further question his change of heart. But the moment pointed out to her just how far from each other she and Marcus had strayed, that she was so giddy over so mundane a thing. The question was, had they become so adept at hiding from each other that they'd lost their closeness forever, or were they finally on their way home?

"I'll meet you at your office. We can walk up together." His blue eyes met her brown ones and he actually smiled at her.

For the first time in a long time, Lisa allowed herself to believe in their future.

"How much rest is enough?"

Lisa lay on the examining table and bit the sides of her cheeks to hold back her smile. Marcus had been grilling Debbie Crutchfield ever since she'd entered the examining room.

Debbie exchanged a glance with Lisa, hiding her grin behind the clipboard she took a sudden interest in. "Everyone's different, Marcus," she said, obviously used to the vagaries of expectant fatherhood. "Lisa's body will tell her when she needs to rest. I suggest you lay off those books a little. Having a baby is a completely natural process. Just let nature do its job."

"Books?" Lisa asked. *What books?*

Marcus looked a little sheepish. "I'm going a little overboard, huh?" he asked the doctor.

"What books?" Lisa asked again. Debbie slid Lisa's top up almost to her breasts and stretched a tape measure across the slight mound of Lisa's stomach.

"I assumed you and Marcus had bought out the local bookstore with all the questions he's been asking," Debbie said, stretching the tape across Lisa's stomach at another angle.

"My secretary picked up a couple for me," Marcus admitted.

Lisa grinned up at him then. He was reading books about pregnancy. "You told Marge?" she asked.

"A few weeks ago," he replied absently, his eyes on what the doctor was doing. "What's the purpose of that?"

"We monitor the baby's growth by the growth of Lisa's stomach." Debbie went on to explain to Marcus the different ways they'd be keeping track of Lisa's condition throughout her pregnancy, while Lisa lay between them, a spectator at her own party.

She stared at her husband, wondering if she was reading too much into his announcement to Marge, into his willingness to be a father, at least publicly. Was she only lying to herself by believing that his reading all those books pointed to a more private commitment? Happiness bubbled up inside her, in spite of her warnings to herself to wait and see. Happiness and a relief so powerful she felt light-headed as she lay there, grinning from ear to ear.

"What about intercourse?"

Lisa's grin vanished and she felt herself turn ten shades of red. She was a doctor, too, for God's sake. Couldn't he have saved that question for her?

"What about it?" Debbie asked, her hand hovering over Lisa's exposed belly.

"I was under the impression it might be slightly, uh, risky."

Lisa wanted to pull the paper on the examining table up over her head.

"Not normally. I would think the risk of dying of frustration would be the more serious one," Debbie said, smiling. She was obviously used to such questions, unlike Lisa who didn't discuss sex much on the pediatrics ward.

Marcus looked down at Lisa, his eyes sizzling with a heat she hadn't seen there in weeks. "Good."

Is that why he hasn't touched me in all these weeks? He's been worried about the baby?

"Are you taking your vitamins?" Debbie asked Lisa.

Lisa nodded, struggling to pay attention to what the doctor was saying. All she could think about was getting her husband alone.

"And how's the morning sickness?"

"Better. The soda crackers helped."

Debbie pulled a pair of double stethoscopes from her pocket. "By the size of things I suspect we might just get to hear this determined character today," she said.

"Really?" Lisa popped up.

"Lie still and we'll see," Debbie said, pushing gently against Lisa's shoulders until she was flat on the table again.

Lisa barely felt the chill of the stethoscope against her stomach as she studied the concentrated look on the doctor's face, waiting while Debbie listened for the baby's heartbeat. She held her breath, afraid the sound of her breathing would drown out the fainter sound Debbie was seeking.

The doctor froze suddenly, holding the stethoscope just to the left of Lisa's belly button. "Don't move. It's right here," she said, sounding excited. "Here, Marcus, let's put your mind at ease. You come listen first." She held out the other set of earpieces.

Lisa looked over at Marcus, impatient for him to hear their miracle, to share with him the most exciting moment of their lives. Hoping to see her favorite smile lighting his features, warming his serious blue eyes, she was shocked at the brief glimpse she caught of his face before he turned, and without a word walked out of the room, closing the door behind him with a definitive click. Her new, oh-so-foolish hopes shriveled and died right there in the examining room, to be replaced by the fear that had become too common a companion these past months. Fear for herself, for her baby, but most of all, fear for Marcus. Was he never going to allow himself the happiness she was trying so desperately to give him?

At Debbie's urging she listened to the faint steady beat of her baby's heart, but rather than the elation she'd expected to feel, she felt only despair. What had she done? Dear God, what *had* she done?

CHAPTER EIGHT

LISA GOT THROUGH the rest of the doctor's appointment as people usually get through a crisis, simply because she had no other choice. She made some inane excuse for Marcus, something about his being embarrassed showing emotion in front of people, and while she was sure Debbie didn't buy it, the woman was too kind to say so. And while she listened to Debbie's orders for more exercise and vegetables over the coming month, her mind was on Marcus, on the depth of despair she knew that frozen look of his hid, on whether or not he'd be waiting for her on the other side of the door—or anywhere.

She almost wished he'd just leave her and get it over with. The thought panicked her, devastated her, but she honestly didn't know how much longer she could go on walking on eggs, afraid to upset the fragile peace under which they'd been going about their days, wondering when he might reach his threshold of endurance and walk out on her again.

She held her breath as she left the examining room, hoping Marcus would be waiting for her, ready to tell her he'd just become so overwrought with joy that he'd needed a moment to compose himself. Or that he'd had an instant of panic as it finally hit home what a mammoth responsibility they'd undertaken by bringing a new life into the world. Anything. She'd accept anything. As long as he was waiting there.

He wasn't waiting outside the door. Bracing herself for whatever the next hours might hold, Lisa said goodbye to Debbie, avoiding the pity she knew she'd find in the doctor's eyes, and took the elevator back downstairs to her office, telling herself to hold it together at least until she got home. She'd think about Marcus then. Just let her get home.

He was waiting for her in her office, his overcoat already on, but unbuttoned. He looked so solid and male and dependable. Relief flooded through her in that first second when she saw him standing there, but one glance at his face, and the knot in her stomach returned, tightening painfully.

"Can you leave?" he asked, his jaw clenched with the effort it was taking him to contain whatever emotions were roiling within him.

Lisa nodded, collected her keys and slipped into her winter coat. Picking up the phone to call her receptionist, she cleared her calendar for the day, with orders to send any emergencies to the pediatrician on call, and followed her husband's forbidding back out to the parking lot, where they climbed into their respective cars.

She drove home dry-eyed, a cloud of dread pervading her, and pulled the Mercedes into the garage beside Marcus's Ferrari, closing the automatic garage door behind her. She felt trapped as she sat there, not wanting to follow him into the house, not wanting to find out how bad things really were. And she was trapped by her own body, too, by the life growing within her from which there was no escape. Trapped by the dreams that made this child so essential to her happiness.

He was sitting in the middle of the velvet brocade couch in the formal living room, his overcoat tossed carelessly over the back of the matching Queen Anne chair. The coat frightened her. It was unlike Marcus to leave anything lying around.

Unless he was planning to go out again.

He stared up at the portrait of his father that hung over the fireplace. His face was no longer a frozen mask. He looked sad, defeated. Lisa felt physically ill, watching him.

She'd done this to him.

He reached out his arm to her as soon as he noticed her standing there. "Come. Sit with me," he said, helping her off with her coat.

He didn't sound like Marcus at all, lacking the pride, the self-assurance, that had first attracted her to him all those years ago, when he'd informed her that day outside her new sorority house that he'd carry in the rest of her boxes.

She thought of those few crucial seconds in Beth's examining room and wished there was some way she could undo them. She'd meant to give her husband back his dreams. Instead, she'd taken away his self-respect.

"I'm sorry." The words weren't enough, not nearly enough, but she meant them with all her heart.

Marcus slid his hand beneath hers, curling his fingers around her palm. "No, I'm sorry, Lis. I'm sorry I can't give you the children you need but—"

"No, Marcus," she interrupted, needing to make him understand once and for all. "You can't take responsibility for what happened. You can't keep blaming yourself for the negligence you suffered as a child. *I* don't blame you. *I* don't love you any less for it. Your sterility is something that happened to both of us, equally, just as if our house burned down, or we lost all of our money on Wall Street. It was just a piece of bad luck."

His jaw clenched, and Lisa wished she could know what he was thinking.

"—but I'm sorrier still for what I'm about to say," he continued as if she'd never interrupted him.

Lisa went cold at his words, her hand still locked with his.

"I love you, Lisa, far more than anyone or anything else in my life. And I'll stand beside you until the day I die, as long as that's where you want me to be."

"Always, Marcus. I want you there always," she said, running her free hand along his cheek. How she loved this man!

He pulled away from her caress. "Let me finish," he said, then paused, as if composing himself.

She sat still, the silence agonizing while she waited for him to go on.

"We can't keep skirting around each other, Lis. I don't want hiding from each other to be our way of life." He took his hand from hers.

"Neither do I. You don't know how much I've missed sharing your thoughts."

She needed to touch him, but wasn't going to make the mistake twice. He was talking about bridging the silences between them, yet he'd never seemed farther away.

"I understand, you know. I know why you enlisted Beth's help, and I've long since forgiven you for what you did, though I'm not even sure that it required forgiveness, that your going to Beth was in any way wrong. I just know I'm okay with it now. I want you to have your baby, Lisa. I want you to be happy."

Tears pooled in Lisa's eyes for the first time that day. There was more. She heard it coming. And she wasn't ready for it. She didn't want to know.

"But I cannot, and never will be, a father to that child."

No! Lisa sat silently beside him, holding back sobs with every ounce of strength she had left.

"I can't have you expecting it of me, Lis, or hoping that someday I'll change my mind. You'd only be setting yourself up for disappointment, and it wouldn't be fair to either of us, or to your child."

He sounded more like himself, in control again. And it was that more than anything that convinced Lisa he meant what he said.

"Do you want me to leave?" she asked.

"Not unless you want to. Our marriage can continue just as it always has."

"You're saying you want us to live together, all three of us, only one of us gets ignored by another one of us all his life?" She was incredulous.

Marcus was silent, staring straight ahead, obviously digesting her words. Surely he'd see how unfair that was, how deplorable to bring up a child that way. Surely he'd—

"I won't ignore the child, Lisa, any more than I'd ignore anybody living in our household. I just can't be a father to it. I can't rejoice in the little things parents get happy about. I can't take pride in the child's accomplishments. They aren't mine to take pride in.

"I went to your doctor's appointment today because of you, because I want to know everything you're going through, because I want to help keep you safe and healthy—not because of the baby."

Lisa couldn't stand it. "You're cheating yourself out of so much, Marcus. It's like you're punishing yourself for your sterility, denying yourself a joy you've wanted all your life. You could have listened to that heartbeat this morning. You would have felt the wonder. I *know* you would have, if you'd only given yourself a chance."

Marcus stood up, walking over to stand with his back to the fireplace, to the portrait of his stern-faced father. Lisa was frightened by how much the two of them looked alike at that moment.

"I've discovered something these past few months, Lis. First, I was presumptuous enough to think I was doing what was best for you by making plans to move to Chicago. And then you had yourself inseminated, partially because you thought you knew better than I what was best for me. But the truth is, we were both doing each other a grave injustice, taking away each other's basic rights to decide for ourselves. Only *you* know what's best for you, honey, and if you think having your baby and having me, too, is your best shot at happiness, then I'm behind you one hundred percent. But *I* have to do what's best for me, too, and that's to accept that some things will never be. I can't claim what isn't mine. I can't spend the rest of my life pretending. Not even for you."

His gaze was filled with his love for her, and it broke her heart. "I want us to grow old together, Lis, just like we planned, but only if you can be happy without a father for your baby."

Tears filled her eyes, but she blinked them away as she continued to hold his gaze, truly seeing inside him for the first time in months. Marcus was such a proud man, a man who stood by his convictions. She'd always loved those things about him. She'd never dreamed they might put an end to his dreams.

She ached for him, for his inability to allow himself the happiness that was his for the taking, for the insecurities that made it so hard for him to accept anything he didn't provide for himself. And she ached for the child she was carrying, who might never have all the benefits of his father's great wealth of love.

"I love you, Marcus, with all my heart. And if this is what you need, we'll find a way to make it work," she said, falling apart inside.

His eyes narrowed as he looked at her from across the room. "You're sure?"

"I'm sure." But she wasn't. Not at all. Not for herself. Not for their baby. But most of all, not for the man she loved. Marcus was meant to be a father; he was a natural care giver with a heart bigger than the state of Connecticut. And she feared that he'd never be happy if he continued to deny himself this chance.

"YOUR FATHER-IN-LAW is returning your call on line six, Marcus." Marge's voice on his intercom interrupted Marcus's reverie about his wife. In the week since he and Lisa had talked, he seemed to spend more time thinking about her than about the work at hand.

He pushed a button on the intercom. "Thanks, Marge," he said. He picked up the phone. "Hello, Oliver."

"Marcus? Is something wrong? Is Lisa all right? And the baby?"

Marcus chuckled. "Everything's fine. We're just a little concerned about you. We haven't heard from you since the day after Thanksgiving. Lisa's starting to get worried."

"Ah, you know how it is, Marcus. I always lose touch a little bit as finals draw near."

"That's what I told Lisa, but she worries, anyway. Especially now. Was Barbara emotional when she was pregnant?"

"I'll say she was," Oliver said. "I came home one day when she was pregnant with Lisa and found her crying because I'd bought a green teddy bear for the nursery, instead of the yellow one she'd wanted. I tried to convince her that one was just as nice as the other, but she wouldn't hear it. Said it didn't match the wallpaper."

"So what'd you do?" Marcus asked, thinking of Lisa's disappointment when he'd accidentally brought home chocolate-chip ice cream, instead of the fudge ripple she'd asked for the previous night.

"I returned the green teddy, of course."

Marcus settled further into his chair and smiled. He'd gone back for fudge ripple, too.

"Seriously, son, things okay with you two now?"

"They're better. We've reached an understanding that I'm confident will work."

"An understanding?"

Oliver was family. He was going to have to know. "We're staying together, but not pretending I'm the child's father."

"So what are you?"

"Lisa's husband."

"And the child?" Oliver sounded doubtful.

"Her child."

"And you're sure you'll be able to handle this? Sharing her with the baby but not sharing the baby with her?"

Marcus wasn't sure yet, but he was working on it. "I love her, Dad. I want her to be happy."

"I know, son. But it isn't wrong to want a little happiness for yourself, too, is it?"

Marcus didn't know what happiness was anymore. "I'm happy," he said.

"You want to tell me how you do that?"

"Do what?" Marcus picked up the gold pen Lisa had bought him when he'd graduated. They'd had so many dreams back then.

"Convince yourself to be happy with what you have when you want more. I'm thinking I could use the lesson."

Marcus sat up, concerned. "Why? What's up?"

Oliver chuckled, but there was no joy in the sound.

"I've just been thinking about the next twenty years of my life and wondering which part I'm looking forward to."

"Meaning?"

"I've had the love of my life, Marcus. I've reached the pinnacle in my career." He paused. "I've been starting to question where I go from here."

"Where do you want to go?"

"I'm not certain yet. Let me ask you this. Do you consider fifty-three too old to begin thinking about starting over?"

Marcus couldn't think of a career that suited Oliver better than the one he had, but he knew it wasn't for him to make that determination. "Not if that's what you really want to do."

"You wouldn't think I was just being an old fool?"

"Never. You're the least foolish person I know, Oliver, and if there's something out there you want, then go get it."

"I'm not sure I can, son, but, thanks. You've given me something to ponder."

Marcus wasn't at all clear on what they'd just been talking about, but he was glad to have been able to help someone else, since he couldn't seem to find a way to help himself.

Shortly after hanging up the phone with Oliver, Marcus packed it in. Wednesday was Lisa's early day, and he'd been driving her to and from work most of the week. They'd often traveled to work together back before Marcus's diagnosis. It was something he'd missed when they'd started working such crazy hours.

Something he was enjoying doing again when he could.

He also enjoyed the massages he gave Lisa each night before dinner to help ease the cramps in her muscles. And he looked forward even more to the lovemaking that always came later. He'd made love to Lisa every night since the doctor had given him the okay to do so, and he still couldn't get enough of her. All she had to do was look at him in that way, or he at her, and they started undressing. He'd wondered a time or two if maybe they were falling into bed so much because that was the only part of their relationship that was working, but decided that if that was the case, he was just grateful that *something* was working.

Surprisingly enough, he was even finding himself turned on by Lisa's expanding belly. Regardless of how the baby came to be inside her, she looked so womanly to him, so sexy, growing big with child. He was awed by her physical ability to do that which he, a mere man, could never do.

And he was awed by the things he was finding out he could do. It was hard to feel like a failure when all it took to make his wife stop crying was for him to walk into the room.

He arrived at the medical complex a few minutes early, and not wanting to bother Lisa while she was working, decided to pay a visit to little Willie Adams while he waited. The convalescent center was at one end of the medical complex, and he'd been in to see Willie a few other times during the boy's long recuperation, finding himself drawn to Willie's cocky self-assurance against all odds.

"Hi, Mr. C. I just saw Dr. C. this morning. It's pretty cool, you two having a kid and all," the boy said as soon as Marcus walked into his room. He'd offered to pay for a private room for Willie, but the boy preferred to have the company of other children, and so shared a room with two other long-term orthopedic patients. He was alone that afternoon, however.

"Dr. C.'s been wanting one a long time," Marcus said. He was learning to think of the baby only in terms of Lisa, hoping that would eventually make the whole thing easier somehow.

"Yeah, she'll prob'ly be a great mom, too, for a woman." Willie grinned, his red hair and freckled skin standing out against the stark white sheets of the hospital bed.

"I hear you've been doing pretty well yourself," Marcus said, sitting down on the end of the bed. "Dr. C. tells me you've taken a few steps without any assistance."

"I got to if I'm gonna be runnin' by next summer," Willie said, his chest expanding importantly.

"Just don't overdo it, fella. Dr. C. and your other doctors are doing everything they can to get you ready in time, so don't go messing up all their hard work by rushing things." Lisa had told him just the other night that Willie had been caught trying to get out of his bed by himself over the weekend to practice walking.

"I only did it once, Mr. C., honest. They canceled my therapy Saturday morning, and I didn't want to waste a whole day of getting better."

"They canceled your session because of some

swelling in your muscles, Willie. I guess you pushed yourself a little hard on Friday, huh?''

"I guess.'' The boy looked contrite for all of two seconds and then grinned up at Marcus. "But I was awesome, Mr. C. You shoulda seen me. I made it all the way across the bars, only stopping once.'' Marcus knew a lot of Willie's workouts consisted of forcing his legs to move forward in walking motions while he supported his weight with his arms on the bars on either side of him.

"I'm proud of you. Keep up the good work, and you and I'll hit the batting cages before you go to camp next summer. Can't have your hitting rusty when you're playing with those older guys.''

"Cool! You mean it, Mr. C.?''

"Yep. Just as soon as Dr. C. says you're ready.'' He glanced at his watch. "And now I've got to get over to her office before she gets mad at me for being late.''

Willie's eyes opened wide. "She really gets mad at you?''

"Yeah, but I can handle it,'' Marcus said, ruffling the boy's hair affectionately.

"Hey, Mr. C.?'' Willie called just as Marcus reached the door.

"Yeah?'' he looked back at the boy, thinking how small and defenseless he looked in the bed.

"Your new baby sure is gonna be lucky, having you for a dad and all.''

Marcus felt the sting of the boy's words clear down to his soul.

THE FOURTH MONTH of her pregnancy was both the best and the worst time of Lisa's life. In some ways she and Marcus had never been closer. She cherished their love, knowing what an incredible gift it was.

And she was pregnant, soon to have the baby she'd always wanted. Her morning sickness had subsided and she felt great. She was even starting to show enough to need some of the maternity clothes she'd already purchased, with Beth's help, one Saturday afternoon. And she spent a lot of time daydreaming about the months to come. She was scheduled for her first ultrasound during her four-month checkup and might even then know the sex of her baby.

Everything would have been perfect if Marcus had shown any interest whatsoever in the life her body was busy creating for them.

She'd chosen the bedroom across the hall from them to use as the nursery, instead of the room Marcus's parents had used farther down the hall, and by the fifteenth week of her pregnancy, she was well under way with plans for decorating it. She and Marcus had always said they'd decorate the nursery themselves, piece by piece, rather than hire a professional as his mother had done when she'd been expecting him. And though Lisa longed for Marcus's help, she settled, instead, for remembering as best as she could the opinions he'd had when they used to talk about the nursery they'd have someday. He'd wanted colors, lots of them, all primaries, and balloons, too. He'd also wanted a race-car motif, but she was holding out on that, waiting to see whether the baby was a boy, or a girl who might prefer something a little softer, like the teddy bears she'd always wanted.

Marcus had also always wanted a Raggedy Andy doll. It was something he'd confessed to her one night after they were first married, and only after having had a couple of drinks. One of his earliest memories was of wanting the doll because of a cartoon he'd seen where the boy, Andy, had saved a little girl's life. And that was one of the few times he'd received his father's complete attention. The old man had blasted Marcus for wanting a doll, any doll. Cartwright boys didn't play with dolls.

Lisa's first purchase for the nursery was a pair of two-foot Raggedy Ann and Andy dolls.

She'd looked through scores of books of wallpaper samples and had settled on a pattern of red, yellow, blue, orange and green balloon bouquets, all floating on a background of soft white clouds. She bought her supplies, but waited until Marcus was at the office one Saturday to begin the actual transformation. She wanted the conversion to be as painless for him as possible.

She managed to sand down three of the walls rather quickly, but was having trouble getting the old wallpaper down from the fourth wall. Turning off the electric sander, which just seemed to be smoothing the wallpaper into the wall, she grabbed a hand sander and started in on the wall with good old elbow grease. Twenty minutes later, she was blinking back tears of frustration, mingled with drops of sweat. She was only about a tenth of the way done with the wall.

"What in hell do you think you're doing?"

Lisa jumped, dropping the sander on her toe.

"You scared me," she accused, standing before him in her plaster-spattered leggings and one of his old shirts, her hair pulled back in a ponytail.

"I'm sorry," he said. But he didn't sound it. "With all this racket going on, you must not have heard me come in. What are you doing, Lis?" He asked the question as if he thought she'd lost her mind.

"Decorating the nursery. What's it look like?"

"It looks like you're in danger of hurting yourself. What were you thinking, tackling a job like this all by yourself? You're pregnant, Lisa. You're smarter than this."

Lisa resented his high-handedness. And she'd had enough of sanding a wall that didn't want to be sanded, of carrying a baby that its own father didn't want.

"And who was I going to ask to help me with it, since the father of my baby has refused to have anything to do with him?" she hollered at Marcus.

She wanted to take the words back the minute they were out of her mouth. Marcus's face froze into that awful mask again.

"I'm sorry," she said, leaving the mess behind her as she walked over to her husband. She laid her head against his chest, sliding her arms beneath his jacket. She hadn't wanted to hurt him. Hadn't meant to hurt him. But she was hurting so damn badly herself the words had just slipped out.

"I'm truly sorry, honey," she said again as his silence rent the room. "I'll hire someone on Monday to do the job."

He didn't put his arms around her, didn't reach for her at all, except to push her away from him. ''Give me time to get changed and I'll do it,'' he said, turning to leave before she could read what was in his eyes.

But she *could* read the posture in his back as he crossed the hall into their bedroom. His shoulders were slumped, his gait slow, as if he'd just fought an important battle—and lost.

CHAPTER NINE

THE NURSERY GOT PAINTED. And papered. Marcus tried not to look at the colorful balloons when he pasted them up, which was a little difficult since he had to match the strips as he hung them side by side. He tried not to care that Lisa's choices were making a room so like what he'd pictured for his own children back when he'd thought he'd have some. He tried to concentrate on her satisfied smiles, instead, as they worked on the room together every evening that week. And was never so thankful in his life as he was the day he finally put the supplies away for the last time. The job was done, and now they could get back to normal—at least for the few normal months left to them.

He took Lisa to dinner Friday night to celebrate.

"Here's to a finished nursery," she said, smiling across their intimate table for two at one of New Haven's elite restaurants. It was a place frequented more by his parents' generation than his own, but it was quiet.

Marcus tapped the edge of his glass of whiskey to the apple juice she held up to him. "To a finished nursery," he said wholeheartedly.

"Marcus! Lisa! Goodness, we haven't seen you in months!"

Marcus cringed when he heard the voice of his mother's best friend behind him. Soon after his parents' death, he'd cut most of his ties with the superficial society they had flourished on, but Blanche Goodwin kept reappearing once or twice a year, like a flu bug he couldn't shake.

He stood, holding out his hand to Blanche's silent husband. "Blanche, Gerald. It's good to see you again." Gerald's handshake was slightly unsteady.

Blanche bobbed her silver head importantly. "You're looking good, Marcus. We read in the paper that you'd acquired Blake's department stores. Your father would have been proud of the way you've taken charge of the business." She spoke before her husband could get a word in edgewise.

"I hope so, Blanche," Marcus said politely, angry with himself for the immediate pleasure he felt at her words, for the fact that his father's approval still mattered.

"Are you still toiling down at Thornton, Lisa?" Blanche asked next, making it sound as though Lisa scrubbed bedpans.

"I am," Lisa said, smiling graciously at the older woman.

"Let's leave the kids to their dinner, Blanche," Gerald said, his words a little slurred. Marcus was pretty sure he was drunk.

"Oh, my, yes, of course. I'm sorry. Your food must be getting cold. It was good to see you again, Marcus," she said, shaking Marcus's hand. "And Lisa…"

She held out her hand to Lisa, far enough away that Lisa would have to stand to reach it. Marcus recognized the sort of power play meant to make Blanche feel superior.

The bitch, Marcus thought, watching Lisa stand. She looked beautiful in the dark blue maternity dress she'd donned for the occasion. Beautiful and—

"Oh, my God! You're pregnant!" Blanche said, loudly enough for all the tables around them to hear. Marcus had actually managed to forget for a few brief minutes.

"Yes, I am. Sixteen weeks today," Lisa said gently, looking at Marcus.

He smiled at her. He'd prepared himself for the fact that their many acquaintances would naturally assume that Lisa's baby was his. He could handle having to claim the child in public situations. After all, he'd been handling Marge's questions for weeks, and had managed to relay information about his wife's child just fine without thinking about it in terms of himself.

Blanche inspected Lisa's stomach once more before looking at Marcus as if he'd just amassed another million. "Oh, Marcus, congratulations. A Cartwright heir! Your mother and father would have been so pleased."

He felt like he'd been slapped. He wasn't ready for this. Not by a long shot.

"Thank you," he said, forcing himself to continue smiling as Lisa answered Blanche's questions about the due date and late-night feedings. And watching his wife's animated face, it came home to him just how much he was missing. Lisa was living their dream. He was on the outside looking in. And always would be.

HE HAD TO WORK the next morning, but remembering the trouble Lisa had gotten herself into the previous Saturday, he handled only what absolutely had to be done before Monday morning's meeting with his executives. He drove home with his head full of plans for a drive up the coast that afternoon. Maybe he and Lisa could stop at some seaside place for a late lunch and then spend the night at Haven's Cove. Remembering their anniversary, the glorious idyll of forgetfulness they'd found in the little cabana there, he called from his car phone to make a reservation. And maybe they'd even get some snow while they were there, making it impossible for them to return.

Recognizing in his high-handed approach to planning their lives a hint of desperation, Marcus pushed it away. He and Lisa were talking again. And though they were facing a very unorthodox situation, somehow they would make their marriage work. They loved each other too much not to.

"Lisa?" he called, shrugging out of his overcoat and pulling off his tie as he walked in the front door. He'd left the Ferrari out front. It should only take him a couple of minutes to change into jeans and help Lisa pack an overnight bag.

"I'm up here!"

Marcus took the steps two at a time, eager to share his plans with her. The more he thought about it, the more he knew that a weekend away was just what they needed.

"Pack a bag, Lis. We're—" She wasn't in their bedroom.

"Lis?" he called, back out in the hall.

"In here."

Marcus looked at the door across from him. The door he'd been avoiding. What was she doing in there now? He'd finished everything up in there so they wouldn't have to go in again. At least not for a while. With reluctance, he approached the nursery.

His good spirits evaporated when he saw what was inside. An entire room full of boxes—and his wife standing in the midst of them, dressed in a new pair of designer maternity jeans and a silk-embossed sweatshirt, grinning from ear to ear.

"I knew you'd be mad if I tried to put this all together by myself, but please hurry and change, Marcus. I can't wait to see how it all looks in here. I think we should put the crib over there. What do you think?"

Marcus blanched, his plans for the weekend fading as he surveyed the number of boxes in the room. There was barely room to walk.

"If that's where you want it, Lis," he said, calculating the hours it was going to take him to get all that stuff put together. "I'll be right back."

Swallowing his disappointment, Marcus canceled the reservation he made for the night. Lisa was trying hard to make their marriage work. To allow him to help her, even though she knew he was only doing it for her, not for the child she carried. He couldn't afford to waste her efforts.

Pulling on a pair of sweatspants and a T-shirt, he decided to tackle the crib first, sensing his wife's impatience to see it assembled, in spite of the fact that she'd never mentioned the furniture to him. Other than when she'd answered Blanche Goodwin's questions the night before, she hadn't mentioned the baby since last week, when he'd caught her sanding the nursery all alone.

"I already brought up the electric drill and all the screwdriver bits," she said. Marcus hoped he remembered how to use it. They had a shed full of tools, but they were for the gardeners and whatever handymen Hannah occasionally hired.

Lisa's excitement was contagious, and as they pulled the various pieces of the crib from the box and slowly put them together, Marcus started to relax.

"Remember that waterbed we bought when we were first married?" he asked, grinning as he thought back to those invincible days.

"What a mistake *that* was," Lisa groaned, sliding the long plastic covering on the top bar of the crib. "It would've been nice if they'd told us beforehand that it was really nothing more than a million pieces of plywood."

"Or if we'd had any idea that the only real stability the thing had was *after* it was filled with water. But it was still kind of fun putting it together, wasn't it, Lis? You were so damn cute strutting around with that tool belt on."

Lisa slid the plastic tube on the top bar of the other side of the crib. "I probably would've enjoyed it a whole lot more if I hadn't just started medical school. All I could think about was how many hours it would be until I could get some sleep," she said.

"I wish I could've helped you more, honey. You practically killed yourself that first year, and I was so busy climbing my own ladder I didn't even notice how tired you were half the time." He tightened a bolt on the bottom of the crib.

"Oh, no, Marcus! You were wonderful! Most of my classmates were working, and some were even raising families. Compared to them I was spoiled rotten. I had a wonderful home, no financial concerns, all the time I needed to study—and a lover who could always be depended upon to take my mind off whatever ailed me. You were what got me through medical school." She handed him another bolt.

"That's not the way I remember it. You wore yourself out."

"I was a woman in a predominantly male class. Whether it was true or not, I always felt like I had to do everything better than the rest, to prove I deserved the place I was taking up."

Marcus glanced at her, loving her more than ever. "It wasn't just that. You had to learn everything there was to know, didn't you, hon? So you could save all the little Saras in the world."

"I just needed to do my best," Lisa said, rubbing her belly protectively. *Soon,* he could almost hear her saying. Soon her home would be filled with childish laughter again. And Marcus understood, more than ever, how much his wife needed the child she was carrying.

"Hold this while I get the bar to slide into this end," Marcus said suddenly, cursing himself for reminding her of painful times.

Lisa's breast brushed against Marcus's hand as she moved to the other side of him. He fondled her nipple between two of his knuckles almost subconsciously for a second before she grabbed the edge of the headboard where he'd indicated. Her eyes were smoky as they met the sudden question in his.

"Later, buster. We've got work to do," she said, but she was smiling again.

"Slave driver," Marcus grumped cheerfully, filled with new incentive to get the job done. He could think of nothing better than losing himself in Lisa's love-making.

Inspecting the sides of the crib before he attached them to the frame, he assured himself that the bars were close enough together that a baby's head couldn't slip through.

"How come you're setting those springs so low?" Lisa asked as he was about to screw the bed together.

"There's going to be a mattress on top of them, Lis. You don't want the baby to fall over the top when it starts to stand."

She grinned, warming the cold spots within him. "We can lower the springs later, as he grows. See, they're adjustable. And at first, when he'll only be lying down, I'll need the mattress higher so I can reach him to lift him in and out."

Marcus looked over the crib again, picturing, for a second, a newborn baby lying there and Lisa trying to get to it. He raised the springs. For Lisa.

He finished tightening the last screw and stood up, releasing the catch on the side of the crib to make certain that it lowered and raised as it should. Lisa pulled the mattress over and stood with it propped up against her leg.

"It looks great. And you didn't even swear!" she said, admiring his handiwork.

Marcus glanced over at his wife. "Was I supposed to?"

She grinned again. "I don't know. It's just that I always hear people talking about how guys swear putting cribs together."

"Oh, but I'm not 'guys,'" Marcus said, coming over to relieve her of the mattress. "I do a lot of things differently from most."

"I'm holding you to that," Lisa said, her voice husky.

He lifted the mattress easily, laying it on the springs he'd just fixed into the bottom of the crib, and was shocked by the surge of strange emotion that struck him. He was leaning over the crib just as he'd pictured Lisa doing a moment before. Except that this crib wasn't his for leaning over. He wouldn't be lifting a baby off this mattress. He'd never have a child of his own to tend to in the middle of the night. Clamping down on the raw agony that shot through him, he was filled with the old anger again, the cancerous rage that was as irrational as it was hopeless.

"I'm going down to get a beer. You want something to drink?" he asked Lisa, straightening abruptly. He had to get out of there before he ripped the damned mattress apart.

She was opening the package that contained the crib sheet. "Ice water would be nice," she said, smiling her thanks. Her smile turned to a frown when she saw his face.

"What's wrong?" she asked, immediately concerned. Her hands stilled.

"Nothing. I'm just thirsty. I'll be right back." He wiped the sudden sweat from his brow as he headed for the stairs. He hadn't had such a destructive surge of anger in weeks. He'd thought he was done with all that, that he'd come to terms with himself, his place in Lisa's life. Now he was beginning to wonder if he ever would.

"MARCUS!" LISA WAS calling, and Marcus reached out, but there were too many people around for him to get to her. All he could see was a flash of white. There were too many lights. The flurry of people made him dizzy with fear.

Someone screamed. Lisa, he thought, but as he pushed forward, knocking over the people in his way, he heard the doctor calmly order him outside. It took three sets of strong arms to arrest his progress, but they couldn't get him to leave.

"I need to operate," the doctor said, and the flurry increased. The noise was too loud, hurting his ears, and then suddenly all he could hear was crying. Lisa crying. Or was it him?

Marcus sat up, his body drenched with sweat, which cooled his skin in the night air. His gaze flew to Lisa. She was breathing softly, regularly, her lovely face nestled in a corner of his pillow.

His gaze strayed to the mound Lisa's belly made beneath the covers. *Please, God, let us get through this. All of us.*

LISA WAS IN THE DEN, reading literature she'd just received on a new strain of flu virus, while Marcus was on the telephone in their office. They'd both been in the office until Marcus's conversation with George Blake had distracted Lisa to the point where she couldn't concentrate.

It was Monday, one week before Christmas, and she and Marcus were planning to go Christmas shopping. But first she had a presentation to prepare. She was going to be speaking at the free clinic staff meeting on Tuesday about this new strain of flu, and she wanted the staff well-informed. There had only been a couple of cases in New Haven thus far, but in other parts of New England the virus was rampant. The free clinic was bound to be hit the hardest.

It usually started with a headache followed by— Lisa stopped reading as she felt a peculiar jolt in her belly. Her heart rate practically doubled as she sat completely still, waiting to see if it would happen again. It did. Another little jolt. And then another.

Grinning from ear to ear, Lisa ran down the hall toward the office, bursting with joy at this, the first definite movement of her baby. She had to tell Marcus.

He was still on the phone, but she rushed in, anyway, hoping he'd get a chance to feel the miracle, too. He looked up at her, a question in his eyes, and it was in that second it dawned on Lisa. He wouldn't want to know her news. Marcus didn't want to be his baby's father. He wasn't going to share in the little joys that parents share. Shaking her head at him, she turned and left the office, the rumble of his voice on the telephone nearly drowned out by the roaring in her ears.

She couldn't stand it. Dear God, she couldn't live a lifetime of having every cause for celebration turned into a moment of sadness. What would happen when her child said his first word, took his first step, made the school play or hit a home run? When he came running into the house to share his news only to have his bubble burst by an indifferent father?

Lisa wandered upstairs, telling herself it wouldn't be like that, it wouldn't be that bad. Marcus wasn't heartless the way his own father had been. He'd come around. She went into the nursery, the room she and Marcus had built together—so much like they'd planned that she'd actually forgotten for a time that Marcus had done it all for her, not for their baby.

Sitting down in one of the rockers they'd brought over from their bedroom, she picked up the Raggedy Andy doll and hugged it against her.

"Don't worry, little one. Your daddy's a good man, a fair man, and a very loving man. He'll come around for you. You'll see."

The baby chose that moment to kick her again, harder than the first couple of times. Hard enough that Marcus would for sure have been able to feel it if he'd put his hand there. Lisa buried her face in Andy's soft cloth chest, using the toy to stifle her sobs.

BETH HADN'T SEEN much of Lisa in the weeks since the anniversary of John's death. True, her professional services for Lisa were done. And she was really very busy, with more and more couples seeking the services of the fertility clinic. Furthermore, she knew how important it was that Lisa and Marcus have as much time as possible alone together as they passed through this crucial adjustment period in their marriage.

But she was avoiding Lisa.

Beth sat in her office late on Friday, the Friday before Christmas, and faced a few more home truths.

Oliver wasn't coming. The holiday was only two days away. She'd already told Lisa she wouldn't be spending the day with them, that she was driving upstate to see her cousin again, but she'd bought something for Oliver, anyway. It was nothing momentous, just a tie she thought would look good with the tweed jackets he favored, one that was just a little bit wider than the ones he had. She pulled the gaily wrapped package out of her desk drawer, staring at it as if it had answers to the questions that were eluding her. Oliver had missed two out of the last four Fridays. Both of them since they'd sat together in his gazebo.

She was disappointed. More disappointed than she had any business being.

Oliver had been John's colleague. He was her best friend's father. He was fifteen years older than she was. He was still in love with his wife. And Beth still tingled whenever she thought of the way he'd kissed her.

Which was often. More often than she cared to admit.

She looked at the clock on her wall one more time. It was an hour past the time Oliver usually stopped by. No. He definitely wasn't coming.

Picking up her purse, Beth shrugged into her coat, locked up and headed home. To the memories of her dead husband.

She was glad Oliver was backing off from their friendship. He wasn't right for her. Not at all.

"MERRY CHRISTMAS, sweetheart."

"Merry Christmas, Lis. I didn't hurt you, did I?" Marcus asked, concerned that he'd been a little too inventive. He wasn't sure what had gotten into him lately. It was almost as if, now that the pressure was off him to give Lisa the baby she wanted, now that he didn't have to feel guilty for his inability to give her that child, he was free to really let his passion loose.

"Uh-uh." She shook her head lazily, her eyes slumberous as she smiled up at him, her long dark hair in disarray across both pillows. There was a blizzard outside, making their large bedroom seem almost cozy. "Not that I have much to go on, mind you, but you've got to be the best lover in the world."

"I'll bet you say that to all the guys," he murmured softly, gazing down at her naked body. They'd shared most of the holiday with Oliver, and Marcus had enjoyed every minute of it, but it was these moments alone with Lisa that he'd been waiting for.

"You *are* all the guys in my life." She looked as if she wanted to say more, but wasn't sure she should. "Can I tell you something?"

"Of course, Lis."

"I lied to you."

His heart started to pound with dread. "When?"

"Remember that first time we made love?"

"At the cabin? Of course. I'd thought I'd died and gone to heaven."

Lisa smiled, though a little nervously. "Remember, right before, when you asked me if I was a virgin?"

"Sure." Marcus wondered if this was another one of those pregnancy things, where she got a little irrational for no reason he could figure out. "You explained about that other guy, Lis. It was only once. You were of age. I've never thought anything of it."

"There *was* no other guy, Marcus." She looked away again, as if embarrassed. "I lied to you. I was afraid you'd go all noble on me and stop if you knew it was my first time."

Marcus propped himself up on one elbow. "You should have told me, Lisa. I wouldn't have stopped—we'd come too far for that—but I could've made it easier on you. I must've hurt you." He didn't know whether to feel angry with her for putting herself through that, or elated that she'd never been with another man.

Lisa shrugged. "It hurt a little, but at that point, I didn't care. And you made me forget about the pain soon enough."

He leaned over, wondering what he'd ever done to deserve this woman. "I'm still sorry I hurt you," he said, running his hand along her brow and down over her cheek. "But, God, Lis—I'm the only one?"

Her tentative nod freed something inside of him, a sense of security he'd never known before. His fingers brushed the sensitive spot on the side of her neck. She'd just given him the best Christmas present he'd ever had.

Lisa shivered, and Marcus continued the caress, down over her shoulders to her breasts and below.

Lisa's belly had expanded to the size of a small basketball, and he caressed the taut skin. She was his Madonna. She was his angel sent from above.

Marcus began to make love to Lisa again, his movements more careful than usual—as if she were a virgin, showing her how it should it have been for her all those years ago. When it was time, he entered her slowly, with the ease of familiarity, but also with a hesitant exploration, learning her anew.

He loved her as slowly as he could, until he was certain he wasn't going to last another second. And then he plunged into her fully. But just as he reached his hilt, something jerked against him, from within her, as if protesting his invasion.

Marcus flew off Lisa and away from the bed so fast he almost hurt himself, staring at his wife as if he'd never met her before. He couldn't believe what had just happened.

Lisa's baby had kicked him. Where it counted. Another man's baby was inside his wife telling him to go away.

What if the baby did that after he was born, too? Told him to go away? Would it come in between him and Lisa? Force her to choose between the two of them?

"Marcus?" She sounded close to tears as she sat up, staring back at him.

Lisa's baby had kicked him.

There really was a little human being growing inside her. One she was going to give birth to in the not-too-distant future. And he'd felt it move. In the most intimate way possible.

He knew her baby in a way no other man ever would.

Yet…it changed nothing. Still didn't make Marcus the father of Lisa's baby. But suddenly he found that he was no longer jealous of the man who *had* fathered her child. Envious as hell, yes. Definitely. Always. But no longer jealous. Marcus knew that baby far more intimately than *that* man did.

LISA SLEPT LITTLE that night, tormented by the look of horror she'd seen on Marcus's face when the baby had kicked him. He'd come back to her, finished what he'd started, tenderly drawing a response from her as he always could, but the minute he'd fallen asleep, her tears had come, sliding silently down her cheeks to sink into the pillow beneath her head. So much for a merry Christmas.

Lying in bed beside Marcus, listening to his steady breathing, she despaired of their future. How could she raise a child with a man who hated it? What would it do to their son or daughter to live in a house with a man who was repulsed by the child's touch? What right did she have to subject *any* child to that kind of life?

Getting out of bed, Lisa wrapped herself in the big furry bathrobe Marcus had given her for Christmas that morning and sat in the bathroom trying to make sense of the tangle that had become her life. The man she adored hated her baby. What was she going to do, torn as she was between the baby she'd come to love so dearly, the baby she needed so badly, and the man who was her other half? How could she possibly keep all three of them happy?

She didn't know, but she could no longer hide from the fact that something had to be done. She couldn't raise her baby in a house full of resentment or indifference. The poor child would grow up feeling unloved.

Much as Marcus had done.

And as confident as he was, when it came to loving, Marcus still blamed himself for the fact that his parents hadn't loved him enough to find time for him. He believed that he was lacking, that he was unlovable. And, God help her, she didn't think she could ever leave him and, in his mind, confirm that belief.

CHAPTER TEN

OLIVER WAS CONCERNED about Lisa. She'd invited him to dinner one Sunday in the middle of January, and by the end of the afternoon, she looked awful. Her skin was white, her eyes dull, and she had almost no energy at all.

"I'm just tired, Dad," she said when he became too worried to keep silent about it.

"Dr. Crutchfield said to expect this," Marcus added later as he walked Oliver to the door.

Oliver wasn't a doctor. And after losing one daughter and a wife, he knew he tended to overreact a bit sometimes, but he'd still rest better with the reassurance of someone who would know just what she was talking about. Someone who wouldn't sugarcoat things for him if, indeed, there *was* something wrong with his daughter.

He hadn't seen Beth at all over the holidays and was certain he'd recovered from whatever middle-aged foolishness had overcome him. At least that was what he told himself when he made a detour by Beth's office on his way home from the university on Tuesday.

"Oliver! Come in!" She sounded happy to see him. He'd been half-afraid she'd show him the door.

"You busy? I can get back to you another time," he said, noticing the huge stack of files on her desk. She looked tired, too. Maybe it was just something that was going around.

"No! No. Come on in. Have a seat. I've missed you these past several Fridays. Not that you have to come by or anything. It's just that I'd gotten kind of used to seeing you."

She was babbling. Oliver liked it. A lot.

"I've been pretty busy lately," he lied, shrugging out of his overcoat. He hated lying, but even more, he couldn't stand to hurt her with the truth. He'd been out with another woman the last Friday, a volunteer at the hospital like he was, a woman his own age. "There's always so much to do when the new semester starts up."

She smiled, looking relieved. "That's all right. I probably wouldn't have been much company, anyway. I've been busy, too. Last Friday I was asleep by eight o'clock."

He could just picture her all curled up in bed. He'd bet she wore a nightie, not pajamas. "Have you seen Lisa lately?" he asked, reminding himself of the reason for his visit.

"Not in the last week or two. She's been spending all her free time with Marcus. But I've spoken with her doctor. Why?"

Oliver shrugged, feeling better already. "I had dinner over there Sunday. She looked tired. Wan."

Beth grinned. "Wouldn't you be feeling kind of tired yourself if you were lugging around all that extra weight? She's gained almost ten pounds."

Oliver considered the grandbaby his daughter was going to present him with. "I guess I would," he said. He was suddenly happier than he'd been in weeks. "And Lisa's small-boned, too, like her mother. Though I don't ever remember Barbara looking so sickly."

"I'll take a look at her, Grandpa. Would that make you feel better?"

"It would," Oliver said, feeling deflated. *Grandpa.* What would a woman Beth's age ever find of interest in an old codger like him?

And why was he even thinking such things again? He'd been cured of all that.

LISA WAS ANEMIC. Debbie Crutchfield recommended that she cut down her working hours to part-time until she was fully rested and had regained her strength.

"I think you should quit working altogether, Lis. At least until after you have your baby," Marcus said as soon as they left the doctor's office. He helped her into her coat, pulling it up over the sleeves of her suit jacket before he tied the belt across her expanding belly.

She was glad he was there. He'd missed one of her checkups because he hadn't wanted to accompany her to the ultrasound that immediately followed the appointment.

"I'll see what I can do," Lisa said, her arm through his as he walked her back to the car. If she had to quit work, she would. She was willing to do whatever it took to have a healthy baby. She just didn't know what she was going to do after the baby was born. She was almost into her seventh month. That gave her three more months. Three months to decide what would happen when she had another life to consider before her own. Would she still be able to lean on Marcus then?

He'd just said it again. *Your* baby. Not *our* baby. He couldn't make it plainer that the baby she was carrying was hers and hers alone. And she was growing more and more afraid that was just how she was going to be raising it. Alone.

"We haven't talked about afterward, Lis," Marcus said later that night. They were in the den, sitting in front of a roaring fire, waiting for the eleven o'clock news.

"What do you mean?" she asked, her heart leaping. Had he read her mind? Did he know that he and her baby couldn't live as strangers in the same house? That she might be forced to choose between the two of them?

"Your work, for one thing. Do you plan to go back after the baby's born?"

Oh. "I guess I just assumed I would, once he's old enough for me to leave him."

Marcus's eyes narrowed. "You keep saying 'he.' Do you know you're having a boy?"

"No." Lisa shook her head. What an insane conversation to be having with the father of her child. If he'd been with her during the ultrasound, he'd know. Or if he'd cared enough to ask her at any time during these many weeks since. "The baby was lying on his stomach and it was impossible to tell."

Marcus nodded, looking about as interested as if

they'd been discussing the weather. "So you plan to hire a nanny to care for it?"

It. Not him or her. *It.* "Yes. I've already made some inquiries at the hospital." She plucked at the bottom of the lounging pajamas she'd put on as soon as they'd arrived home.

"I think that would be preferable to day care," he said.

Lisa froze, not certain she wasn't reading more into his casual statement than was there—as she had a tendency to do these days. But it had sounded like Marcus had just expressed a personal opinion where *her* baby was concerned.

"I thought I'd only work part-time, for the first year at least," she said tentatively.

"That sounds like a good plan. A child should have its mother with it as much as possible during those first years."

As he, Marcus, had not. Lisa heard what her husband wasn't saying. *Oh, Marcus, please let yourself be loved as you were meant to be loved. Not just by me. But by your new family, too.*

"I don't think I'll be able to leave him more than that, anyway," she said, chuckling. "I'm finding I have some rather possessive motherly tendencies."

Marcus smiled. "I'm glad."

He reached for the television control and flipped on the news, which effectively put an end to the conversation. But Lisa was smiling when she went to bed that night. Was Marcus finally starting to thaw? Could it be that she'd be able to have her baby and her husband, too? Was it possible she'd gambled—and won?

SHE WAS STILL ASLEEP when Marcus left for work the next morning. He left her a note on his pillow, telling her good-morning, rather than waking her. He was happy to see that she was finally getting some rest. With her nights constantly interrupted by trips to the bathroom, getting up at the crack of dawn had become too much for her.

He'd be relieved when the whole thing was over, he thought as he drove through the old and elegant streets of New Haven, beautiful even with the gray skies overhead and the slush on the ground. As much as he enjoyed watching Lisa's body blossom, he was growing increasingly more worried about her as her pregnancy progressed.

Of course, he had his share of apprehensions for afterward, too. Would Lisa still have time for him? Would her baby resent his place in Lisa's life? She was going to be a very devoted mother, which pleased Marcus, but would she need him around once she had her baby to love?

Disgusted with himself for harboring such fears, Marcus attacked his work that day with a vengeance. He had another meeting with George Blake, and he was going to get the deal done. It was time to quit being Mr. Nice Guy.

Blake and his team arrived fifteen minutes early, but Marcus was ready for them. He led them to the executive conference room down the hall from his office then waited only until Marge had served coffee before beginning the meeting.

"Gentlemen, I think what we've worked out here together should just about take care of the future of

Blake's department stores," Marcus said, cutting to the chase. He held up a copy of the latest proposal for a fifty-one/forty-nine percent merger, allowing Blake's the fifty-one percent and Cartwright Enterprises the management privileges, all of which were specified in minute detail.

"I have just one suggestion about page fifteen, item one, young man," George Blake said, "under software implementation for inventory control."

Marcus stifled a groan. He'd known the old guy was going to find a way to make this difficult. It was time to play hardball. "What would that be, George?"

"I'm not sure that it's fiscally wise to invest so heavily in a system that will be outdated by the end of the year."

Marcus's rebuttal died in his throat. "Oh?" he said. He'd had to fight for months to get George to allow him to put computers in the Blake's enterprise at all because the old man hadn't known the first thing about them and, thus, didn't trust them.

"CD-ROM, all of that, will be a thing of the past before we know it," George said, tapping the pages in front of him. "If we were buying this two years ago, I'd agree that it would be worth the investment, but at this late date, I say we buy a system that will allow us to move into the future, a system that we can expand on, rather than replace."

Marcus felt like giving the old man a hug. He grinned, instead. "I'd say that's sound advice, George. I'll have my team on it first thing in the morning."

OLIVER WAS BUSHED. He stopped by Beth's office after volunteering on Friday, needing to see her in spite of the anger tamped down inside of him. They'd lost another kidney patient that week, one who probably could have been saved if they'd had the new dialysis equipment he'd been campaigning for. Thornton had the money. They just chose to spend it in other places. Such as Beth's clinic. A few lives gained for one lost, he thought with uncharacteristic bitterness.

"You up for dinner?" he asked, poking his head around her door.

"You bet." She turned off her computer, grabbed her coat and locked up behind her, watching him all the while.

"What's wrong?" she asked.

They were walking briskly out to their cars, hunched over against the cold.

"Rosie Gardner died today."

He could see the instant understanding in her eyes as she slowed to look at him. It was hard to blame her for taking the dialysis-equipment money when she looked at him like that.

"I'm sorry." She linked her arm with his so naturally that he shouldn't even have noticed. Except that he did. His whole body noticed.

"If we'd just had that damned equipment," he said, reminding himself that it was better if he stayed at least a little bit angry with her. Except that he wouldn't have a grandchild on the way, an extension of Barbara, if it wasn't for Beth's clinic.

"Have you asked Marcus for help?" she asked, standing beside her car while he unlocked the door for her. He could see her breath in the frosty air.

"Of course not. I'd never ask Marcus for money.
Too many other people do that every day of his life.
The boy already thinks his money is the only reason
most people care about him. I certainly don't want him
thinking that about me."

Beth smiled, her full dimples twinkling up at him.
"I didn't mean personally. I meant Cartwright Enterprises. If you get your money from a private source,
it has to buy only what it was donated to buy. The
hospital no longer has a say in designating how the
funds are spent. And it's not unheard of for private
companies to donate to hospitals, though the way hospitals have become big businesses themselves, it's not
done as often anymore. Still, it's a great tax write-
off."

"You're sure the hospital has no means to direct
the spending?" Oliver asked. He'd understood that everything that was used in the hospital had to be hos-
pital-sanctioned.

"They can direct only insomuch as determining
which machine they deem most suitable to their needs,
but all the money either has to be used for the desig-
nated purpose or returned."

Oliver followed Beth to a steak house around the
corner from the hospital, mulling over her suggestion.
It might work. It just might work.

Beth was one smart woman. Which was one of the
reasons he enjoyed the time he spent with her.

It had nothing whatsoever to do with the fact that
her lips were made for kissing.

"OH, LOOK AT THIS ONE! It's so tiny." Lisa held up
the cutest little T-shirt she'd ever seen.

"I think your baby's already too big to fit into that," Beth said, grinning at her.

"Nah," said Crystal, a maternity nurse from the hospital. "She's hardly showing yet. Just wait another couple of months. Then he'll be too big."

"Don't even talk about it." Lisa rubbed the front of her navy blue maternity dress. "Another couple of months and I'm not going to be able to walk."

Everyone laughed and Lisa was suddenly glad Beth had arranged the baby shower for her. She'd missed her friends.

"Have you guys picked out names yet?" Nancy, a doctor from ER, asked.

"Sawyer if it's a boy," Lisa said. "Sara Barbara if it's a girl." The names had been picked so many years ago she didn't even have to think about it.

She opened another gift, a pair of tiny designer tennis shoes. And looked up just in time to see Marcus standing in the doorway. He was supposed to be in Storrs at a meeting for most of the afternoon. Which was why she'd agreed to Beth's suggestion that the shower be at her, Lisa's, house.

He was gone before anyone noticed him, before Lisa had a chance to call him back, but not before the look on his face had torn her heart in two. Raw longing had blazed from his eyes as he'd looked at the tiny pair of shoes she held. Longing and agony. Her husband still wanted a child of his own. And it was killing him that she was having one without him.

SHE TRIED TO PULL AWAY from Marcus, to make herself, and her condition, as scarce as possible after seeing his face that day of her shower. She just couldn't bear to hurt him anymore.

But staying away was almost impossible. Everywhere she went, everything she did, he was right beside her, watching over her. Protecting her. Loving her. And her foolish heart began to hope again. Marcus's pain would vanish if he could only allow himself to believe that the baby she was carrying was his.

But how did she make him believe?

"LET'S GO FOR A WALK," Marcus said one Sunday during the seventh month of her pregnancy. It was one of those sunny February days, still cold but dry, and perfect for walking. He looked disgustingly energetic in his jeans and corduroy shirt.

"I'm too tired." Lisa was lying on the couch reading the paper and perfectly content to stay that way.

"Come on, Lis. You heard Debbie. The more walking you do, the easier the birth will be on you."

Lisa threw down the paper. "Fine. We'll walk," she said, hauling herself up to go put on some warmer clothes and some shoes. She was getting tired of everyone else knowing what was better for her than she did.

Marcus waited more than fifteen minutes before he started to get concerned and went up to check on her. What could possibly be taking her so long?

She was in the bedroom, stomping her foot on the carpet and crying like a baby. She only had one tennis shoe on.

"Lisa? What is it, hon?" he asked gently.

"Nothing," she said petulantly, sounding more like

a child herself than a woman preparing to give birth to one.

He crossed to her and took her in his arms. "Something must be wrong, Lis. Please tell me what." He wasn't sure he was ever going to become accustomed to her unpredictable mood swings.

Laying her head against him, she sniffed noisily, then muttered something inaudible.

"Hmm?" he asked, stroking her hair.

"I can't tie my shoe," she said more loudly.

He had to use every muscle in his face to hold back the grin that threatened to burst forth as he took stock of the situation. His beautiful talented wife could no longer reach her arms around her expanding belly to get to her feet.

"Then I guess it's my job to do it for you, huh?" he asked once he was sure he had his smile under control.

She pulled back from him. "I guess," she said, holding her foot out dejectedly.

She teetered a little when Marcus bent to his task. "Maybe you better sit down." He nudged her backward to the bed.

Kneeling, he tied the shoe and then slid the other shoe onto her other foot, tying that one, as well. Just as he was finishing, he felt her foot quiver, spasms that were repeated throughout her body, even shaking the bed.

Damn. If she was sobbing that hard she really had it bad.

"It's okay, Lis," he said, running his hand gently along her calf. He glanced up at her, wishing he could do more to help her—and couldn't believe what he saw. She wasn't crying. She was laughing so hard her whole body shook.

"I'm s-s-sorry," she said, through her mirth. "It's just…seeing you down there…" She broke into another peel of laughter.

Feeling alive and in love, and very relieved to see his wife had regained her sense of humor, Marcus took her into his arms, sharing her laughter and her love.

Their walk was postponed until later in the afternoon.

THE SHOWER WAS RUNNING. Marcus could hear it when he came in from work one Thursday during the last week in February. Dropping his briefcase in the office, he climbed the stairs, a grin on his face, one he could definitely share with his wife. It must not have been one of Lisa's more energetic days if she was only just getting around to showering at four o'clock in the afternoon. It amused him how much a lady of leisure she was becoming as each day seemed to add another pound for her slight frame to carry around. He loved having Lisa pregnant.

There were still times when his laughter stuck in his throat, when he thought about what might have been if Lisa's pregnancy had been as real for him as it was for her. But he'd learned to ignore those moments. Most of them.

He could see her through the steamy glass door of the shower enclosure. Her head was back, her hands running through her hair as the water ran across her face and down over her shoulders. Marcus's gaze followed the route the water was taking, stopping at Lisa's ripe breasts. Her nipples pebbled as the water caressed them and then streamed over her rounded belly.

His own body hardened with desire and with sheer male pride as he watched her. *His woman.* The baby she was carrying wasn't his, but the woman was. He was the only man who would ever know this particular sight of her, naked and wet and swollen with child. Marcus had never been more grateful for anything in his life.

Stripping off his clothes, he joined her in the shower, greeting her with a wet heated kiss.

"Nice greeting," she said, wrapping her arms around him. "I'm glad you're home."

He licked a drop of water off from her chin. "Had a rough afternoon?"

"I seem to have slept most of it away," she said, grinning at him.

Marcus took the bar of soap from its dish and began a leisurely exploration of Lisa's curves, caressing her shoulders and then her breasts.

"Mmm. This was worth getting up for." Lisa's eyes were closed, her lips smiling and moist. Marcus bent to kiss them as his soapy hands moved down to caress the stretched skin of her belly.

He touched her so tenderly, his big hands almost reverent in their attention, that Lisa thought she'd die of love for him. The water grew cold and Marcus turned it off, never missing a beat as he continued to kiss her. Wrapping her in a big fluffy bath towel, he lifted her and carried her to their bed.

But later that night, when the loving was done, she

couldn't help wishing that the wealth of tenderness Marcus was showing her included the child she carried....

BETH STOPPED to see Lisa the next day on her way home from work.

"How ya doing, Mama?" she asked, giving Lisa a hug.

"I don't know," Lisa said, returning the hug.

Beth's stomach sank. "You're not feeling well?" she asked, searching Lisa's face for any sign of pain, pallor, anything she might have missed when Lisa had opened the door. Lisa looked great, every bit the healthy mother-to-be in her maternity blouse and slacks.

"I feel as well as can be expected physically." Lisa shrugged. "You want some tea?"

"Sure." Beth followed her friend to the back of the house, to the huge homey kitchen she knew Lisa adored. Oliver had told Beth that Lisa and Marcus were doing fine. Better than fine, according to Marcus. So what was up?

"I'm glad you stopped by," Lisa said. "I've missed you." She put water on to boil and pulled a couple of herbal teabags out of a canister on the counter.

Feeling uncomfortably guilty, Beth reached for the cups. "I've missed you, too. It's not the same not having you at work."

Lisa gave a small grin. "I don't miss it as much as I thought I would. Of course, that's probably because it's such an effort just getting out of bed in the mornings I can't imagine having to handle a crisis."

Beth smiled. Maybe the normal fatigue that went with pregnancy was all that was bothering Lisa. "Get your rest now, while you can. 'Cause in a couple of months, you'll be lucky to look at your bed, let alone get in it."

Lisa poured hot water over the teabags, still grinning. "I know. I can't wait."

The two women sat down at the kitchen table, sipping their tea, and Beth couldn't help being a little envious. Not of Lisa's beautiful home. Not even of her baby. But of her happiness, her surety of where life was leading her, the closeness she shared with her husband.

"It's probably not going to be all that bad for you, anyway," Beth said. "Knowing Marcus, he'll insist on taking all the middle-of-the-night feedings."

Lisa frowned, looking down into her cup. "I'm planning to breast-feed."

"So he'll get up and bring the baby in to you, always changing his diaper first, of course."

Lisa was silent for a minute before looking up at Beth. "He's not going to have anything to do with this baby," she said softly, her eyes suddenly filling with tears.

Beth covered Lisa's hand with hers. "What makes you even think such a thing?"

"I don't just think it, Beth. I know it." The conviction in Lisa's voice was chilling.

"He's said so?" Beth asked.

Lisa nodded, the tears spilling from her eyes and rolling down her cheeks. "Many times. I thought he'd change his mind, even after he told me not to hope that he would. I thought I knew Marcus. But I guess I don't. As far as he's concerned, my baby doesn't exist."

"Oh, Lisa, I'm so sorry. What are you going to do? Do you want me to try talking to him?"

"Yes. No. I don't know anymore. It wouldn't do any good. I've talked until there aren't any words left. Dad's talked to him, too, though I don't think he has any idea how bad it really is." Beth saw utter despair in Lisa's eyes. "I can't even imagine a life without Marcus," Lisa went on, "don't know where I'd ever find the strength to leave him. But how can I bring my baby into a house where he'll be ignored, treated as if he doesn't exist?"

"Does Marcus know? That you're thinking about leaving him, I mean?"

Lisa shook her head, looking more miserable than any pregnant woman ought to look. Beth got up and took her friend into her arms, her heart breaking in two. This was her fault; she'd ripped apart the lives of her best friends with her meddling. Her tears slowly mingled with Lisa's as she held her, wondering when it was she'd forgotten that she was a doctor and started playing God, instead.

CHAPTER ELEVEN

BETH COULDN'T GO HOME that night. She couldn't face the silence, the recriminations, the "I told you sos" she'd hear every time she looked at John's picture. He'd been after her for her meddling since the day they'd met, telling her to leave other people's business alone. But it was a habit she'd developed early on, growing up with a bunch of younger siblings. She'd been the one to take care of everyone, to prevent whatever disasters she could, to make certain everyone was tended to. She'd had to meddle to keep everyone safe—and she'd been good at it.

But it was an asset that had become a liability as she reached adulthood. This wasn't the first time she'd caused someone heartache because she couldn't leave well enough alone. If only John were still alive. He'd have stopped her from pushing Lisa into this last irrevocable step.

Beth didn't make a conscious decision to seek out Oliver, but found herself pulling into his driveway just after dark, anyway. She wasn't sure how he'd react when he found out how awful things really were between Lisa and Marcus. He'd probably never forgive her for sticking her nose in where it didn't belong.

Remembering Lisa's broken sobs, she didn't think she'd ever forgive herself.

"Beth! What is it, my dear? Come in. What's happened?" Oliver asked as soon as he answered his door and saw her face.

Beth knew she must look a wreck. But it didn't matter. Not when her friend's life was falling apart.

"I've made the biggest mistake of my life and there's no way to fix it," she said bluntly, standing in the foyer of Oliver's home.

Oliver's eyes darkened with concern. "I'm sure it's not that bad. We'll think of something. Come in and sit." He put one arm around Beth's shoulder and led her into his living room.

I don't deserve his concern, Beth thought.

"Marcus refuses to accept Lisa's baby and it's all my fault. I talked her into it. I was so sure it was the perfect answer. But I had a feeling she hadn't told him, and I went ahead and inseminated her, anyway. And now it looks like she's going to have to choose between the husband she adores and her baby. Where do I get off thinking I know what's best for other people when I don't even know what's best for myself?"

"Shh. Slow down. What's this about Marcus and the baby? He told me himself just two days ago that things were great between him and Lisa. He looked happier than he's looked in years."

Beth shook her head. "He *is* happy with Lisa. But he's got some cockamamy idea that he and Lisa can be married while she raises her child herself. Even *I* know that's no way to bring up a child."

Oliver shook his head, sadness mingling with the

worry Beth saw in his eyes. "She's got to give him more time. Wait until he sees the baby. Until she brings it home. I suspect he'll come around then. Marcus has a wealth of love to give. I'm laying odds he'll make the right decision when the time comes."

"And if he doesn't?"

"I'm not ready to consider that possibility. It would kill my daughter to lose Marcus. I know that as surely as I know my own name."

To her chagrin, Beth felt tears fill her eyes. "Oh, God. What a mess I've made of things," she said. How could she have ruined the lives of the two people she cared about most in the world?

"What do you mean? You did your job. That's all."

Beth shook her head. "I wish that was all. I'd been after Lisa for months to consider artificial insemination. I was just so sure it was the right answer. The only answer for them. I couldn't have been more wrong."

"But the final decision was Lisa's, my dear. She wanted this baby, make no mistake about that."

Beth wished she could be so sure. "She said no for months, Oliver. She wouldn't even consider it, because she knew Marcus would react this way. I see that now. But she was so unhappy, getting unhappier every time I saw her, so I kept at her. The week before we did the procedure she came to see me. I'd even picked out a donor for her and told her all about him. She still said no."

Oliver put his arm around her shoulders again. Beth couldn't believe how badly she wanted to snuggle into his embrace, in spite of how wrong that would be.

"She didn't come to you against her will, Beth. Lisa's a big girl with a mind of her own. You, my dear, seem to have a tendency to be a bit too hard on yourself. You're not to blame for Marcus and Lisa's current situation any more than Marcus is to blame for his sterility."

"It's just that I meddle sometimes. I know I do. I try not to, I really do, but before I know it, I'm up to my elbows in someone's problems." Oliver might as well know.

He pulled her against him, right where she so wanted to be. "That's called caring, dear Beth, not meddling," he said softly.

Beth glanced up at the odd tone in his voice, and her blood started to race the minute she met his gaze. He was looking at her with complete honesty, holding nothing back, and the desire she saw in his eyes took her breath away.

"Oliver?" she whispered, knowing they were crossing a line never meant to be crossed, yet unable to prevent herself.

"Ah, Beth. Life's too short, happiness too fleeting, to let this slip away. You feel it, too, don't you? This thing between us. It's not just a silly fantasy of a wishful old man, is it?"

"You aren't old, Oliver. Not by a long shot. And yes, I feel it, too."

As he bent his head and kissed her and she lost herself in the blissful experience of his touch, she hoped John would forgive her for falling in love with another man.

HER BACK ACHED. Drugged with sleep, Lisa rolled over, burrowing into Marcus's side as she tried to get comfortable. But the pain came again, sharper this time, bringing her fully awake. And instantly afraid.

"Marcus?" she said, scared to move, to sit up.

"What is it, Lis?" He flipped on the bedside light, concern in his eyes.

"It's the baby, Marcus. He's coming and it's way too early." Tears stung her eyes, but she was afraid to cry. She lay perfectly still, hoping against all the logic of her doctor's training that if she didn't move, she could keep the tiny life inside her a little while longer.

Another pain gripped her, and Lisa cried out. Something was wrong. Drastically wrong.

"Lis? Do you need to get to the bathroom?"

"No!" she cried. "No. I don't want to move. I'm not going to lose my baby. Not now. Please, God, no." She started to sob softly, as yet another pain shot up her back. She'd been feeling twinges in her back for just over a week, but she'd thought they were perfectly normal.

Marcus was a blur in her haze of pain as he reached for the phone on the nightstand and dialed Debbie Crutchfield. He spoke quickly, then just as quickly hung up the phone and got out of bed.

"I'm going to have to move you, Lis. Debbie's meeting us at the hospital in fifteen minutes."

He pulled on a pair of jeans and a sweatshirt while he talked, shrugging into his jacket and pulling on his shoes in record time.

"Here we go. Just lie still, honey," he said, wrapping the comforter from the bed around her and lifting her, still in her nightgown, into his arms.

He sped down the stairs with her, not even stopping to lock the door behind them as he stepped out into the garage and settled her into the Ferrari.

Lisa felt a rush of warm liquid between her thighs when he lay her back in the seat. "Oh, God, no!" she cried.

"What?" Marcus looked down at the blanket around her, saw the spreading stain. "Okay, Lisa. Just hang on, love. We'll beat this yet. Just hold on."

His words did little to ease the ache in her heart. She was a doctor. She knew what was coming. With her water broken, they wouldn't be able to save the pregnancy. And she was barely seven months along.

She bit her lip and groaned as another pain consumed her. She was losing her baby.

"Hold on, sweetheart. Just hold on another few minutes. We're almost there, and then everything's going to be fine. You'll see, it'll be fine..."

Marcus's soothing words filled the car during the entire trip to the hospital, but Lisa barely heard them as she fought the pain. It was constant now, and building in such intensity she was afraid she was going to tear apart.

Don't go, little one. Please don't go. She repeated the words over and over, as if somehow they could manage to accomplish what she knew medical science could not. She couldn't bear to lose this baby. She couldn't.

A stretcher was waiting for her at the hospital, and

Lisa looked up into Debbie's worried face even before she was inside the emergency-room doors.

She heard Debbie's brisk command. "Take her into delivery, stat."

"No! Not yet. Let's wait and see—"

"It's too late, Lisa," Debbie said, hurrying along beside the stretcher. "It's you we have to be concerned about now. You're losing a lot of blood."

It was *her* they had to be concerned about now. Did that mean...? No. It couldn't. She'd felt the baby move only a couple of hours ago. He'd kicked her hard, twice, when she'd climbed into bed. She'd rubbed her hand over him, soothing him, until he'd fallen asleep. She'd whispered good-night to him, just as she had every night since she'd found out she was pregnant.

She was rushed into a room filled with bright lights and people. Things were happening so fast, orders coming so quickly, Lisa couldn't keep track of it all. She was in agony, both mentally and physically, and soon the only thing she was conscious of was Marcus standing beside her bed, dressed in surgical greens.

"We'll make it through this, Lis. You just hang on for me, you hear?" he said, holding her hand while the doctor and nurses got an IV going, examined her and hooked her up to a couple of different monitors. In one part of her brain, Lisa knew everything they were doing. And she knew why. She knew she'd have given the same orders Debbie was giving were their positions reversed.

Yet she hated the doctor for taking away her dream. As the minutes passed and the pain didn't relent,

Lisa focused more and more on Marcus. On his steady strength. His hopeful words. He was telling her what she wanted to hear. What she needed to hear. That everything was going to be all right. And because he was saying it, she tried to believe him.

Marcus thought that this was what it was like to lose one's mind. He was finding it increasingly difficult to concentrate. To focus. As the medical personnel rushed around Lisa, peeling the bloodstained blanket away, he sank further and further into a blind panic.

"Get me the blood, stat," Debbie Crutchfield hollered at one of the orderlies. "She may be hemorrhaging."

It was his worst nightmare coming true. Lisa was in trouble. And all he could do was stand by and watch as the team of professionals tried to save her. And pray. Marcus had never prayed harder for anything in his life as he did then, standing beside his wife, horrified as he watched the blood flow out of her.

Only Lisa kept him sane. Lisa and her need of him. Marcus refused to let her see his fear or hear the worry in his voice. He reassured her over and over, knowing how desperately she needed the words of encouragement. He would pull her through this with his strength alone if he had to. He wasn't going to lose her. Not now. Not like this.

Lisa gave a sharp cry and Marcus's heart missed a beat. He glanced at Debbie, looking for reassurance, but Debbie's face was a study of intense concentration as she worked between Lisa's legs.

And suddenly Marcus knew a new fear, an unfamiliar fear, as he considered the life his wife was trying so desperately to save. Not her own. But the life inside her. For the first time he noticed the mirror set back behind the doctor. And as he glanced up, he saw a flash of a tiny head, a swatch of hair, and then the full head, as Lisa started to push the baby from her body.

Her fingers were clutching his so tightly he lost circulation, but he continued to hold her, to soothe her, his eyes glued to the mirror behind the doctor.

There were the shoulders. And with one last groan from Lisa, the tiniest body he'd ever seen emerged into the brightly lit room. Marcus's gaze flew to Debbie's face. Waiting.

"She's alive."

He hadn't even realized he'd been holding his breath until he heard the words. *She's alive.* His gaze darted from the too-tiny body to his wife's face, and then, medical personnel be damned, he gathered Lisa into his arms, holding her against him.

LISA HAD BARELY a glance at her daughter before Debbie snipped the cord and they whisked the little body away. She didn't even get a chance to see if the baby had all her fingers and toes, seeing only that she had a full head of dark hair, this child she'd waited so long to have, yet had way too soon.

She buried her head against Marcus, no longer able to hold back the sobs that tore through her. She was a doctor. A children's doctor. She knew.

The baby couldn't have weighed more than two pounds. And she hadn't cried, indicating that her lungs weren't fully developed—if at all. Her chances of surviving were slim.

There were so many things that could go wrong, that could already be wrong. Lisa wished she could still the voices in her head.

She knew what she'd tell the parents if she was the attending pediatrician. And she couldn't bear to hear the words. This time she was the parent. And that hopelessly tiny silent baby was her daughter. Sara Barbara Cartwright. She had a daughter. Who was to have had a perfect life.

And suddenly Lisa knew that any decision she had to make had already been made. If Marcus could not be a father to their daughter, she couldn't live with him. Because if the baby survived—and she would if Lisa had to breathe life into her every day until she could breathe on her own—she was going to be raised in a house of love.

Debbie finished with Lisa, making way for the nurse to prepare her to go to her room, and Marcus stood aside while they did what they had to do.

"You came through this just fine, Lisa. Much better than I expected, as a matter of fact. I suspect you'll be released sometime tomorrow." The doctor didn't smile, didn't attempt to sugarcoat her words. She was fully aware that Lisa knew exactly how grave the situation really was.

Lisa could go home the next day. The baby wouldn't be going home for a long time. If ever.

Tears streamed down Lisa's tired face and Marcus wiped them away. Turning her face into his palm, Lisa kissed him. In spite of the decision she'd made, she needed him desperately. Needed his strength. His warmth. She wasn't going to get through the next hours without him.

"I've ordered something to help you sleep as soon as you get settled in your room," Debbie said, pulling off her gloves.

"I don't want to sleep. I have to see her, see what they're doing. I have to know."

"Listen to the doctor, Lis," Marcus said, his hand on her shoulder.

"You have to be sensible, Lisa." Debbie stood on the other side of Lisa's bed. "For the baby's sake, as well as your own. You just came through a rough birth, you came close to hemorrhaging, and you need your rest if you're going to do that young lady any good later. And they won't let you in with her right now, anyway. You know that. Randal Cunningham is with her. He's the best there is. Let him do his job."

Marcus stayed with Lisa until she fell into an exhausted sleep. It was more than an hour after the birth, and she'd fought sleep with every bit of strength she had, waiting to hear about her baby, but the sleeping pill Debbie had prescribed had finally done its work, allowing Lisa the rest she so desperately needed.

Marcus rubbed his hands down his face as he sat beside Lisa's bed, more exhausted than he'd ever been in his life. What a night. The most frightening night of his life.

He shuddered when he saw again all that blood soaking the blanket around Lisa. He'd never been so afraid of anything as he'd been during that trip to the hospital and the minutes immediately following.

Standing, he took one last look at his wife, and then headed out into the silent corridor of the sleeping hospital. He needed to get home, get some rest, if he was going to make it back by the time Lisa awoke in the morning.

Stopping only long enough to notify the night nurse that he was going home and that he expected to be called if Lisa so much as turned over in bed, he continued on down the hall toward the elevator. Most of the rooms he passed were in darkness or lit only by a soft night-light, but there was a window down by the elevator that was glaring with so much light it spilled out into the hospital corridor.

Marcus found out why when he reached the window. It was the nursery. He told himself to keep on walking, that there was no reason for him to glance that way, but as he passed he heard the plaintive wail of a newborn baby and turned his head instinctively. It wasn't Lisa's baby he heard.

Hers was the one everybody was working on in a separate part of the nursery. Marcus could barely see the tiny body in the sea of medical personnel surrounding the funny little crib in which she lay. It was a box not more than two feet long and maybe eight inches wide, with huge bright lights hanging above it. He winced as he saw the many hands, which looked so big next to such a small body, working over it so quickly.

Marcus moved around the corner, entering a viewing room with a couple of couches and chairs that had another window into the nursery, a window closer to the peculiar bed with the miniature baby. From there he could see the card that hung at the end of the crib. *Cartwright Girl.*

His gut clenched as he looked again. *Cartwright Girl.* That tiny baby girl had his name.

He knew he needed to go, that he had to get some rest before he collapsed, but he couldn't make himself leave the window. Lisa's baby was barely the size of his hand. He didn't see how it could possibly have all the working parts necessary to sustain life. He knew the baby was still alive. There would be no reason for anyone to be working over her if she wasn't. But that bit of news didn't tell him anything about her chances to survive.

One of the nurses moved away from the crib for a moment, reaching for something on a tray, and Marcus had a clearer glimpse of the baby. A tube wider than her arm was taped to her mouth with what looked like a big Band-Aid. The other end of the tube was connected by a series of contraptions to a ventilator machine. She wasn't breathing on her own.

He had no idea what the rest of the many tubes and wires applied to her minute body were for, but knew it wasn't good that they took up more room in her bed than she did. Other than the medical paraphernalia attached to her, the baby was naked, her diminutive bottom lying on an open disposable diaper. Her tiny head wore a blue-pink-and-white-striped cap, covering up the thatch of hair that was the first sight he'd had of her. Her eyes were closed. He wondered if she was actually sleeping through all of the ministrations, or if she simply couldn't open her eyes.

She appeared to have all her fingers and toes.

The nurse returned to the crib, blocking Marcus's view, and he slumped back into the chair closest to the viewing window, watching as the specialists worked. *Cartwright Girl.* He'd kept himself so apart from the life Lisa had been creating these past months that he'd never even considered there would be a name for the child. His name.

He wondered what else Lisa planned to call her baby. But he already knew. Sara, for her beloved little sister. And Barbara, after her mother. Sara Barbara Cartwright. The name had a familiar ring to it. Sara. He hoped Lisa was calling her Sara. They'd always said they'd name their first girl Sara.

Personnel came and went from the baby's crib for most of the night, and as the hours passed, Marcus continued to sit, to watch. He wondered about the baby's father. Was he a young college student who'd given a donation to the sperm bank for a quick buck? Or a good samaritan who wanted to make dreams possible for women who couldn't have children any other way? Maybe he was in the medical field. If so, Lisa's baby was going to be one smart little girl. If she survived.

And suddenly Marcus knew without a shadow of doubt just how badly he wanted the child to survive. Lisa would never be the same if her baby died. After all she'd been through, after all the lives she'd saved and the ones she'd lost, she deserved this chance for herself. And the baby deserved it, too. She was Lisa's baby. That alone made her the most special child in the nursery.

The tall silver-haired doctor who hadn't left the baby's side all night finally turned away from the crib, stripping off his gloves. Marcus's heart caught in his throat as he waited for some sign that the battle had been won—or lost. The doctor spoke to a nurse who'd remained beside the crib, and the nurse nodded several times before pulling a chair up to the side of the crib and sitting down to watch the baby's monitors. It was then that Marcus noticed what he thought was some kind of heart monitor, set way off behind the baby. The marks he saw were wavery. But they were there.

Marcus heaved a huge sigh of relief. He thought again of the father of Lisa's baby, wondering if the guy would care that his daughter was lying there, so tiny, fighting impossible odds for her life. The guy was a first-class bastard if he didn't.

Marcus was appalled at all the gadgets surrounding the tiny body, the IV taped to her skull, the catheter in her right arm, which was strapped to a board. He hated that someone so small had to endure so much discomfort. And aside from all the wires and tubes, her entire body was wrapped in what looked like a big piece of cellophane. She lay there silently, her eyes still closed. Marcus hoped she was sleeping peacefully.

He was still there early the next morning when Beth came in to see the baby.

"Beth!" He shot upright. "Oh, my God. I never even called Oliver. How'd you know where to find us?"

Beth didn't turn from the window, her gaze glued on the box that was Lisa's crib. "Crystal called me an hour ago. Lisa was awake and asking for you, and they couldn't reach you at home, but she's asleep again now,'' she said. Crystal was the night nurse working Lisa's floor. ''Crystal said Lisa had the baby shortly after one. Have you been here all night?''

''I didn't realize how much time had passed,'' Marcus said, turning toward the baby again. She hadn't moved a muscle in all those hours. He knew. He'd been watching every second for any sign that she was taking control of her life.

''Has anybody been out yet to tell you anything?''

''No.''

''Crystal said she's holding her own.''

''But she's not breathing on her own.''

''Not yet. But that's to be expected for now.''

''What're her chances, Beth?'' He'd spent the night avoiding the question, but he had to know.

''Twenty-five percent. Maybe thirty.''

''That's all?'' His heart sank.

''Her lungs aren't developed. But the machine can do their job until they are,'' she told him.

''Is everything else all right?'' he asked.

''It's too early to tell,'' Beth said, still watching the baby. ''Her digestive system isn't fully developed yet, either. But again, that's expected. There's a fairly good chance of brain damage and deafness. Mental retardation, too.'' Her voice caught in her throat and Marcus knew she was feeling a lot more than she was letting on. Her bedside manner could only cover so much. And Marcus knew Beth well.

''But isn't there a chance she'll be perfectly normal once she grows up to size?'' He was asking for all their sakes. Including the baby's. The baby's most of all.

Beth shrugged. "A slight one."

"What about her kidneys and other organs?" he asked, wondering for the hundredth time how a body so small could actually sustain life.

"It's too early to tell. She'll be fed intravenously for now, glucose only. After a few weeks, if they can, they'll begin tube-feeding her. It'll be a while before they know if her excretory system's working."

Marcus heard the qualifier. *If* the baby lived. They both stood silently, keeping their vigil.

"It killed her to do this without you, you know," Beth said.

It took Marcus a second to understand what she meant. He didn't reply. He couldn't. He'd put all that behind him now.

"I found her in the bathroom afterward, being sick to her stomach. She said she was going home to seduce you, that her baby was going to be conceived in love one way or the other, and that you were going to be the one to provide that most necessary ingredient. The love."

Marcus remembered that night, remembered the way Lisa had met him at the door. Desperate for him. For his love. He'd given it to her, too. Just as he'd always given her everything she wanted. Except the one thing she'd wanted most.

"How long's the baby going to be in that special crib?" he asked, looking at the child Lisa and Beth had created that day, needing to make Beth stop talking about things that were past.

"It's a warming bed, and that depends completely on her. One of the reasons she's there is so they can get right at her, but also because her body's unable to maintain enough heat to stay alive. The warming bed simulates the mother's uterus, maintaining a temperature of ninety-eight point six rather than normal room temperature of seventy. And based on her size, I'd say she could be in there for six weeks or more before she's moved to an incubator."

If she lives. Damn. She *will* live. Watching the still form in her bed of plastic wrap, he said, "She's going to make it, Beth."

"I hope so, Marcus. I sure hope so." Beth turned from the window to face him.

It was then that Marcus saw the tears running slowly down her face. He pulled Beth into his arms, offering what comfort he could, taking from her the silent solace she had to give.

CHAPTER TWELVE

LISA AWOKE with a feeling of dread and she reached for Marcus automatically, thinking even through her groggy confusion that whatever was wrong was manageable with Marcus beside her. Her hand bumped against the cold rail on the side of her hospital bed, instead. And it all flooded back to her. Her baby! Oh, God, was she...

Fumbling frantically, she found the call button for the nurse among the covers on the side of her bed, depressing the lever immediately and continuously. A young nurse she barely knew flew into the room, her short dark hair framing a no-nonsense face.

"Yes, Dr. Cartwright? Do you need help?"

"My baby. How's my baby?" Lisa asked, clutching her bedcovers.

"She's alive, Doctor."

Lisa released the breath she'd been holding. "She made it through the night. That's a good sign," she said almost to herself, while visions of underdeveloped lungs and kidneys filled her mind. There was so much that could be wrong, that could take her baby from her at any moment. Her chest tightened.

The nurse smiled shyly, her features softening into

prettiness. "You've got a fighter there, Doctor," she said.

Lisa nodded, trying to smile. Trying to be strong.

"Your husband brought some clothes for you. I can help you get ready to go if you like. Dr. Crutchfield will be here to release you shortly." The nurse picked up an overnight bag from the floor at the foot of her bed.

Lisa heard one thing through her panic-induced haze. "Marcus is here?"

The nurse nodded. "Dr. Montague's been here, too. Your husband just left to get some coffee, at her instigation, and I'm willing to bet he'll wish he hadn't. He really wanted to be here with you when you woke up. I wish my husband were half that besotted with me," she confided.

Lisa smiled, barely hearing the nurse's small talk. Marcus was here. She just had to hold on a few more minutes and he'd be with her. And then she'd face whatever news was waiting down the hall in the nursery. She'd find out what kind of battle her tiny baby was fighting.

There was a knock on the open door, and Lisa turned her head to see her father standing there, holding the biggest teddy bear she'd ever seen.

"Hi, honey," he said, his eyes only for her.

"Let me know when you're ready to get dressed," the nurse said softly, and slipped out the door as Lisa opened her arms to her dad.

"Oh, Daddy..."

Dropping the teddy bear on the end of the bed, Oliver pulled her into his arms and held her tightly, wordlessly, telling her with his touch what no words could convey. They'd both lost so much. They needed Lisa's baby to fill the voids left in their lives.

"Have you seen her?" Lisa asked when Oliver finally pulled away to sit on the side of the bed.

He nodded. "She's the prettiest one in there," he said. But his eyes, moist with unshed tears, frightened her.

"She's going to make it, Dad," Lisa promised. She'd been too young to save his Sara, but she'd save her own. Somehow.

Oliver nodded and patted her arm. "I know, honey. Now, did I hear the nurse say you could get dressed?"

Lisa nodded. "They're letting me out of here. It's supposed to be better, you know, under the circumstances, for me to be at home as soon as possible."

"Then I'll leave you for now, sweetie. Call me when you get home, okay?"

Lisa nodded, and he bent to kiss her head. "I love you."

"I love you, too, Dad."

Lisa called for the nurse again the minute Oliver left. She couldn't stand the silence in her room that allowed her medical knowledge to torture her. A body that small fighting against the world of disease into which it had been born. Why, even a simple cold could—

"You ready to get dressed?" The nurse was back. Thank heaven.

At Lisa's nod, the young nurse helped Lisa lift herself from the bed.

"You okay here, or would you like me stay?" the nurse asked as she let go of Lisa in the bathroom.

Lisa swayed on her feet for a moment and then took a step, moving cautiously as she felt the pull from her stitches. "I'm fine," she said as soon as she knew it was true.

"Feel free to take a shower, then, and call if you need me." The nurse closed the door behind her when she left.

Lisa was just soaping down in the shower when she heard the door open again.

"Lis? You okay?"

Marcus. "Yes." *Now that you're here.* "Would you mind waiting, though, just in case?"

"I'm right here, sweetheart. How do you feel?"

"Physically a lot better than I thought I would," Lisa called back. She finished rinsing and shut off the water. Marcus handed her a towel as she pulled open the shower curtain.

His blue eyes warmed her instantly. "She's alive, Lis."

"I know." She wanted to ask him if he knew any more than that, but she couldn't. Not now. Not yet.

Debbie Crutchfield came in as Lisa was pulling on the loose denim jumper Marcus had brought her, and after a quick look at Lisa's stitches, announced that Lisa could go home whenever she was ready.

"I've ordered an injection to dry up your milk," she said, as she was signing off Lisa's chart.

"No!" Sara was going to need that milk.

"It's going to be quite a while before your baby's even able to suck, Lisa, if ever. You'll be miserable."

"I'll pump six times a day if I have to. My milk will be better for her than anything else once she's ready for oral consumption."

Marcus walked over, putting his arm around Lisa's shoulders. "Will it cause Lisa any harm to do as she wishes?" he asked.

Debbie shrugged. "No harm. Just a lot of discomfort."

"I have a feeling," Marcus said, "that the discomfort you refer to will be nothing compared to what it would do to Lisa to miss this chance."

Lisa smiled up at him. Her knight in shining armor. She could only imagine what this was costing him, being a part and yet wanting no part of the tragic events of the past hours. But he was here for her. Just as he said he'd be. How was she ever going to find the strength to send him away?

Just as Debbie was leaving, Randal Cunningham arrived. The silver-haired doctor gave Lisa a report too detailed for her mother's heart to handle. Not her baby. How could he just sit there and discuss her little Sara's chances, or rather, lack of them, like that? Like she was just another case.

Except that, even as her soul protested, Lisa's doctor's mind understood that Randal was handling things in the only way he could—impartially, professionally. He couldn't allow himself to become emotionally involved with his patients. It could mean the difference between life and death, the making of a tough decision that could save a life—or lose one.

And so Lisa listened to the things she needed to

know, her mind already jumping ahead to probable crises and ways to fight them.

"Because of the risk of infection, it's best that only the few personnel taking care of her be near her right now, but I'm not going to tell you you can't go in there, Lisa. I will ask, however, that it not be for more than an hour twice a day."

Lisa nodded, realizing the necessity for Randal's request. But one hour twice a day! It seemed like a prison sentence.

Please, dear God, don't let it be a lifetime one.

Marcus helped Lisa gather her things together as soon as Randal was gone, putting Oliver's teddy bear in her lap as she got settled into the wheelchair the nurse had left outside the door. He began to push her slowly down the hall.

"I need you to take me to her, Marcus," she said, afraid he'd freeze on her again. But her need to be with her baby was too great.

"I know. That's where we're headed."

He wheeled her down to the nursery window and then turned the corner, entering the nursery viewing room. He let go of her chair, and Lisa panicked, afraid he was going to leave her. She needed to draw on his strength to help her through whatever she might discover when she looked through that window.

"Don't go." She was breaking his rules.

"I'm right here." But he was looking at her, not the window.

Lisa held his gaze for another second and then slowly turned. Her eyes found her daughter instantly, knowing just which part of the nursery housed the neonatal babies. *Cartwright Girl*, she saw. *Sara. Her name is Sara.*

They were going to have to change that card.

And then she brought her gaze to the minuscule body lying so quietly in the cellophane-wrapped warming bed.

Forgetting everything, even, in that moment, her husband standing behind her, Lisa rose from her chair, motioned for a nurse to let her in and went through the door into the overly warm nursery. She saw nothing but the baby in front of her. Her baby. Her Sara.

Mindless of her own discomfort, she scrubbed at the sink by the baby's crib and tied a mask over her face, her eyes still on her daughter. She had a daughter. She was finally a mother.

With tears in her eyes, gloves on her hands and more than nine hours after giving birth to her, Lisa finally touched her baby. She couldn't hold her, couldn't take her away from the healing warmth of her crib, but she touched her.

"Hello, my precious," she whispered through her tears, running one finger lightly along the baby's side.

Sara was lying on her back, completely still, breathing only with the help of the tube taped to her mouth.

Careful of the various wires and vials attached to the baby's body, Lisa lay her hand against Sara's belly, needing the contact, needing her daughter to feel her touch, despite the gloves she wore and the plastic covering the baby. Her baby. Her Sara. Lisa had never felt such an overwhelming rush of love in her life.

"Mama's here, my Sara," she said, her voice

stronger. "You be a good little girl and do just what the doctor tells you, you hear?"

Lisa stood beside the crib for the entire hour she'd been allotted, rejecting the rocker a nurse brought over to her. She wanted to be as close to Sara as she could possibly get.

And throughout the hour, one eye on the monitors attached to Sara, she talked to the baby, bonding with her new daughter, not in the usual way, but bonding with her just the same.

The nurse told her when her hour was up, and Lisa nodded, running her hand along Sara's side one more time. "You're going to be just fine, Sara. Just fine. Mama's going to be watching over you every second now, so don't you worry."

"She's a strong one, Doctor. If ever a preemie had a chance, it's this one," the nurse said, smiling down at Sara.

"She hasn't opened her eyes, has she?" Lisa asked, still watching her daughter.

She knew the answer even before she heard it. "No. It could take weeks."

Lisa nodded. "I know," she said. But they'd be blue when she did. They were meant to be blue. Like Marcus's. Except that he couldn't allow himself to claim them.

"Her pulse and blood pressure are fluctuating," Lisa said, glancing again at one of the monitors attached to her little darling.

The nurse nodded. "It's something we expect at this stage."

Glancing at the monitors, the nurse took a small

blood-pressure cuff from a tray beside the crib and lifted the plastic around the baby enough to fit the one-inch-long cuff around the baby's arm. Sara's arm was barely as thick as the nurse's middle finger.

Lisa couldn't bear to watch anymore.

"I love you, Sara," she said one last time, bending to brush her masked face against the tip of the cap covering the baby's head. Sara didn't respond.

Stopping only long enough to ask that the baby's nameplate be changed, Lisa stripped off her sanitary garb and went out to find Marcus, more afraid than she'd ever been in her life.

She practically fell into the wheelchair he had waiting for her, only then becoming aware of how much she ached, thankful she didn't have to make it down to the car on her own. She wasn't sure she had the strength even to make it out to the hallway. Nor the will. She'd just left her heart with a tiny bit of humanity who couldn't so much as open her eyes. Or cry when she was hurt.

Marcus didn't once look toward the nursery as he helped her into her coat and wheeled her out, and all during the drive home, Lisa waited for him to say something, anything, about the child they were leaving behind.

She waited in vain.

MARCUS DROVE Lisa back to the hospital that evening for her second hour with her baby. He hated the toll this premature birth and resulting vigil was taking on Lisa, the panic that came to her eyes every time the telephone rang. He hated, too, his helplessness to make things better.

This was supposed to have been a happy time for her. One of the happiest times of her life. Instead, she'd cried when Hannah had met her at the door with an uncharacteristic hug. And she'd cried over the cards and flowers and gifts that had been arriving steadily all day—from her colleagues, from his, and from the matriarchs of the families on New Haven's social register.

She'd cried when she'd talked to Beth on the phone. And she'd cried when he'd carried her by the door to the nursery they'd decorated, too. Her heart was breaking, and there wasn't a damn thing he could do about it.

He waited outside the hospital nursery while Lisa visited the baby, though a well-meaning nurse had invited him in, too, with the provision that he scrub and dress as Lisa had in the sterile garb. He saw the look of hope in Lisa's eyes, but she didn't ask him to come. He wanted to be there for her, to fulfill her wishes, but he just couldn't cross that final line. He'd be there for her, but outside the nursery.

The entire time Lisa was in with her baby, he watched the child, as he had the night before, thinking that her color looked a little better, though she was still awfully red. Most of the tubes and wires were just as they'd been that morning. Marcus didn't know if that was good news or bad. Still, he prayed for the child. Prayed she had what it took to win with the impossible hand she'd been dealt.

He noticed, too, that her nameplate had been

changed. *Sara Barbara Cartwright.* She still had his name.

OLIVER PICKED BETH UP from work the next evening. After spending most of the afternoon with Lisa, he needed a means of forgetfulness. They drove straight to his house and she was barely in his door before he took her in his arms. Not with passion, that would come later, but with warmth, seeking and giving comfort.

"I've needed this since the hospital called yesterday," he said.

"Me, too. I'll bet you barely made it home in time to get Marcus's call. We're going to have to tell them about us, you know," Beth said.

"Yes. But not yet." Oliver was afraid to trust the happiness that had begun to bloom in him again. It seemed so delicate, so fragile.

"Not until we know more about Sara's condition?"

"Right."

"You think Lisa's going to take our relationship hard?"

"Maybe. What do you think?" Oliver had been wanting to ask her that since the first time he'd kissed her. Beth was Lisa's best friend. In some ways she knew his daughter better than he did.

"I think she's going to be shocked," Beth said. "And I'm sure she doesn't need to hear about it now."

"Then we'll have to be careful for a while."

"Right." She kissed him gently, almost innocently.

"I'm a grandpa."

She smiled at him softly. "I know. She's beautiful."

"She is, isn't she? Prettiest one there. And the strongest, too. She'll be making more noise than all the others combined before we know it."

Beth pulled out of his arms, turning her back as she moved to the front window and looked out. "Her chances aren't very good, Oliver. You realize that, don't you?"

He stood his ground. "I hear what they're saying."

"This is one time I wish I didn't know even half of what I learned in medical school." She shivered. "The things that could go wrong... I can't even imagine the hell Lisa must be putting herself through."

Oliver hated to think of the anguish his own little girl must be suffering. He'd watched her torture herself all afternoon. It was just too much. First she'd lost her baby sister. And then her mother.

They weren't going to lose Sara Barbara, too. They just weren't.

SARA'S HEART CONTINUED to beat. As the hours turned slowly into days, the baby lay in her warming crib, relying on a respirator for her every breath, but still alive. Her oxygen level fluctuated, her body temperature fluctuated, and she slept constantly. But she was alive.

A week after the baby's birth, Lisa's doctor ordered Lisa back to work. Part-time only, and nothing but office calls, but back to work. Debbie was worried about Lisa's mental state and said that working would not only give Lisa something to do other than anticipate what could go wrong with Sara, it would also bring her closer to Sara for more hours during the day.

Marcus agreed with Debbie's reasoning, knowing that being near her baby would bring its own measure of comfort to his wife.

He returned to work himself, though only part-time, as well. He wasn't going to leave Lisa home alone any more than he had to. Nor was he going to have her sitting in the nursery viewing room for hours every day letting her fears eat her alive. Instead, he bought her a ship-to-shore radio and took her to the *Sara*. He picked up several romantic comedies at the video store and sat through them with her, although he had to take cold showers after every one of them. He missed making love to his wife.

And daily, he told her how strong she was, how capable, hoping that if she ever needed to rely on that strength, she'd know it was there.

He also held her when the anguish was too much for her and she could no longer hold back her sobs.

As the days passed, one after another, he found himself thinking about the tiny little girl lying across town in her funny little bed. He worried about her. Almost constantly. And almost every evening, on his way home from work, he stopped by the hospital and stood at the nursery window watching Lisa's baby wage her battle for life.

The baby was eight days old when he noticed a new catheter in her foot. He knocked on the nursery window, getting the attention of Regina, Sara's personal night nurse.

"You want to come in, Mr. Cartwright?" she asked,

peeking her head out the door that was always kept secured.

He shook his head. That was always her first question. "What's the new catheter for? The one in her foot?"

"It's not new. It's just been moved. Her veins are too fragile for us to use any one site for too long."

Marcus didn't know what Regina thought of his refusal to get close to Sara and he didn't care. All that mattered to him was that the woman keep his visits there to herself. If she found his request that she do so odd, she was professional enough not to say anything, and professional enough, as well, to agree to keep whatever gossip his visits might at some point incur away from Lisa's ears.

"And what about the longer vial?" Marcus asked now.

"We've upped her fluid intake."

"A step forward?" he asked, his hands in his pockets as he rocked back on his heels.

The nurse shrugged. "Her diaper weighed almost an ounce more this morning. That means her excretory system's working. Your daughter's a fighter, Mr. Cartwright."

She wasn't his daughter. Marcus wasn't even sure why he had this insatiable need to know every little thing about that tiny life lying just beyond the window. But if he was somehow going to give Lisa's baby the strength to live, he had to know what they were up against.

LISA KNEW SOMETHING was wrong the minute she walked off the elevator. There was too much commotion in the nursery. Praying that her baby wasn't the cause, even though she knew she was, Lisa rounded the corner, her gaze straining frantically for her first glimpse of Sara's crib.

All she could see were the medical personnel surrounding it.

Lisa ran the last couple of yards to the nursery door, pounding on the secured entrance with all her might. She had to get in there. Her baby was in trouble. And she was a doctor.

The door opened immediately when one of the nurses inside recognized Lisa.

"She's developed some congestion in her chest, Dr. Cartwright. They're giving her a treatment right now."

Lisa scrubbed quickly, donning her garb faster than she'd ever donned it before, never taking her eyes from the figures bending over her daughter's crib.

She almost cried out when she finally got to the side of the bed herself and saw what they were doing to her child. The mask on the baby's tiny face was bad enough, but when they had to start chest percussion, someone had to lead Lisa away. There was nothing she could do to help, and if she stood there any longer, she was going to stop everyone from doing anything. It was too terrible to watch. By the time she reached the nurses' station, the mask she was wearing was soaked with her tears.

"She's so tiny!" she wailed. "Too tiny to have to endure so much!"

"It's her only hope, Doctor," one of the nurses gathered there reminded her.

And with that, Lisa was silent, her gaze once again glued to the mass of bodies surrounding Sara. Her only hope. *Oh, please, God, let it work. Don't take her from me now.* But even as she prayed, Lisa wondered if she was being fair to the tiny being she'd brought into this world. How much suffering was too much? When was life no longer worth the agony?

Lisa sat there for another fifteen minutes, every muscle in her body tensed against the pain Sara must have been in. Until finally, one by one, the therapists and nurses surrounding Sara moved away, pulling off their masks, until only one nurse remained, resealing the cellophane that was Sara's only blanket.

Lisa felt the constriction in her chest loosen just a little. They'd finished. For now.

"She's better, Dr. Cartwright," Jim, one of the therapists, said, stopping by the station where Lisa sat. "That's one tough cookie you've got there, ma'am."

At Jim's words, Lisa felt the rest of her strength drain out of her. They'd made it through another crisis. Everything was okay. For now. But as she drove home later that afternoon, she couldn't help wondering how many more crises there'd be. And how many more she could ask her child to survive.

CHAPTER THIRTEEN

MARCUS DIDN'T TALK to Lisa about her baby. Her father, Beth, and all her colleagues did that, he knew. His job was to distract her from the trauma just enough to keep her going. But he continued to visit the child, although he did so without Lisa's knowledge. Not because he wanted to keep secrets from her, but because he couldn't let her get her hopes up that he was in any way seeing himself as a father to the child. He wasn't.

He wanted the baby to survive. He wanted to bring her home. For her sake, and for Lisa's. Not his own.

They didn't talk about the baby, but Marcus could always tell, even without having visited the hospital himself, when Sara had taken a turn for the worse or not gained the weight Lisa had hoped or not made any of the other progress Lisa watched for daily. He could tell the minute she came in the door, and his heart ached for her. And for the baby trying so valiantly to live.

"Let's have dinner at Angelo's," he said one night almost four weeks after the baby's birth. He knew the child had lost a couple of ounces over the past day and a half, and Lisa was worried sick. She'd dropped her briefcase by the front door as she came in from work, barely looking at him.

Lisa shook her head. "I'm not hungry." Continuing on through the house to the kitchen, she fell into a seat at the kitchen table, staring aimlessly into space. Just as she'd done the night before. And the night before that. She didn't even kiss him hello anymore.

"You ready to give up your fight, Lis?" he asked softly from the doorway behind her. Her apathy alarmed him.

"No!" She swung around, jumping up out of her chair. "Why would you even say such a thing? Is that what you want? For me to give up? Let her go? That would suit you just fine, wouldn't it, if it was just you and me again. Isn't that what you really want?"

Her words stung. "Of course I don't want that, Lisa. I'm not heartless."

"Aren't you?" she cried. "Aren't you? What do you call it, then?" She stepped closer. "Our daughter's barely big enough to fill your hand, let alone a cradle. She may be dying. She's certainly hurting, and still you don't claim her. Damn you! Why don't you claim her?" she screamed, hitting him in the chest with her fists.

The pain her words inflicted far surpassed that of the physical blows. "I can't, Lis. I've tried, but I just can't." Grabbing her wrists, he held her hands still against him. "She isn't mine to claim."

She could have no idea just how much he wished, every minute of every day, that the tiny baby fighting so stalwartly was his to claim. But that choice had been taken out of his hands long ago.

"She is so yours! She's your daughter, Marcus, just as much as she is mine." Her voice broke. "You're just too damn stubborn to see it." Tears dripped slowly down her cheeks, the fight going out of her as she gazed up at him.

"I wish she was, Lis. More than you'll ever know, I wish she was," he said, wrapping his arms around her to hold her close to his heart. He wanted to make love to her, to sink into her velvety depths and find forgetfulness for both of them. To reaffirm that they were still part of the same whole. But she wasn't ready. It was still too soon after her baby's birth.

The child was less than a month old, and already she was coming between them.

LISA HAD THOUGHT, back when they'd first found out Marcus was sterile, when her marriage had been disintegrating right before her eyes, that things couldn't get any worse. She'd thought she'd reached the depths of despair and couldn't hurt any more than she'd been hurting. She'd been wrong. Because these days she'd discovered a whole new realm of despair where the pain was so fierce, so frightening, it rendered her powerless.

Never in her worst nightmare could she have imagined anything like the situation she was facing. Her life's dreams were warring against each other. Eventually one had to lose.

"I figured I'd find you here."

Lisa turned away from the window of the nursery viewing room to see Beth sit down beside her. "I'd be in there if I wasn't so damned worried about infection," she said, looking back at the familiar two-foot box, the only home her daughter had ever known.

Beth's arm slid through hers. "I know."

"She's not gaining like she should," Lisa said, forcing herself to face the truth.

"I know."

"I've been pumping my milk four times a day for a month, sure that she'd soon be needing every drop. My freezer's so full that yesterday I had to throw some out."

"Are you thinking about drying up?" Beth's question was hesitant.

Though no one talked to her about it, Lisa figured it was what everyone wanted. Debbie Crutchfield thought Lisa was making things harder on herself, but this was one time that Debbie Crutchfield didn't have a clue. "No."

Beth surprised her by nodding. "Good. Your daughter's held on too long to be robbed of any single chance she has. And once she's ready to digest it, your milk will be the best thing for her."

Lisa blinked away sudden tears. "Thanks, friend," she said, squeezing Beth's hand. "You know, I'm a mother, but I'm not. It's like I'm still pregnant, waiting for her to be born, but instead of feeling my baby growing inside me, I have to watch her development through a maze of wires and tubes and plastic, watch other people taking care of her, changing the diaper underneath her, doing the things I should be doing. About the only time I feel like a mother is when I sit by myself with my breast pump. And someday, she's going to be ready for all those nutrients I'm providing. I have to believe that."

"You bet you do," Beth said, squeezing Lisa's

hand back. "That little fighter in there deserves to have all of us believe in her. She's already come farther than anyone predicted. And she's going to need the support from all of us even more in the months ahead. There'll be a lot of lost time to make up for."

Thinking of what lay ahead, the least of which was the developmental catching up her baby, her fatherless baby, faced, Lisa felt a fresh surge of tears. "I know."

"Lisa?" Beth looked at her, her brow lined with concern. "What is it? What'd I say?"

Lisa shook her head. "It's nothing you said." She met Beth's gaze, knowing she had to face facts if *she* was going to survive. "If Sara lives, I have to leave Marcus."

"No!" Beth shook her head in confusion. "I thought he'd finally come around. He's been wonderful through all this, anticipating your every need, cutting back so much at work..." Her voice trailed off.

"I know," Lisa said again, smiling sadly. "He's been the best. Which just makes everything worse. I love him so much it hurts, Beth, but he isn't going to accept Sara. Not as his own. And if I ever get to bring her home, it can't be to a father who rejects her. It just can't. Can you imagine how awful that would be for her?"

She paused, then went on, "In every way that matters, Marcus is her father. She was born into our marriage. She has his name. Can you imagine how much his neglect would hurt her? Because she'd know, if we were living with him, that it was *her* he didn't want. But if we're divorced, she'd be just like any other kid in a single-parent home. Not the best situation, God knows, but at least she wouldn't feel personally rejected.''

Beth stared at Lisa, obviously shocked. ''But I thought... I mean he...the night she was born, he...''

''He what?'' Lisa asked. She and Marcus had never talked about that night, other than for Marcus to tell her how awful he felt for her, how sorry he was this had happened.

''He was here, sitting right on that chair, all night.''

''Marcus was here?''

''Uh-huh.'' Beth nodded. ''Watching Sara. I found him here about four o'clock in the morning just staring at her crib. And other than when he left me to go call your father, we sat here together until the six-o'clock shift change. He left then just long enough to go home and get your bag.''

Hope bubbled up in Lisa as she listened to Beth. Marcus had been here. He'd watched over their daughter for the whole night. He *did* care. He *was* the man she'd thought him to be. She'd gambled on him and won, after all. Her thoughts sprang ahead to the dreams that might yet come true, the years of living and loving that might be waiting just around the corner.

But they slammed to a halt when she remembered his words to her in the kitchen several nights before.

''That must have been what he meant when he said he'd tried,'' she said softly, sadly, almost to herself. She hadn't thought it possible for her heart to break any further. ''He told me he'd tried to accept her, but he just couldn't.''

She looked through the window at Sara, still sleeping silently in her odd little bed, seeing her as Marcus must have seen her that night. Knowing him as she did, she could just imagine the torture he must have put himself through as he watched his wife's baby, unable to get beyond the fact that her tiny features, her little fingers and toes, genetically belonged to another man.

Remembering the agony she'd seen on his face that day he'd walked in on her baby shower, she could almost feel the anguish he must have suffered sitting through an entire night of watching her baby. And as she sat there suffering in sympathy, she finally understood that Marcus wasn't ever going to come around, not because he didn't want to or wouldn't let himself, but because he *couldn't*. He had as little choice in the matter as she did. And knowing that, she couldn't go on hurting him. She couldn't force him to live the rest of his life watching from the outside. Bringing Sara home to him wasn't only unfair to Sara, it was unfair to Marcus.

"Maybe if he had some counseling," Beth suggested somberly, her gaze fixed, like Lisa's, on the infant on the other side of the glass.

Lisa shook her head. "Marcus isn't confused. He sees things clearly. Too clearly, really. It's just that his vision is different from mine. I think being a father starts with the heart. He thinks it starts with the body. It's an argument no one can win."

"I can't believe this." Beth rubbed her hand down her face.

"Me, neither," Lisa whispered. "Every time I pray for Sara, I know that the answer to my prayer means the death of my marriage. If my baby lives, I lose the other half of myself.'' Lisa started to cry. ''Oh, God, Beth, what have I done?''

Beth's arms wrapped around her, and Lisa lay her head against her friend's shoulder, taking the comfort that Beth gave so willingly, the same comfort Beth had taken from Lisa those months immediately following her husband's death.

''It's not what *you've* done, Lisa. It's what *we've* done. I'm so sorry I ever talked you into this.''

Lisa pulled back, shaking her head. ''Don't be sorry, Beth. Don't ever be sorry.'' She looked toward the nursery again and the tiny baby lying there. ''I wouldn't trade her for anything,'' she said, swiping at the tears spilling from her eyes. ''I just wish Marcus could feel as I do. I wish he could find a way to accept the gift I've tried to give him.''

''The man's a fool,'' Beth said, but Lisa could tell she only half meant it. If Marcus was a fool, if he was wrong, if she could be angry with him, it wouldn't be so hard to do what she had to do. But he wasn't wrong. He was simply a man who had strong convictions and who lived his life as his conscience dictated. Even now, even in this, he was the man Lisa had fallen in love with.

She and Beth watched the baby silently for a moment, both women considering the magnitude of what they'd set in motion that morning so long ago.

''Have you told Oliver that you're leaving Marcus?'' Beth asked a few minutes later.

Oliver? He'd always been ''Dr. Webster'' or ''your father'' in the past.

Staring at her friend, Lisa shook her head. "I haven't even told Marcus yet. Sara's still got a long way to go, and I'm just not strong enough, or maybe it's that I'm not unselfish enough, to leave him before I have to," she said, wondering if there was something *else* going on she should know about. She'd been so wrapped up in Sara these past few weeks that she'd barely been aware of a world outside home and the hospital.

Beth nodded, saying nothing more, but Lisa had the most uncomfortable feeling that she was missing something. It was the way Beth had said her father's name, the *familiarity* in it. Lisa didn't like it. She didn't like it at all.

A nurse came in to put a new diaper under Sara's bottom, and Lisa and Beth watched as the young woman took the diaper over to the counter to weigh it. But Lisa sneaked a couple of surreptitious glances at her friend, as well. The years of missing John had taken their toll on her friend, adding lines around her eyes that hadn't been there before, lines that had nothing to do with the smiles Beth wore so easily.

Lisa shook her head. She was really losing it if she thought Beth had any interest in her father. The two hardly knew each other. And not only was her father a generation older than Beth, but her friend was still in love with the husband she'd lost so tragically. Thinking of her father and Beth together was ludicrous. Ashamed of herself, she apologized silently to both of them.

But as she walked back to her office later that day, her thoughts drifted to her father once again. Was it possible he would someday take an interest in another woman? Lisa had never really thought of him as a man before, only as a father, and she found it unsettling to do so now. She supposed a lot of women would find him handsome. And, in his early fifties, he was still relatively young. Certainly young enough to have sexual interests. Except that he was still so in love with her mother.

Thinking of Barbara, of the mother she'd lost too soon, Lisa felt the familiar pangs of loss and regret. And she knew her father felt them, too. He might be young enough to begin a relationship with another woman, but Lisa knew he wouldn't. He'd already had the best.

SARA BARBARA CARTWRIGHT was one day short of five weeks old when she finally opened her eyes for the first time. Marcus heard all about it the minute he got to the hospital that night. Regina rushed over to him as soon as she spotted him outside the nursery window.

"Dr. Cartwright was here when it happened," she said, grinning as she recounted the joyous moment.

"Lisa was in the nursery with her?" he asked, wishing he could have been there to see Lisa's face. To share her elation with her, just as, together, they'd shared so much sorrow.

"Yep." Regina nodded. "From what I heard, she was standing there talking to her like she usually does, and suddenly the wee one just opened her eyes and stared straight at her."

Looking at Lisa's baby through the window, Marcus

could feel Lisa's excitement almost as if it had happened to him. "Was she awake long?"

"I guess it was only for a minute or two, but Dr. Cartwright carried on like her kid had just graduated from Harvard. Not that I blame her, of course. I'd have done the same thing, and the mite isn't even mine." She leaned her head a little farther out the nursery door. "I've been watching her ever since I came on shift, hoping to catch a glimpse of it myself. But so far she's sleeping tight. My luck, she'll wake up when I'm at dinner."

Marcus chuckled, but his eyes never left the baby in her funny little bed. He, too, had a surprisingly strong urge to witness the phenomenon. To look into the child's eyes, to see the little person who'd been living so silently in a world of her own.

He stayed an extra half hour that night, on the off chance the child would wake up. He knew he should go, that Lisa would be waiting at home for him, but like a gambler mesmerized by the gaming table, Marcus couldn't seem to tear himself away. He kept thinking that the next minute would be the one.

He took one final look as he was turning to leave, and as if she'd known this was her last chance, the baby opened her eyes. Just like that. With no warning, no fanfare, her little head turned, and she was staring right at him. His breath caught in his throat as he returned her stare, feeling exposed, as if she was taking stock of him, maybe finding him wanting, even though he knew she couldn't be, that she probably couldn't even focus yet.

She was more beautiful than he'd even imagined.

But there was something odd about her eyes. Marcus continued to stare at her, unable to put his finger on what was wrong. Their shape was perfectly normal, amazingly normal considering the circumstances, nice and round and big. But something wasn't right.

He felt sick to his stomach when he realized what it was. All along, he'd assumed that Lisa's baby would one day look at him with Lisa's warm brown eyes. But Sara didn't have brown eyes at all. Hers were clear blue, like a bright summer sky. They were someone else's eyes. Another man's eyes. Because she was another man's child.

Marcus turned and left.

AT LISA'S SIX-WEEK checkup, Debbie pronounced her well, even going so far as to say she didn't expect there to be any problem if Lisa ever wanted to have a second child. Nevertheless, Lisa left the doctor's office feeling vaguely out of sorts.

Debbie had suggested again that Lisa allow her milk to dry up. And she was beginning to wonder if maybe the doctor was right. Sara was six weeks old and still not taking any nourishment other than the glucose they continued to shoot into her veins. Lisa was throwing away more milk than she was keeping. And while she'd known all along that Sara's good days would be mixed with bad ones, the ups and downs were getting harder and harder to take.

Debbie also told Lisa that she and Marcus could make love again. Lisa couldn't believe how much she missed the intimacy with Marcus. Not just physically, though she was certainly hungry for her husband's body, but she missed the emotional connection their lovemaking provided. She missed that feeling of one-ness, a togetherness so intense it seemed nothing could come between them. A time when only the two of them existed.

A time she knew was slipping away.

Needing a pick-me-up, she detoured from the route between Debbie's office and her own for a quick stop at the nursery. She'd already spent her hour with Sara earlier that morning, but another dose of her darling baby was just what she needed.

"Dr. Cartwright, we were just calling your office," one of Sara's day nurses said when she arrived at the nursery door.

Lisa's stomach dropped. "What's wrong?" She knew they'd been toying with the idea of removing the baby's ventilator for a trial period, but surely they wouldn't have done it without notifying her.

The nurse grinned at her. "Nothing's wrong, Doctor. They're about to take Sara off the ventilator, and Dr. Cunningham said to get you up here."

"He'll let me be there?" Randal was a tyrant when it came to playing things his way. And having a mother standing next to him when he was facing a life-and-death situation with a child was something he never allowed. Not even if the mother in question was a damn good pediatrician in her own right.

"Just as soon as you're scrubbed," the nurse confirmed, standing aside as Lisa rushed by her.

Lisa's hands were shaking as she scrubbed them, and she had to accept the help of one of the aides to get into sanitary garb. She'd never been more nervous in her life.

She approached the familiar crib on rubbery legs, for once wishing she could make use of the rocking chair that was kept beside Sara's bed. Standing where Randal instructed, she watched as a technician pulled the cellophane away from Sara's body and carefully, slowly, removed the tape holding the tube to the baby's mouth.

Lisa held her breath, her gaze glued on her daughter, waiting to see if the infant lungs would take over for the respirator. The air surrounding the warming bed was filled with tension as the seven adults watched that tiny body, waiting...

Sara shuddered, her muscles protesting against the hands holding her down. Her big blue eyes were wide open at first, and then they scrunched closed as she objected, silently, to the attention she was receiving.

The tube was taken away, and the machine wheeled backwards. At the sudden silence, Sara opened her eyes again and uttered a small sound. Sara's muscles twitched, as if she'd surprised herself, and the sound came again. A little louder. A thin wail of disapproval, followed by a sigh.

Sara was breathing on her own.

A nurse slipped a rocker behind Lisa, and she sank onto it, tears blinding her to the smiles on the faces of the other adults. But she heard the relieved sighs of all of them.

Wiping her tears, Lisa looked around her at the staff of medical professionals that had been helping her daughter to sustain life for these six long weeks. There wasn't a dry eye among them.

"Well, Mama, you ready to hold her?" Randal asked, wiping his arm suspiciously across his own face.

Lisa's heart thumped heavily. "You'll let me hold her?"

Her stern colleague actually smiled. "Her temperature's been steady all week. I think it's safe." He reached into the bed, careful of the catheter in the baby's foot, slid his large hands beneath her and gently lifted her.

With quivery arms, Lisa reached for her baby, her heart soaring with a joy she'd never known before, in spite of the danger she knew Sara still faced.

The little girl weighed less than four pounds and was more a warmth than a weight against Lisa's breast as, six weeks after she'd given birth to her, she held her baby for the first time. The baby snuggled against her, her little chest shuddering again with the unfamiliar burden of breathing. And then, tired out by her new chore, she fell promptly asleep.

THE NURSERY WAS STILL buzzing when Marcus arrived before dinnertime that night. Regina was just coming on shift, and she met him at the viewing-room door.

His glance shot immediately to the box that served as a crib for Lisa's baby.

"Where's the ventila— She's breathing?" He stared in astonishment at the almost steady rise and fall of the tiny chest.

"Yep. Has been all afternoon. You can come on in and hold her, but the doctor says only for ten minutes at a time until he's more confident that she's maintaining her body temperature on her own."

Marcus felt something closing in on him. He could hold her. He could take that little body into his arms and make certain that nothing ever harmed it again. Regina said he could.

"Come on, Mr. Cartwright. You'll do fine. Fathers are always a little timid at first. Especially with the preemies."

Fathers. He wasn't one of those.

"I'll pass."

"Okay, but I'll leave the door unlatched in case you change your mind," she said, turning to go.

He'd disappointed her. "Regina?" he called.

"Yeah?"

"Has Dr. Cartwright held her?" Suddenly it was very important that she had. That the child know she had a parent who loved her unconditionally.

"Yep. She was here when they removed the respirator. They said she just broke down and sobbed, poor thing."

Marcus stared at the baby, concentrating on containing the emotions that threatened the control he'd been maintaining so carefully since he'd recommitted himself to Lisa and their marriage. "Thanks, Regina," he said. The nurse nodded and left.

The baby moved her head, looking in the direction of the door as it closed behind Regina. He wished he'd been there that morning, sharing those first moments with Lisa. He wished they were his moments to share.

And he was angry with himself for doing what he'd promised himself he'd never do again. Wishing.

The baby moved again, flinging her unobstructed arm up, and Marcus found himself moving to the window for a closer look. He couldn't tell if she had fingernails yet. He looked at the nursery door. The unlatched nursery door. And looked away. Why did he have to torture himself with what could never be? Was this his fate, to be always on the outside looking in?

Cursing at himself, or the fates who'd played such a cruel joke on him, he yanked open the nursery door, strode to the nurses' station and asked for instructions on how to sanitize himself enough to be near Lisa's baby. He didn't yet look at the child. He didn't ever intend to touch her. But he wasn't going to be afraid of her, either. She was going to be living in his home.

He had to know whether or not she had fingernails.

Regina appeared from a small room off the nurses' station. "Here, put this on—" she handed him a gown "—and come with me."

She led Marcus over to the sink he'd seen Lisa use the day after the baby was born, waited while he washed his hands, then showed him how to apply the elastic gloves that covered not only his hands, but his wrists. "I'm glad you changed your mind," she said now, leading him to the baby's part of the nursery. "It's really not so bad once you get used to it. Holding her isn't that much different from holding a football. Did you ever play football, Mr. Cartwright?"

Marcus nodded, though he wasn't sure what she'd asked. His attention was on the impossibly small body squirming around not six feet in front of him. He couldn't believe she was that small.

"How on earth does she stay alive?" he asked Regina as they drew nearer to the baby's box.

The nurse shrugged. "That's for God to determine. Medical science has no explanation for how she's managed to accomplish as much as she has so far."

"Does this mean she's out of the woods?" Marcus asked. Was this it, then? Had they really made it?

Regina shook her head. "I wish I could say it did, Mr. Cartwright, but there's still so much that can go wrong. She's not even eating yet."

"What's that she's listening to?" They'd reached the crib. "That sounds like my wife," he said, recognizing the soft soothing voice. "Where's it coming from?"

"Here." Regina showed him a small tape recorder tucked in among the baby's other technical paraphernalia. "Shortly after the baby was born, Dr. Cartwright recorded stories and songs on cassettes, and we play them for Sara twelve hours a day. We use it to help set her biological clock so she'll know the difference between night and day, but more importantly, so that she'll learn to recognize her mother's voice first and foremost, and to bond with it."

Marcus nodded, his gloved hands stiff at his sides.

"Would you like to hold her now?" Regina reached for the baby.

"No! I'd rather not, no," Marcus said. "I'd just like to stand here a few minutes, if I may."

"Certainly, Mr. Cartwright. You can stay an hour

if you'd like," she said, pushing a rocking chair closer to the bed before she moved away.

Marcus ignored the chair. He ignored his own longings. He ignored everything but the baby girl lying stark naked in front of him. She'd been alive six weeks and still hadn't had so much as a diaper around her bottom.

"You just wait, little one," he said softly, leaning over just enough to be sure she could hear him. "Your mother is a clotheshorse, and she's already got a closet full of designer duds for you. Just as soon as you split this joint, she'll be changing you so often you'll wish you could go around naked as a jaybird again. Don't worry, though. She's got great fashion sense. You'll be the prettiest little girl on the block."

At some point over the next half hour he pulled up a stool, which allowed him to sit very close to the baby. She'd fallen asleep in the middle of his recitation, but he kept talking to her, anyway.

"You have to be strong. Your mama needs you so much. More than she needs me, I think." He stopped, looking over his shoulder to see if anyone had heard him make such an asinine comment. It probably wasn't something a grown man should say to a kid. Even if it was true.

To his relief, the nurses were all keeping a respectable distance.

"I know this is all kinda rough right now. I know you must really hurt sometimes. But your mama will make it up to you. No little girl will ever be loved more than you are. But your mama won't smother you with it. Not her. Nope. She's really good about that.

She'll be there for you, supporting you, always trying to understand, doing what she can to make your dreams come true. But she won't be one of those parents who try to live their own lives vicariously through their children's. She'll let you have your own. 'Cause she has her own, too, you know. She's a doctor. A fantastic one. She takes care of sick kids, too. And she's also my wife. But don't let that bother you any. We've got that all worked out.''

Marcus continued to prattle on to the baby, unconsciously relieving his mind of things that had been running around inside it for months, until a full hour had passed and he knew it was time to go. Pushing the stool back into the corner where he'd found it, he stood over the crib one more time to say goodbye, then dropped his hospital attire in the basket Regina had shown him earlier and let himself out the door.

CHAPTER FOURTEEN

"I DON'T THINK this is going to work."

Beth's heart froze. She'd been a fool to believe that anyone as experienced, as distinguished, as Oliver Webster would take more than a passing interest in her. A fool to think she could find love more than once in a lifetime. "Why not?" she said anyway.

They were sitting outside on his patio, barely finished dressing from the latest of their afternoon rendezvous. Oliver leaned forward in the lawn chair he'd pulled up close to hers and took her hand in both of his.

"Because, my dear, it's getting harder and harder to let you go each day. I don't just want stolen moments with you. I want to share dinner with you every night, to see your face next to mine when I wake up in the morning."

"And that's bad?"

"I find myself wanting more than I can have, and I think we should stop before things get out of hand."

They'd been lovers for weeks. Wasn't it already out of hand?

"So you want us to stop seeing each other." She'd been prepared for this from the beginning, hadn't she?

Oliver was endearingly old-fashioned, and they had too many strikes against them.

He nodded. "It might be for the best."

"Do I get any say in this?"

He looked at her, his eyes sad. "Of course."

"Well, good," Beth said, something deeper than reason driving her on. "Because I think we'd be fools to walk away from the happiness we've found. I know you feel guilty about Barbara sometimes. I feel guilty about John, too, but do you really think either one of them would begrudge us a little more happiness and love? Are we supposed to walk around half-dead because they're no longer with us?"

Oliver frowned, deepening the lines around his eyes. "Of course not, but—"

"I'm not ever going to take anything away from Barbara, Oliver. The part of you that she has she'll always have, just as the part of me that I gave to John will always be his. But I have other parts of me, some I'm only just discovering. I'd like to give them to you, if you want them."

"Oh, I want them, honey. Don't ever doubt that." His eyes were fierce now with self-condemnation. "I want them so much I've acted like a dirty old man."

Beth smiled in spite of the tears forming in her eyes. "You aren't old, Oliver. You're twenty years younger than Ronald Reagan was when he ran for his first term as president. And what about Charlie Chaplin? He was fathering children in his seventies."

"But that's just it, my dear. I've fathered my children. I've raised my family. You haven't even started yours.''

"I raised my family when I was still a child, Oliver. My mother died when I was eight, leaving me five younger brothers and sisters to care for. When the last one finally made it into college, I knew I'd be hard-pressed to give up my freedom again. I figured out a long time ago that I'm much happier being an aunt than I would be being a mother.''

"But I'm a grandfather!''

"So?''

"I know that a lot of people today are happy to just live together, but I can't do that, Beth. Not to you or to myself. It leaves too many doors open.''

"I understand,'' Beth said. And she did. She just didn't like it. She was tired of living alone. Of eating alone. Of waking up alone.

"I guess we're just going to have to be patient a little longer until I can talk to Lisa. I can't ask you to marry me until I've at least warned my daughter that I've rejoined the living.'' His sheepish grin charmed Beth—and then his words sank in.

"What?'' she squeaked. Had he said *marry* her? She hadn't even dared consider such a thing. Whenever she'd looked into their future, she'd just assumed Oliver would want her as a long-standing "friend.''

"She's my daughter, Beth. I have to tell her.''

"Did you just ask me to marry you, Oliver, or did I miss something?'' Beth asked, hoping she didn't sound as young as she felt.

"Not yet. But I intend to. Just as soon as I have a

talk with my daughter. Little Sara's getting better every day, so we shouldn't have to wait too much longer."

Beth worried a moment as she thought of Lisa's likely reaction to the news. She was not at all sure her friend would be happy for them. Especially when her own marriage was in so much trouble. She hadn't told Oliver about that last conversation she'd had with Lisa in the hospital, when Lisa had said she was planning to leave Marcus as soon as she brought her baby home. But in any case, she knew her own happiness wasn't worth causing Lisa more distress.

"Maybe we should wait at least until Sara's home." She entwined her fingers with his.

He nodded. "You're right. Lisa's a strong woman, as was her mother, but everyone has a breaking point and I can't risk putting any more on her shoulders just now."

"Lisa always said her mother could handle anything. She envied that," Beth said, looking out over the lawn that still showcased the gardens Barbara Webster had cultivated.

Oliver squeezed her hand. "Thank you, my dear."

Beth smiled. "What for?"

"For allowing me my memories."

And suddenly Beth understood. "You never have to worry about mentioning Barbara around me, Oliver. No more than I ever want to have to worry about talking to you about John. I can't go through life being threatened by the past. Nor do I want to lose the beautiful memories I have of it."

"I love you, Dr. Montague," Oliver said. He leaned over to kiss her, and for the first time since John's senseless death, Beth felt real hope for the future.

"Tell me something," Oliver said several minutes later as he walked her out to her car.

She grinned up at him. "Anything."

"When I do get around to asking, is your answer going to be yes?"

"THIS IS BETH MONTAGUE. I can't come to the phone right now, but if you'll leave a message, I'll—"

Lisa hung up the phone with a frown. That was the fourth time she'd tried to call Beth in the past week and found her out. Not that Beth wasn't free to go away, of course she was, but over the years, Lisa had become so familiar with Beth's schedule that she almost always reached her friend on the first try. She called Beth's office to make certain Beth had been showing up there, to assure herself that Beth was at least all right. Then she put a call through to her father, asking if he was going to be home for the next hour because she wanted to stop by. She knew he had a faculty meeting that evening, but Sara had been breathing on her own for almost four hours. She had to share her news with someone!

Oliver looked great when he opened his door to her fifteen minutes later. "How's our little one?" he asked immediately.

"She's breathing on her own, Dad! Has been for over four hours now." Lisa could barely contain her excitement.

"She's off the respirator?" he asked, pinning her with his no-nonsense gaze.

Lisa nodded. "Yes!"

"And she's getting enough oxygen?" Oliver was well versed on every aspect of Sara's progress.

"Her counts have been out of the danger zone."

"Well, I'll be damned!" He grabbed Lisa up and swung her around.

She noticed a new bounce in his step as she followed him out to the enclosed back patio for a quick cup of tea. It had been years since she'd seen her father look so happy. She was glad to see that he was finally getting over the loss of her mother.

"Guess what else?" Lisa asked, sipping her tea.

"What else?" her father asked, mimicking a game they used to play when Lisa was a little girl.

"I held her today."

Oliver's mouth fell open and he sat forward, taking Lisa's hands in his own. "You took her out of her bed?"

Lisa's eyes brimmed with tears as she nodded. "For ten whole minutes."

"That's great, honey. That's just great!" His eyes were moist, too, as he shared her joy. Other than herself, Oliver was Sara's only living blood relative. It did her battered heart good to know that he cared for her daughter as much as she did.

"I imagine Marcus was standing in line to hold her," Oliver said thirty minutes later as he and Lisa walked back through the house to the front door. He had his meeting to get to, and she had a husband who'd be waiting for her at home.

Lisa stopped, unwilling to face that part of her life, but knowing she couldn't put it off any longer.

"Marcus doesn't know, Dad. He hasn't had a thing to do with the baby since the day she was born, or even before, really."

Oliver stopped in his tracks. "Nothing?" He frowned.

"He says he can't pretend." Fresh tears gathered in Lisa's eyes.

"Oh, honey, still?" He pulled her against him. "I'd hoped he'd worked his way through all that after Sara was born. Why didn't you say anything?"

"I kept hoping he'd come around, too," she said. It sounded so feeble when she said it aloud, but that tiny thread of hope had been keeping her going for months.

"I'm sorry, honey. So sorry."

Lisa squared her shoulders. "If Sara lives, I think I'm going to have to leave him, Dad."

Oliver nodded, the happiness in his eyes dimmed. "I understand. You can't bring the baby home to his house if he doesn't accept her."

Hearing her father say the words made them all that much more real to Lisa. Had she been hoping he'd disagree with her, try to talk her out of it?

"Can I bring her here, Dad? Just at first? Just until she doesn't need round-the-clock supervision?" Lisa hated even having to ask. Moving home was the last thing she wanted to do.

"You bring her here and stay here, young lady. I'll not have you off someplace caring for her all by yourself. You, me and Sara, we'll make a great family."

"I'll need to get a place of my own at some point."

"We'll worry about that later," Oliver said, dismissing her concern. But Lisa promised herself she'd start looking for a home for herself and Sara right away. She'd stay with her father as long as the baby's safety depended on having extra ears and eyes around, but she was going to have a home waiting for them when they were ready. She had to if she was ever going to believe that her marriage to Marcus was over.

"I can't imagine that Marcus is taking this sitting down," Oliver said, walking with her out to her car.

She took a deep breath. "I haven't told him yet."

Again Oliver nodded as if he understood. "Time's getting close, though," he said, echoing the thoughts she'd been trying not think ever since she'd left the nursery several hours before.

"I know." Lisa was filled with a sudden urge to get home to her husband, to grasp whatever last minutes she could with him.

"YOU OKAY?" Lisa asked Marcus over the pizza they shared later that evening.

He'd had the idea on the way home to take her to their old stomping grounds, the pizza parlor they'd frequented during their years at Yale. They had something to celebrate, even if she didn't know he knew that.

"I'm fine. Why?" He smiled at her. She really was a beautiful woman.

"I don't know. You just seem different."

He felt different. "I'm fine," he repeated, unable to explain to her what he couldn't understand himself. Nothing had happened. Nothing had changed. He just didn't feel quite his usual self.

She took another bite of her pizza. "Anything happen at work today?"

"Nothing out of the ordinary." He wanted to tell her about his trip to the hospital. He wanted her to tell him how it felt to hold Sara. He wanted to know how significant she thought it was that they'd removed the respirator. But he knew it wouldn't be fair to her. She'd accepted the situation as it had to be. He mustn't let her get her hopes up, allow her to start expecting things from him he wouldn't be able to give.

"I saw Debbie today," she said casually.

"You did?"

"Uh-huh."

He watched her through narrowed eyes. Could Lisa really not have any idea how desperately he'd been waiting for her to be ready for him again? How hard it had been to lie beside her each night these past weeks and keep his hands to himself? Did she not know that he'd have had her *before* dinner if he'd realized he could?

"And?"

She grinned at him, and Marcus dropped the piece of pizza he'd been about to devour. The minx knew exactly what she was doing to him. He gestured at her plate. "Are you done there?" he asked.

She continued to grin. "That depends," she said.

"On what?"

"On how quickly you can get me home."

"Good answer, woman." Marcus threw down a wad of bills, then took his wife's hand and practically dragged her from the restaurant.

FOR ALL HIS HASTE, Marcus took his time making love to her. He undressed her slowly, then caressed every inch of her while she lay beside him on their bed. He forced himself to be patient while she reacquainted herself with his body, as well.

"You turned every college boy's head in that joint tonight," he whispered, his lips against her neck.

Touched by his nonsense, Lisa laughed softly. "I did not. To them I'm an old lady."

He nipped her earlobe. "Hardly. I'm telling you, honey, every male eye in the place was on you as you sashayed your sweet butt out of there tonight."

"I did not sashay."

"Sure you did, Lis." He moved to her other ear. "You always do."

He captured her lips, and she returned his kiss passionately. She was desperate for Marcus. For his touch. For his tenderness. For him. Desperate because even while she made love to him, she knew it was all slipping away.

Her swollen breasts ached beneath his tender ministrations as he ran his fingers lightly over them, discovering their new hardness. A drop of milk leaked out, rolling down one side of her breast. Marcus caught it with his fingertip.

"Are you saving all of it?" he asked, staring at the path the drop of milk had taken.

She shook her head, oddly embarrassed. "Not anymore. There's too much."

"How long does it keep being produced?"

She tried to turn over, afraid that he found her milk repulsive, but he was half on top of her now and didn't move. "As long as I keep pumping," she finally said. He was still her husband. He had the right to an answer.

He ran his hand lightly over her again. "Does it hurt, this pumping?"

"Not much. It's supposedly a lot worse than nursing, but I don't really mind."

Her breast dripped again, and Lisa bit her lip. She'd had no idea that being with Marcus would stimulate her milk glands. Again Marcus caught the drop on his finger, and this time he brought it to his mouth.

Marcus cherished her that night, loved her in ways he never had before, and when he finally entered her, bringing them both to a climax that seemed to go on and on, Lisa gave him more than her body and heart. She gave him her soul all over again. At least for one more night.

And later, when he lay sleeping beside her, she gave him her tears. Because for everything she'd given him that night, she'd lost just as much. She couldn't fool herself any longer. Marcus wasn't going to come around. Sara was breathing on her own. It was time for Lisa to find her daughter a home.

MARCUS DIDN'T EVEN STOP at the viewing-room window the next afternoon on his way home from work. He proceeded right to the door, and then on to a set of scrubs as soon as Regina answered his knock. He had business to attend to.

"Hello, Sara," he said, settling himself beside the warming bed on the stool he'd used the night before. "My name's Marcus."

A nurse he'd never seen before walked by, and Marcus leaned down a little closer to the crib. "I'm married to your mama."

The baby was awake, but she appeared to be studying a scratch on the side of the bed opposite Marcus. He fought the urge to turn her little face toward him. He wasn't going to touch her. Only the medical professionals and her parents were supposed to be touching her. He was neither.

"Here's the thing. I love your mama very much. And pretty soon, as soon as you get to know her, you're going to love her, too. And she loves both of us. So you and me, we're going to have to share her."

He paused, giving her time to digest his words. One of her inch-long feet kicked in the air.

"Well, I just wanted you to know that I'm okay with that now, sharing her with you, I mean. I'm sorry it took me so long to come around. But it'll work out fine, you'll see. I have an office at home, and I can always work in there on the nights you need her to help you with homework, or if she's teaching you to sew or something. And then she can get a sitter some nights and go out with me, too.''

It wasn't ideal. But it could work.

"But, uh—'' Marcus looked around him before leaning in just a bit closer "—unless you're sick or something, I get her nights.''

The baby didn't cry. Marcus decided that was a good sign. "Okay. Now that that's done, I'll go get someone over here to change that diaper for you.'' He looked around for Regina.

Marcus backed up while Regina moved the cellophane covering Lisa's baby and slipped a dry diaper beneath her. She plopped the old diaper on a scale, wrote something on the baby's chart and came back with a doll-size pacifier in her hand which she attempted to place in Sara's mouth. The baby spit it out, and Regina put it back in, all the while watching a bottle of milky solution drip into the baby's catheter.

"Should she have that thing if she doesn't want it?'' Marcus asked. He'd read that pacifiers were bad for babies' teeth.

"Before she can nurse, she has to learn how to suck,'' Regina said, patiently forcing the pacifier back into the baby's mouth. Sara spit it back out.

Marcus grinned. The baby was as stubborn as her mother. "Maybe it'd be better to try her again later,'' he suggested.

Regina shook her head. "We give it to her only when she's eating so she'll learn to associate sucking with the full feeling in her stomach.''

Marcus looked at the baby's apple-size stomach. "She's eating?"

"Yep." Regina nodded toward the bottle she was watching. "She's taking about an eighth of a cup every four hours. We're just about ready to try her on breast milk."

Thinking of the night before, Marcus had a sudden urge to go home and make love to Lisa again.

"My wife will be glad to hear that," he said, instead.

"She was. We called her about an hour ago. She's going to bring in the first four ounces in the morning and hold Sara while we feed her."

Marcus felt a pang as he thought about being there to watch Lisa feed her baby for the first time, but he knew better than to torment himself—or Lisa. So he settled for watching the nurse continue to offer the baby the pacifier, until Sara finally gave in and accepted the unfamiliar object in her mouth. She sucked for about a minute and then fell asleep.

"I'm a little concerned about her temperature," Regina said, feeling the baby's face with the back of her hand. "She's getting feverish."

Marcus's stomach tightened. "Is that normal?"

Regina frowned and called out to another nurse. "See if Dr. Cunningham's still in the building, Susan." She kept looking from the baby to the dials on one of the machines beside the warming bed. "Her temperature's climbed a full degree in an hour. And no, that's not normal," she said to Marcus.

They were the last words anybody said to him during the next fifteen minutes as a full team of medical personnel went to work on Lisa's baby. Marcus watched from the viewing-room window, just as he had for all those weeks. And when the team finally came away from the baby's bed, Sara was once again hooked up to the respirator.

They were right back where they'd started.

CHAPTER FIFTEEN

URGENCY FUELED his blood as Marcus drove home. He wanted to be with Lisa in case the hospital called. He didn't want her home alone when she heard the bad news. When he walked in the door, he could smell Hannah's crab Alfredo coming from the kitchen. Lisa was in their office, working at her desk. She looked up at him when he came in, saw his worried expression.

"What's wrong?" she said, rising. Her face got that pinched look he'd come to dread.

With his arm around her shoulders, Marcus led her to the leather couch that dominated one wall of the office. "Sara's got some kind of infection, Lis. A nurse noticed her temperature rising when she was feeding her dinner. They had to call Randal Cunningham."

"Oh, my God. Oh, no. Not now." Lisa started to get up from the couch. "I've got to go."

Marcus pulled her back down beside him. He was giving himself away, but seeing Lisa through this crisis was the only thing that mattered right then. "It's okay for now, honey. They managed to stabilize her. The nurse said she'd call immediately if there was any change. The soonest they'll let you in to see her is tomorrow morning, anyway, until they're sure the antibiotic is working."

Lisa's big brown eyes stared at him, begging for reassurance that it wasn't worse than he was telling her. He looked away.

"They had to put her back on the respirator, Lis."

"No!" she cried, tears brimming in her eyes.

Marcus hated having to be the one to bring that frightened look back to her eyes, and he hated being powerless to make everything better. "She wasn't getting enough oxygen, honey. I'm sorry."

Lisa jumped up and began pacing in front of the couch. "She was doing great this morning. I can't stand this. I can't stand that her life is in question from minute to minute. She's fine one minute and then in terrible danger the next. There's never a time when the worry quits."

His hands hanging uselessly between his knees, Marcus watched her pace. "I know, Lis. But you of all people know that as quickly as infections crop up, they go away, too."

She nodded, and Marcus saw the exact moment she switched from the baby's mother to an award-studded pediatrician. "Did they say what it was?" she asked brusquely, stopping in front of him.

"They didn't know yet. When I left, Randal was sending blood to be tested."

She nodded again, assimilating God only knew what in that quick brain of hers, but whatever it was, it panicked the mother in her. Her face crumpled and

Marcus grabbed her hand, pulled her down beside him and into his arms.

"She's beaten all the odds so far, Lis. Don't give up on her now."

"I'm n-not. It's just so...so hard." He felt the sobs that racked her body as he held her, the tears that wet his shirt, and could only marvel that she'd held up as long as she had. She was one helluva strong woman to be able to go to that nursery every day, to sit with her baby, to see the catheters they'd inserted into her scalp, her tiny feet, knowing all of the things that could easily go wrong.

Her tears stopped suddenly, and she pulled slightly away from Marcus, staring at him.

"How did you... Why were *you* there?" The hope in her eyes clawed at him.

"I, uh, only stopped by because I assumed you were there. I called here before I left work and you didn't answer." It was weak. He knew it was weak. But he still couldn't allow her to hope for something he couldn't give her.

"I was in the shower," she said, studying him like a specimen under a microscope.

"I was going to offer to take you to dinner, but it smells like you've already put Hannah's casserole in the oven." *Smooth, Cartwright.* Why did he suddenly feel like he'd been caught with his hand in the cookie jar?

"It's almost ready," Lisa said, linking her arm through his and laying her head against his shoulder.

Marcus allowed himself to relax a fraction. She was going to let it go.

"Is it really all that bad that she's back on the ventilator, Lis, other than that she's lost some of the ground she gained? Ground she can regain?" he asked. He'd wondered about it all the way home from the hospital. And since Lisa knew he'd been there, anyway, he didn't see the harm in asking her a couple of things.

She hugged his arm to her side. "I wish it was that simple," she said, her voice small and worried. "But the longer Sara's on the ventilator, the more chance there is of other things going wrong. Not only is there increased risk of brain damage, but her hearing and internal organs can be affected, too."

He digested her words in silence. Did the worrying never stop?

"There comes a point when she's just plain been on the machines too long."

Brushing back her hair, he kissed her gently on the top of her head. "That's not going to happen, Lis. You have to believe that, believe in her."

"Did you see her, Marcus?"

He nodded, and then realized she couldn't see him with her head pressed against him. Swallowing the lump in his throat, he answered, "I saw her."

"She's so tiny."

"But she's strong."

"I don't know the night staff well, other than the brief phone conversation or two I've had with them. I think I'll call now, just to make sure they know what they're doing." She started to get up, but Marcus put a hand on her arm, restraining her.

"They knew what they were doing, Lis. They had Randal Cunningham there within minutes. Save your worries for the real stuff. They said they'd call if anything changes. And they will."

Lisa was silent for a couple of minutes. "They must've thought it odd that you were there," she finally murmured, and Marcus felt another prick of guilt. He wondered how she explained his supposed absence in the nursery to her colleagues. Or how she would explain it at other functions in the years to come.

His chest constricted, leaving little room for him to breathe. He needed to go out, get away, not just out of the room or the house, but out of her life. Except that he couldn't. Lisa was his life.

"I've been there before, Lis." He cursed when he heard his words. He was only going to hurt her more in the long run.

"You have?" Her neck practically snapped in two when she looked up at him, and the hope he saw in her eyes confirmed his doubts. Because at some point, if not tonight, then tomorrow or next week, he'd only succeed in killing it again. She wanted something from him he didn't have to give.

"Like I told you before, Lis, I'm not heartless. I love you. And she's a very important part of you. I've been keeping tabs on her progress."

Confusion clouded her eyes. "Then why didn't you ever say anything? Do you have any idea how many times I've needed you, needed to be able to talk to you about her, to know that you care?''

His heart was heavy as he pulled her closer. ''You've always known how much I care for you, Lis. I didn't say anything about the visits because I knew you'd start hoping again, and I couldn't let you do that to yourself. Nothing's changed. I'm not deluding myself into thinking I'm the child's father. I go there merely for you, honey, not for myself.''

She leaned against him silently, and Marcus would have given the Cartwright fortune to know what she was thinking, what she was feeling. More than anything, he hated the way she'd learned to close herself off from him. The barrier that came up between them terrified him. His life wouldn't be worth a nickel if he lost Lisa.

''Since you've been going, anyway, will you go with me to see her in the morning? I'm so scared for her, Marcus. Please come. For me?'' Lisa broke the silence with her soft question.

The next day was Saturday. He didn't have to work. And Lisa was at the end of her tether. Looking at the frightened expression still marring her face, he sensed that she didn't just want him there, she needed him there. ''All right,'' he said.

But he was going for Lisa. Period.

IT WAS WORSE going the next morning than Lisa had thought it would be. She was trembling even before she got off the elevator. Though she'd known all along it could happen, she wasn't ready to face Sara's setback.

"She'll be fine, Lis," Marcus said, taking her free hand as they headed together toward the window in the nursery viewing room. "She's got you to rely on."

His words gave her the strength it took to look through the window. But even so, her stomach churned and she felt a wave of nausea as she saw the ugly tube once again taped to her baby's mouth. She didn't know how much more Sara could take.

The nurses hadn't noticed her yet, hadn't come to the door to let her in. Clutching the sterilized bottle of breast milk she'd brought, Lisa watched her daughter, looked at the unbelievably long lashes against Sara's tiny cheek. Lisa's lips quivered as she fought back tears.

"Her color's good, Lis. She was kind of flushed yesterday."

Unable to speak, Lisa just nodded, holding on to Marcus's hand for all she was worth. Almost immediately her stomach started to settle down. It still amazed her, even after more than ten years of living with Marcus, how much his mere presence was able to calm her.

The nurse finally noticed them standing there and came to the door to meet them. "I'm sorry, Dr. Cartwright, but Dr. Cunningham said no visitors for twenty-four hours. Not until he's certain we've got the infection under control."

Lisa nodded. She'd half expected as much, but still she'd hoped. Yesterday she'd held Sara against her heart. Today she couldn't even be in the same room with her. She felt Marcus's arm slide around her shoulders. "Can we see her tonight?" he asked. "That would be twenty-four hours since she started the antibiotic."

The nurse shook her head. "The doctor said twenty-four hours this morning."

"Can we speak with him?" Marcus asked.

"It's okay, Marcus," Lisa said before the nurse had a chance to reply, though she appreciated his willingness to go to bat for her. "We don't want to put Sara at risk." She turned to the nurse. "Can we still give her this?" she asked, holding out the bottle.

The nurse smiled and nodded as she took the bottle. "We've been waiting for it. She hasn't had her eight-o'clock feeding yet." It was almost eight-fifteen.

They watched the nurse take the bottle of breast milk away. "I'm sorry you can't be in there sharing it with her, honey," Marcus said, moving with her back to the window.

Lisa hooked her arm through his. "I'm just glad I have you here with me." If she couldn't be with her daughter while the baby took her first mother's milk, there was no place else she'd rather be than with her husband.

The nurse came back into the nursery with a vial filled with Lisa's breast milk and hooked it up to the tube that would send the milk into the baby's stomach. Lisa stared at the vial as the milk slowly disappeared.

"She took it all!" Marcus exclaimed a short while later.

Lisa smiled for the first time that morning. She was thankful for every small victory she had. And she'd just had two. Sara had had her first real feeding. And Marcus had exclaimed over his daughter's progress just like the proud papa he was supposed to be. It wasn't much. But it was enough to keep Lisa going. At least for another day.

SHE WASN'T SURE just when she knew she wouldn't give up her husband without a fight. The knowledge just seemed to grow in her over the next few days as Marcus continued to share her visits with Sara. They were allowed into the nursery on the second day after the baby had been put back on the ventilator, and Lisa sang to her daughter through her morning feeding that second day. Sara was taking four ounces of breast milk every four hours. And digesting every bit of it. Lisa could tell that Marcus was pleased at this small bit of progress by the satisfied expression on his face, but that was the only indication he gave. He never involved himself with anything that went on in the nursery, never got close enough to the baby to touch her.

But he was always there.

Marcus was the most heroic man she'd ever met. He was the spice in her life, the warmth of the sun on her face. He was also the father of her child. Somehow she had to get him to believe that. For all of them.

They stood together in the deserted nursery viewing room one evening, having stopped by the hospital for another quick peek at Sara after they'd gone out for dinner.

Lisa saw the way his gaze flew immediately to their baby as they entered the room. Saw the way the lines around his mouth relaxed when he saw that she was resting peacefully.

"You care about her," she blurted, frustrated beyond endurance with his inability to allow himself the wealth of love Sara would bring to him.

His face froze, a look Lisa hadn't seen in months, but she ignored it. She wasn't wrong about him. She couldn't be wrong about him. "I saw you looking at her just now, Marcus. You were worried that she wouldn't be all right."

He shoved his hands into his pockets and hunched his shoulders defensively. "I worry for your sake, Lisa, for hers, not for my own. Don't read any more into it than that."

"I see you look at her, Marcus. You watch everything they do to her so intently. I see you tense when they're hurting her, as if you're taking on her pain yourself. I know you, Marcus. You care about her."

"I care for you, Lisa. Period. Don't do this." His jaw clenched.

"Look at her, Marcus! How can you look at her and not love her?"

"She's not mine to love." His words were clipped, his eyes shuttered.

"She's not those nurses' in there, either, but I can guarantee you that every last one of them have fallen in love with her." Lisa couldn't let it go. Too much was depending on making him see this her way.

Marcus was silent for so long that Lisa dared hope

she'd finally won. Until he pinned her with a stare she didn't even recognize. It was hard. Unrelenting.

"You promised, Lisa. There was to be no more of this. Yes, I care about the child, just as those nurses do as outsiders. That's what I am—an outsider."

Her heart splintered into a million fragments. She hadn't won at all. She wasn't ever going to win.

She sensed rather than saw the softening in him. "But we can be happy, Lis. I know we can."

"Just you and me?" she asked, bitterness the only thing she had to give him in that moment. Was he so blind that he couldn't see the writing on the wall?

"The three of us." He rocked back on his heels, his hands still jammed in his pockets. "I'll never begrudge you the time you spend with her, the days and evenings that will belong to her alone, as long as I have your love. I'll always be good to her, Lis, treat her with gentleness and respect."

She felt herself giving in, even though she knew it would never work.

"It might be unconventional, but so was flying when the Wright brothers decided to give it a try. So was talking over wires before Alexander Graham Bell thought it was possible. And now look—everybody's doing it."

There was wisdom in his logic, but he'd missed one key factor. Emotion. Particularly the emotions of a little girl who'd never know her father's love. Gentleness and respect just weren't enough.

"At least give it a try, Lis. Give us a chance. Let me show you it'll be all right. If you aren't happy or you think for one second that Sara's not happy, I'll leave. But please, give us a chance.''

Too choked up to speak, Lisa nodded, but she knew she'd never be able to follow through on his request. She couldn't gamble with Sara's well-being. If she did as Marcus asked, if she brought Sara to live with him and the child suffered from his indifference, his leaving would be too late. The damage would already be done.

But neither could she handle sending him out of her life tonight. She stood beside him for another fifteen minutes while their daughter slept, oblivious to the turmoil going on in her parents' lives. She stood there thinking about the expression she'd caught on his face when they'd first come into the viewing room that evening, and she stubbornly hung on to a thread of hope she knew in her heart had already been severed.

IN SPITE OF the breast milk she was consuming four times a day, Sara lost three ounces that week.

Lisa's heart sank when Randal Cunningham told her about it Friday morning, Sara's seven-week birthday. They were in the nursery, the baby sleeping in her bed between them. Lisa had just tied a Happy Birthday helium balloon to the baby's blood-pressure monitor. Marcus was at work.

Randal tapped Sara's chart against his hand. ''She's still under four pounds, Lisa. I'd hoped to have her in an incubator by now, but she's got to hit the four-pound mark first.''

Lisa nodded, biting the inside of her lip as she tried

not to cry. "The breast milk isn't helping?" she asked. All her determination to help her baby, all those hours of pumping, just weren't enough.

"Oh, it's helping," Randal said. "It's the infection that caused the weight loss. I suspect she'd have lost a lot more if not for your milk. Now's not the time to be getting discouraged on me, Doctor. If she remains stable over the next twenty-four hours, I intend to try taking her off the ventilator again sometime before the weekend's out."

Worry clutched Lisa anew. If Sara didn't make it the second time off the machine, chances were she never would. "Are you sure?" she asked. As much as she wanted the baby off the hateful machine, she wasn't ready to risk a failure.

The brisk Dr. Cunningham's eyes filled with compassion. "Sometimes we know too much for our own good, don't we, Lisa." He looked at the sleeping baby.

Lisa stood next to him, watching her silent little girl, and nodded.

SHE KEPT HERSELF busy for the rest of the morning, taking the few office calls she'd had scheduled for well-child exams and inoculations, dictating charts, even rearranging a shelf of reference books in her office. Anything to keep her mind occupied and not on Sara. What if they took her off the machine and she didn't make it? There'd be no going back a second time. At least not without certain damage to the baby's vital organs.

By noon she couldn't stand herself any longer. Her

stomach was turning inside out, and every breath was more of a labor than it should have been as she pushed the air past the constriction in her chest. Her panic eventually grew to the point of dizziness, forcing her to do what she always did when her head was running away with her. She called Marcus.

"Hi, hon," he said as soon as he heard her voice. "Is everything okay?"

"She's lost a little weight, but Randal says it's due to the infection and nothing to worry about."

"But you're worried, anyway."

"He wants to take her off the ventilator again this weekend."

"Lisa! That's great, honey." He sounded far happier than "merely for her" should entail.

"I'm scared, Marcus. If she doesn't make it this time, chances are she won't make it at all."

"She's outrun all her other odds, Lis."

Lisa twirled the phone cord around her finger. "I know, but it's dangerous to take her on and off life support. It damages all kinds of things—the respiratory system, the brain, the heart. Deafness is already a concern, and mental retardation, too."

"And we could be struck by lightning the next time it rains."

"I'm serious, Marcus. You have no idea how many very real dangers she's facing. I'm not overreacting here."

"I'm serious, too, Lis. I'm fully aware of the dangers, but you're worrying about things you can't control. Save your energy for handling whatever comes."

"But what'll I do if—"

"You'll do whatever you have to do, Lis," he interrupted her. "You always have."

She felt better after she hung up the phone, though she'd been disappointed to hear that Marcus wouldn't be able to make it for her afternoon hour with Sara. He had a meeting with George Blake.

And by the time her second hour that day with Sara was ending, her panic was back. Determined to fight it, to take what control she had left to her, she walked down to the kidney ward, hoping to find Oliver still there. With the exception of her visits to Sara, she hadn't been at the hospital on Friday afternoons in years, since that was one of the days she volunteered at the free clinic downtown, and she wasn't even sure what her father's hours were anymore.

She was disappointed to hear that she'd just missed him, not more than ten minutes before. Thinking he might stop to see Sara again on his way out, she rushed back upstairs, only to find she'd missed him there, too.

"Damn!" she said, punching the elevator for the bottom floor. She couldn't go home. Hannah was still only working part-time, though she'd offered to come full-time after the baby was home, and Marcus wouldn't be out of his meeting with Blake yet. She knew better than to go home and sit by herself. The empty rooms would only torment her.

Cool April air filled Lisa's lungs and the sunshine warmed her face as she walked across the compound to Beth's office. Just being out of the sterile antiseptic-filled air that permeated the hospital corridors helped. Hopefully Beth was done for the day and could go out for a drink or something. She could use a dose of Beth's cheer. She missed her friend. Missed being an everyday part of Beth's life. Something she hoped would change after she brought Sara home.

If she brought Sara home.

Wherever home was going to be.

Her stomach started to churn again, and Lisa picked up her pace, determined to outdistance her demons. The door to Beth's office was closed, but her light was on, which meant Beth was still working—but not with a patient. Beth never closed her office door with a patient inside.

Relieved far beyond what she should have been, Lisa knocked lightly once and opened the door.

She started to speak, words of greeting on her lips, but no sound came out. Beth wasn't alone. And she wasn't working.

Lisa closed the door before either person in Beth's office even knew it had been opened, so involved were they in what they were doing. Cold all over, Lisa walked away as quickly as she could without attracting attention to herself. She felt like a fool. And alone. And heartsick. She couldn't believe what she'd just seen. She kept trying to convince herself that it wasn't true, that it wasn't what it seemed.

Except that there was no way it could have been anything else.

She tried not to think about it, tried to concentrate on finding her car in the parking lot, counting how many red cars there were in the row in which she was walking. Or blue ones. Or green. But all she could see, over and over again, was Beth, sitting on her desk, her blouse halfway undone, kissing a man.

A man Lisa had thought she knew very well.

Her father.

CHAPTER SIXTEEN

"YOU'RE A GOOD MAN, Marcus Cartwright. If I'd ever had a son, I'd have wanted him to be just like you," George Blake said, shaking Marcus's hand as the two men left the conference room long after everyone else on Friday afternoon. They'd just finished going over the best quarterly reports Blake's had ever known.

"I imagine I'd have grown up a little happier if I'd had you for a father," Marcus said, uncharacteristically open with the older man. He'd had a soft spot for George Blake since the moment he'd met him.

George walked with him down to the elevator, as straightbacked as a much younger man. "Your father was a little rough on you, huh?" he asked.

Marcus shook his head. "He never lifted a hand to me. He just wasn't ever there."

George nodded. "He had a business to run."

"Something like that."

"Yeah, me, too. If I regret anything in my life, it's not taking the time to watch my daughters grow. Girls are baffling little creatures, but they'll leave a mark on you that you'll cherish till the day you die."

Marcus reached out and pushed the button for the elevator. "My wife just had a little girl a couple of months ago. Her name's Sara."

"Well, congratulations, boy! Why didn't I hear anything about it? It wasn't even in the paper, was it?"

"We've kept things quiet for Lisa's sake. The baby was more than two months premature. It's been touch and go. I'm on my way to Thornton Memorial to see her now."

George's brows drew together in a frown, and his eyes filled with compassion. "I'll be praying for her, son. For all of you," he said, clasping Marcus on the shoulder just as the elevator doors slid open.

"Thanks, George."

"I'd like to keep in touch, Marcus, other than to discuss Blake's, if you can find the time."

Marcus didn't hesitate. "I can find the time."

George nodded again and Marcus watched the elevator close on his new friend. He couldn't remember a time when he'd felt so contented.

LISA HAD ONLY BEEN HOME a few minutes when Marcus called from his car to say he was on his way and asked that she put on a pair of jeans and a warm sweater. But he wouldn't say where he was taking her. It had been so long since he'd planned one of the mysterious dates she'd always loved that she'd forgotten how magical they could be. It was just what she needed to take her mind off the rest of her life.

She was ready and waiting when he strode through the door and even had *his* jeans and pullover sweater laid out on the bed for him. She called the hospital with instructions to call her on her cellular if there was any change in Sara's condition, while he got ready.

She was looking forward to whatever diversion he had in mind.

When she climbed into the Ferrari beside Marcus, Lisa caught sight of a couple of bags from Berelli's. Her favorite deli. Things were looking better every minute.

"So where we going on our picnic?" she asked, grinning at her husband.

He merely grinned back, put the Ferrari in gear and roared out of the drive. But Lisa knew where they were going almost immediately. She couldn't have chosen better herself.

She followed him across the dock to *Sara*'s slip, then took his hand as he helped her aboard. It was a beautiful evening, not cold, though there was a nippy breeze blowing in from the ocean. The water was too rough to take the boat out, but Lisa wouldn't have wanted to be away from shore and the hospital, anyway. She was content to sit with Marcus, enjoying the night, with the waves lapping at the boat, away from it all, and yet close enough to not be away at all.

"I went by Beth's office on my way home this afternoon," she said once they were sitting together on the deck, a blanket from down below wrapped around her. Marcus had a glass of wine for his predinner drink. He'd brought her a couple of nonalcoholic wine coolers in deference to her breast feeding.

"How's she doing?" he asked, his arms crossed in front of him as he toyed casually with his wineglass.

"She was making love with my father," Lisa blurted. She still couldn't believe her father would get involved with a woman young enough to be his daughter. It upset her every time she thought about it.

A full minute had passed before she realized that Marcus wasn't saying anything. He was looking out to sea, and Lisa could almost envision the wheels turning around in his head.

"Define making love," he finally said.

"Her shirt was undone. He was...touching her. They were kissing." It embarrassed her to talk about it.

She was shocked when Marcus turned to her and grinned. "Well, I'll be damned," he said.

"You aren't appalled?"

"I think it'll take some getting used to for sure, but think about it, Lis. They've both already had, and lost, their mates. In spite of their age difference, they're at about the same point in their lives, settled in their careers, their homes. They're practically perfect for each other."

"She's young enough to be his daughter," Lisa said. She kept picturing herself with Beth's father, or Marcus's had he still been alive, and she shuddered.

"Not technically," Marcus said, reaching under the blanket for her hand. "She's five years older than you, Lis."

"There's an entire generation between them."

"But if it's not a problem for them, why should it be for us?"

"He loves my mother," Lisa said softly, and suddenly knew where her shame should be directed. Not at her father, but at herself. She was jealous.

"And Beth loved John every bit as much, honey. I suspect they both understand that. It's probably why they were drawn to each other in the first place."

Lisa sighed. "I'm being a jerk, aren't I?" she asked, not at all proud of herself.

"Just being human, love," Marcus said. He leaned over and kissed her.

"Well, it *is* going to take some getting used to," she said when she could finally think coherently again.

Marcus nodded. "It all makes sense now, though."

She frowned. "What makes sense?"

"A conversation I had with Oliver a while back. I thought he was talking about his career, but he must have already been seeing Beth. He was saying something about looking at the years still stretching out in front of him and wondering where to go from there. He asked if I thought he'd be acting like an old fool if he started over."

Lisa's eyes pooled with tears. Marcus's words gave her a whole new insight into the man she'd taken for granted all her life. He was much more than just a father. He was a man with needs and desires, a man who still had a lifetime stretching out in front of him. A man who, despite his loss, was still capable of finding love with the right woman. It was time she recognized that. And loved all of him.

"So you think we should tell them we know?" she asked, suddenly just wanting to get it over with.

"They don't know you saw them?"

Lisa shook her head.

"Then I think we ought to let it be until they come to us. It should be their call."

"I just don't want them to feel as if they have to hide from us," Lisa said, understanding now the change in her friend over the past months, the times when Beth had avoided her. Although, when Lisa had needed a friend, Beth had still been that friend. Lisa was ready to return the favor.

THE HOSPITAL CALLED the next morning. They were removing Sara's ventilator. Randal wanted Lisa present.

Marcus held her hand all the way to the hospital and during the minutes standing next to Sara's bed while the technician removed the tape that held Sara's life support secure. As before, the baby protested the attention, but she didn't seem to Lisa to be putting up as much of a fight. Her little arms and legs weren't squirming quite so energetically. Lisa broke out in a cold sweat while they stood there watching. And waiting.

Marcus stood silently beside her. Lisa wondered if he realized how crucial the next moments were. She wondered if he allowed himself to care at all. And suddenly she didn't want him there. Not if he wasn't there for Sara's sake. She didn't want anybody in the room who wasn't pulling for her baby. Sara deserved a supportive family, not a disinterested bystander.

But before she could do more than release her grip on Marcus's hand, the tube was gone. Sara blinked at the sudden need to pull in her own air. The room was silent. There were no little wails like the last time.

Nothing to indicate that the baby was going to help herself.

Until suddenly Sara's little features scrunched up into the ugliest face Lisa had ever seen, and she let out a wail that reverberated throughout the entire nursery.

"Thank God." The words were Marcus's.

LISA DIDN'T WANT to leave the nursery. She was afraid to go home, to let the baby out of her sight, in case something went wrong. Marcus agreed without any argument and sat with her in the nursery viewing room once their allotted hour with Sara was through. He left just before noon to pick up some lunch.

They'd barely finished the hamburgers he'd brought back when Oliver walked in the door to the viewing room, an apprehensive look on his face. Beth was right behind him. Her eyes darted to Lisa and then away. She looked like she was going to cry.

"Hey, you two," Lisa said, "don't look so glum."

Beth did start to cry then. "I'm so sorry, Lisa," she said. "I had no idea you'd come by."

Oliver coughed and looked down. Lisa looked at her husband. "You called them."

Marcus grinned sheepishly. "I called your father. Beth was there."

"So what was all that about waiting for them to come to us?" she asked, standing up.

"I was wrong. The more I thought about it, the more I realized you were right. I didn't want them hiding from us, either. Besides, I knew you were missing them. That you wanted them beside you today."

Oliver crossed to Lisa, brushing a strand of hair back from her face as he'd done when she was a child. "I'm sorry, baby. I'll always love your mother, you know."

Lisa threw her arms around her father, proud to be loved by him. "I know, Dad. And don't ever be sorry about being happy."

He crushed her to him, and for the first time Lisa was at peace with her mother's passing and her father's moving on. He'd had too much anguish in his life.

And so had Beth. Lisa reached out and hugged her friend as soon as her father let her go. "I love you, Beth. Be happy," she whispered for Beth's ears alone.

"I've missed you, friend," Beth whispered back.

"So when are you going to make an honest woman out of her, Dad?" Lisa asked, one arm still around Beth.

Oliver laughed, a hearty outburst that Lisa hadn't heard in years. She'd missed it. "I guess we have nothing to wait for anymore, do we, Beth? So what do you say? Are you going to marry me?"

"You mean you haven't asked her?" Lisa gasped.

"He was waiting to talk to you first," Beth said, smiling up at her lover.

Lisa hadn't expected such consideration, but she appreciated it. She wasn't losing a father or memories of her mother. She was gaining a new closer relationship with her best friend. It still felt a bit odd. And it would definitely take some getting used to. But she was happy for her father and Beth.

And then she saw Marcus, standing away from the three of them, gazing through the window into the nursery with a frown on his face. Her gaze flew to Sara. The baby was sleeping peacefully, her heart monitor beeping reassuringly. But Marcus's frown remained. Was he, in the face of the love she shared with her father, reminding himself that he'd never have a daughter with whom to share a similar love? His face froze when he caught Lisa looking at him, and she knew she was right.

BETH AND OLIVER stayed for more than an hour, holding hands while they watched Sara breathe. Lisa saw the love brimming in their eyes as they watched her daughter, and she knew that whether or not Sara grew up in her father's house, the child was going to be surrounded by a family who adored her.

Marcus was silent most of the afternoon, frowning more often than not, but when Lisa tried to talk to him after Oliver and Beth left to go inspect the new dialysis equipment Cartwright Enterprises had purchased for the hospital, his replies were nothing more than one or two syllables.

"You don't have to stay if you don't want to," she finally said. They'd been sitting there for more than four hours.

"I'll stay," was all he said.

Lisa didn't speak again until she heard a commotion in the hallway outside the nursery viewing room.

They'd been lucky to have the room to themselves so far, though she knew that the room was rarely used except by the families of preemies. The full-term babies could be seen better from the viewing window around the corner out in the hall.

"So where's this kid I been hearing about?"

Lisa turned her head, recognizing the sassy voice instantly. "Willie Adams. What're you doing up here?" she scolded. She'd dismissed the boy from the hospital a month ago, but he was supposed to be down in physical therapy every afternoon for several hours.

"Look at you, Willie!" Marcus said, turning to watch as the boy walked slowly into the room. His left leg was still dragging a bit, but Lisa could see that his motor coordination had much improved, even from the previous week.

"They say I gotta do stairs, and I figure the real kind are better than that stupid machine they want me to go on. At least this way I get somewhere." His grin went straight to Lisa's heart.

"Besides, I gotta see this kid. Which one is she?"

Marcus put his arm around the boy's thin shoulders, pointing to Sara's warming bed. "She's right there. See, her name's on that plate at the bottom of the crib."

"What's she in that funny-looking bed for?"

"It helps to maintain her body temperature."

"Why don't she just do that for herself?"

"Give her time, Willie, she will. She just has to grow a bit more."

Lisa wondered if Marcus had any idea how much he sounded like a papa defending his young.

"She don't look big enough to grow."

"She's almost four pounds now. You should've seen her when she was born."

Willie nodded, apparently satisfied. "We can skip the batting cages if you want, you know, since you got your own kid to think about now."

Lisa braced herself as she heard the words. Did it hurt Marcus every time people referred to Sara as his, or did he just freeze out their words as he did hers? And how could he possibly think they could go through life living this way?

"I'll have time, Willie. We'll go as soon as you're ready."

Of course he would. Willie wasn't a threat. He expected nothing. Marcus was able to be more of a father to Willie than he was to his own daughter.

SARA'S OXYGEN LEVELS began to drop around four o'clock. She'd only been breathing on her own for just over six hours. Lisa watched as her little chest continued to rise and fall, as her lungs labored for air, worried that each breath might be the baby's last. In spite of the capable medical staff attending to Sara, Lisa was afraid to take her eyes off her baby even for a minute.

"I'll watch her, hon," Marcus said shortly before five. "Why don't you go down and get some fresh air?"

Lisa shook her head. It could all be over before she got back.

"Would you like me to call your father?" he asked.

Again Lisa shook her head. It might be hours yet before they knew anything for sure. Lisa wanted her father to have what unrestricted happiness he could. She was glad that Beth was with him, that if the unthinkable happened to Sara, her father wouldn't be alone.

Sara slept on. The baby hadn't opened her eyes in more than four hours.

Marcus went in with Lisa while she sat through Sara's eight-o'clock feeding. Lisa sang to the child, as she always did when she fed her, but while the baby's body was continuing to accept nourishment, Sara slept through her entire meal.

"She's going to have to go back on the ventilator," Lisa whispered as Marcus led her back out to the viewing room.

"Let's just be patient, Lis. Randal hasn't given the order for that yet," Marcus said. Though his face was pinched, his brows tight with worry, Lisa just accepted that he was worried on her account. The baby's, too, but only in the way anyone would be concerned about another in a life-threatening situation. She wasn't going to read any more into it than that, couldn't afford to waste any more energy hoping for what would never be. For as much as she believed in Marcus's ability to be a father to her child, he didn't believe in himself, and there was nothing she could do to change that.

Randal arrived in the nursery at nine. He checked Sara carefully, not only watching her readings, but listening to her chest and looking under her eyelids. Finally, straightening, he motioned for a technician to bring back Sara's life support.

Lisa started to cry as the machine was wheeled over beside the baby. She just couldn't let them do it. She couldn't put her baby through more pain if it was all going to be for naught.

Randal caught sight of her sitting out there, and Lisa didn't even bother to wipe away the tears that were streaming down her face. She wasn't a professional. She was a mother.

"We're not hooking her up just yet, folks," Randal said, poking his head out the nursery door. "Her levels have been fluctuating a little more this past hour. We'll wait for one more reading."

Lisa nodded, but she knew that at that point the chances of Sara's breathing normally on her own were slim to none. Marcus stood silently behind her, his hands on her shoulders. She leaned back against him, soaking up his warmth. He'd been a rock throughout the entire day, never leaving her side, watching her baby intently, as if he could actually will his own breath into the baby's lungs. She knew, without a doubt, he would if he could.

"Can we sit with her?" Lisa asked. Surely, given the circumstances, Randal would break the rules this once.

The doctor nodded.

"Let me help you with that," Marcus said a few

minutes later. Lisa's hands were shaking so badly she couldn't get into her scrubs. Marcus was already dressed and masked.

He was being a wonderful father. If only there was some way to make him see that, believe it.

Lisa could feel every beat of her heart as Randal approached Sara's crib half an hour later, checked the baby over and then checked her a second time, finally turning to face Lisa and Marcus. His face looked grim.

"Her oxygen levels are up. She's breathing well enough on her own again." He stood by Sara's bed, looking down at the baby. He appeared to be struggling for words.

"What's wrong, doctor?" Marcus asked. He slid his arm around Lisa's waist, pulling her against his side.

"She's not responding to..." The doctor looked at Lisa, his eyes filled with sorrow. "She's in a coma, Lisa."

Marcus caught Lisa as her legs gave way beneath her. A rocker appeared behind him and he lowered Lisa's limp body into the chair.

"What happens next, Doctor?" Marcus asked.

Lisa heard the conversation. There was nothing they could do but wait. She already knew that. The medical team had done everything possible. It was up to God now. They could wait hours. They could wait days. They could wait forever.

Marcus talked Randal into allowing them to remain in the nursery with Sara for the rest of the night.

Lisa dozed on and off that night, her head settled back against the bars of the rocker on which she sat.

And Marcus was in a rocker right beside her, holding her hand, dozing off only when she woke up.

She prayed for all she was worth, but as time slid slowly by with no change from the baby lying so still in her bed, Lisa stopped asking for anything at all. She looked at her baby, all trussed up with wires and tubes and laboring to breathe. Was it right to let her baby suffer so?

She saw Marcus stir, exchanged tired sad smiles with him as they silently changed guard, and settled back to try to get some sleep. She honestly didn't know which was worse. Her sleeping nightmares or her waking ones.

Marcus's soft murmuring woke Lisa sometime in the early hours of the morning. Disoriented and frightened, Lisa struggled to sit up, only to realize that she was already sitting up. And that her neck ached horribly. The shaft of pain she felt when she tried to straighten brought her back to full consciousness. *Sara.*

Her eyes flew open immediately, seeking reassurance that her baby was still alive. Sara's monitors were bleeping, but Lisa couldn't actually see her for the man who was leaning over her crib.

"YOU'VE GOT TO BE strong now, Sara," he said. "It's up to you. Everyone's pulling for you, ready to catch you, but you have to take the jump, Sara. Just take the jump."

The baby's eyes popped open.

Marcus's heart catapulted into his throat when he

saw Sara stare straight at him. He was afraid to move, afraid those beautiful blue eyes were a mirage, a cruel twist of his exhausted mind.

Sara blinked.

He straightened, still watching the baby, holding her gaze with his own, as if he could somehow make her consciousness real by sheer will. She blinked again, and his heart started to pound in double time. The baby was really awake.

"Lisa!" He turned, intending to wake his wife, but the minute his eyes broke contact with Sara's, the baby started to cry, soft thin little wails.

Marcus turned back, frightened, thinking something was wrong. "What is it, little one?" he asked.

The baby stopped crying as soon as he spoke.

Freezing beside the crib, Marcus was aware of Lisa behind him. He knew she was awake because he'd heard her sharp intake of breath when Sara had cried out. But he couldn't go to her, couldn't leave this tiny little girl.

He heard a nurse approach and he shook himself. He was being ridiculous. He had nothing to do with the baby's crying. It was mere coincidence that the child had woken up right when he'd started to speak to her, that she'd stopped crying when he'd turned back to her. Forcing himself to face reality, he backed slowly away from the funny little crib. Sara's eyes followed him until he was no longer in her sight.

And then she started to cry again.

Vaguely aware of the crowd gathering in the nursery, of his wife sitting and sobbing in her rocking chair behind him, Marcus approached the crib again. As soon as Sara saw him, her wails turned into pitying little hiccups. Instinctively, before he even realized what he was doing, Marcus reached down into the warming bed and slid his hands beneath the naked little body staring up at him so trustingly. Careful of the catheter in her foot, he lifted her up to his chest. Sara snuggled against him, obviously not the least bit daunted by his awkwardness.

And in that instant, Marcus suddenly understood what being a father was all about. Just like that, he had his answers.

He'd been such a fool.

He'd allowed his sterility to shake his confidence in himself to the point where he actually thought that if he didn't have what it took to make a child, then he didn't have what it took to care for one. But being a father wasn't about perfection or the ability to do everything. It wasn't even about biology. It was the willingness to struggle, to worry. It was the intense need to provide. To protect. The willingness to give up one's own life, if need be, for the little being dependent on him. Being a father was about loving. And somehow this tiny baby snuggling against him so trustingly had known how much he loved her even before he'd known it himself.

LISA SAT UNMOVING in her chair, tears streaming unchecked down her face as she waited for Marcus to turn around. She wanted to get up, to go to him, but she was trembling so much she wasn't sure she could stand. So she sat. And waited. For what seemed like hours, but was probably only a couple of minutes, while Marcus held his baby.

He turned around slowly and Lisa choked on a fresh wave of tears as she caught her first glimpse of her big strong husband holding their tiny daughter in his hands for the first time. Marcus's palms were resting one on top of the other, supporting Sara's body, but it was his eyes that told her they'd finally found their dream together. His eyes were glistening with tears—and awe.

He walked toward Lisa slowly, lifted the baby away from his chest, kissed her tiny head and slowly lowered her into Lisa's arms.

"I'm a father." His gaze met Lisa's briefly before going back to the baby in her arms. He reached out and ran one finger lightly down the baby's cheek, as if, now that he'd finally held her, he couldn't touch her enough. "I'm a father," he said again.

Too moved to speak, Lisa nodded, as cheers broke out around them.

Marcus watched his wife brush her lips across their baby's brow, and his heart was finally at peace. He'd given Lisa what she'd always wanted, after all. Her dream had not been to have a baby with her husband, but to share one with the man she loved.

And by some miracle, that man was him.

EPILOGUE

THREE-YEAR-OLD Sara Barbara Cartwright was not a happy camper. She kept watching out the window like Mommy had told her, but Daddy's car wasn't coming like Mommy'd said it would. She stomped her foot, trying to make someone notice she wasn't happy, but the sound just went right into the carpet. Mommy didn't even glance up.

Sara looked over her shoulder at Mommy and Aunt Beth, kind of glad they hadn't heard her. She didn't like being naughty. Mommy saw her and smiled and took Sara's mad away.

"You keep watching, Sara baby. Daddy'll be home in just a few minutes."

Sara turned back to the window.

She wondered what "few minutes" was. She'd thought Daddy was coming *now*.

Aunt Beth had her hand on Mommy's tummy, waiting to feel the new baby kick. Sara had gotten to feel it first, so she didn't mind when other people wanted to feel it, too. Especially Aunt Beth. Aunt Beth was married to Grandpa. And she made babies. She made her, Sara. She made her new sister, too. Except she made her new sister bigger than Sara. She was staying in Mommy's tummy longer.

Sara didn't remember being in Mommy's tummy, but she sure wished her new baby sister wouldn't stay in there so long. Mommy couldn't play on the floor so much now. And she slept a lot. One day Sara had even seen Daddy have to tie Mommy's shoe. She wasn't sure why having a baby in your tummy made you forget how to tie your shoes.

She wished the baby would just come out so she could play with her. It wouldn't be so hard to wait for Daddy to get home if she had somebody to play with. Sara stuck her thumb in her mouth, staring out the window. She didn't like "few minutes." It was making Daddy take too long.

Then she heard his car. She couldn't even see it yet, but Daddy drove a really loud car that sounded like the big truck on cartoons. Sara ran to the door.

She started to jump up and down when she heard his key in the lock. "Daddy!" she shouted, barreling toward his legs as soon as the door opened.

"Hi, pumpkin!" he said, swinging her up over his head, and then back down to straddle his stomach. "Did you have a good day?"

She played with the buttons on his shirt. She loved his buttons. They were all the same size. Not like Mommy's, which changed every time she wore different clothes. "I drawed and made cookies," she told him, hoping she wasn't leaving out something else good.

"Cookies? That's great! Did Hannah help you?"

She nodded. "Hannah buyed me gum," she told him, remembering the other good thing.

Daddy carried her into the living room where Mommy was with Aunt Beth. He kissed Mommy hello, and his voice got all soft and gooey like it always did when he talked to her. He said hi to Aunt Beth, too, and then carried Sara with him into the kitchen. They were going to have cookies.

Really, he was going to have some. Mommy wouldn't let her have any of her own because they would spoil her dinner, but Daddy would share his with her. Daddy's cookies didn't spoil dinners.

"You promise to eat all your dinner, pumpkin?" he asked her as he reached into the cookie jar.

"Yes, Daddy." She always had to finish every bite so she'd grow up big and strong.

Mommy came into the kitchen just as Daddy popped the last bite of cookie into his mouth. Sara giggled, trying hard to keep her own mouth shut so Mommy wouldn't see the cookie in it.

"What're you two doing out here?" Mommy asked.

"It's a father-daughter thing," Daddy said. Sara wasn't sure what that meant, but she was glad she had it with Daddy.

"You're the best daddy in the whole wide world," she said, hugging his neck.

Daddy squeezed her. "You've sure made me the happiest one, Sara."

Sara wasn't sure why Mommy got tears in her eyes when he said that, but she supposed it must just be from having a baby in her tummy.

Sara just wished it would hurry up and get borned.

HARLEQUIN SUPERROMANCE®

PROTECTING MOLLY McCULLOCH
by
Dee Holmes

Superromance #732

Hunt Gresham left the police force after deciding that he was no longer in a position to protect anyone. But the indomitable Molly McCulloch has a way of getting to him. When Hunt learns her newfound brother is a hit man for hire, he knows it's time to bury the past and mount his charger one last time.

But with Molly, once is never enough....

Look for *Protecting Molly McCulloch* in March wherever Harlequin books are sold.

Loving
DANGEROUSLY

LOVE-3/97

HARLEQUIN SUPERROMANCE®

There's more to the story...

Every now and then comes a book that defies convention, breaks the rules and still offers the reader all the excitement of romance. Harlequin Superromance—the series known for its innovation and variety—is proud to add this book to our already-outstanding lineup.

#733 SOMEWHERE OUT THERE
by
Connie Bennett

Kit Wheeler doesn't believe in UFOs or aliens or government conspiracies. The former astronaut and now respected TV science correspondent wants nothing to do with the crackpots and their tales. Then an air-force jet mysteriously crashes, and Brenna Sullivan, an expert in her own right, has a convincing theory.

Whether you believe or not, you'll enjoy this wonderful story of adventure, romance and the endless possibilities that exist...somewhere out there.

Available in March wherever Harlequin books are sold.

Heartbreak RANCH

Four generations of independent women...
Four heartwarming, romantic stories of the West...
Four incredible authors...

Fern Michaels
Jill Marie Landis
Dorsey Kelley
Chelley Kitzmiller

Saddle up with Heartbreak Ranch, an outstanding
Western collection that will take you on a whirlwind
trip through four generations and the exciting,
romantic adventures of four strong women who
have inherited the ranch from Bella Duprey,
famed Barbary Coast madam.

Available in March,
wherever Harlequin books are sold.

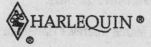

HARLEQUIN ®

HTBK

HARLEQUIN®

Don't miss these Harlequin favorites by some of our most distinguished authors!
And now, you can receive a discount by ordering two or more titles!

HT#25645	THREE GROOMS AND A WIFE by JoAnn Ross	$3.25 U.S. $3.75 CAN.	☐
HT#25647	NOT THIS GUY by Glenda Sanders	$3.25 U.S. $3.75 CAN.	☐
HP#11725	THE WRONG KIND OF WIFE by Roberta Leigh	$3.25 U.S. $3.75 CAN.	☐
HP#11755	TIGER EYES by Robyn Donald	$3.25 U.S. $3.75 CAN.	☐
HR#03416	A WIFE IN WAITING by Jessica Steele	$3.25 U.S. $3.75 CAN.	☐
HR#03419	KIT AND THE COWBOY by Rebecca Winters	$3.25 U.S. $3.75 CAN.	☐
HS#70622	KIM & THE COWBOY by Margot Dalton	$3.50 U.S. $3.99 CAN.	☐
HS#70642	MONDAY'S CHILD by Janice Kaiser	$3.75 U.S. $4.25 CAN.	☐
HI#22342	BABY VS. THE BAR by M.J. Rodgers	$3.50 U.S. $3.99 CAN.	☐
HI#22382	SEE ME IN YOUR DREAMS by Patricia Rosemoor	$3.75 U.S. $4.25 CAN.	☐
HAR#16538	KISSED BY THE SEA by Rebecca Flanders	$3.50 U.S. $3.99 CAN.	☐
HAR#16603	MOMMY ON BOARD by Muriel Jensen	$3.50 U.S. $3.99 CAN.	☐
HH#28885	DESERT ROGUE by Erine Yorke	$4.50 U.S. $4.99 CAN.	☐
HH#28911	THE NORMAN'S HEART by Margaret Moore	$4.50 U.S. $4.99 CAN.	☐

(limited quantities available on certain titles)

	AMOUNT	$
DEDUCT:	10% DISCOUNT FOR 2+ BOOKS	$
ADD:	POSTAGE & HANDLING	$
	($1.00 for one book, 50¢ for each additional)	
	APPLICABLE TAXES*	$_____
	TOTAL PAYABLE	$_____
	(check or money order—please do not send cash)	

To order, complete this form and send it, along with a check or money order for the total above, payable to Harlequin Books, to: **In the U.S.:** 3010 Walden Avenue, P.O. Box 9047, Buffalo, NY 14269-9047; **In Canada:** P.O. Box 613, Fort Erie, Ontario, L2A 5X3.

Name: _____

Address: _____ City: _____

State/Prov.: _____ Zip/Postal Code: _____

*New York residents remit applicable sales taxes.
Canadian residents remit applicable GST and provincial taxes.
Look us up on-line at: http://www.romance.net

HBACK-JM4